THE
ROGUE'S BRIDE

BOOK THREE
THE BRIDES OF SKYE

JAYNE CASTEL

WINTER MIST PRESS

The Outlaw's Bride, by Jayne Castel

Published by Winter Mist Press

ISBN 9780473538743 (paperback)

Edited by Tim Burton

Cover photography courtesy of www.shutterstock.com
Scotch thistle vector image courtesy of Wikipedia Commons.
Map by Jayne Castel

The Wild Mountain Thyme poem, courtesy of
www.rampantscotland.com/songs/blsongs_thyme.htm

Visit Jayne's website: www.jaynecastel.com

**Some things cannot be forgotten—or forgiven.
The widow trying to forge a new life for herself.
The man she once spurned bent on revenge.**

Caitrin is a widow left to rule her husband's territory
alone. The survivor of a loveless, unhappy marriage, she
vows never to let another man control her. Instead, she
finds herself in charge of a vast estate.

Alasdair MacDonald returns from war to discover his
sister-in-law is chatelaine over his dead brother's lands—
territory that now belongs to him.

Caitrin has haunted Alasdair's dreams from the moment
she spurned him years earlier. He's never gotten over it,
or forgiven her for breaking his heart by choosing his
elder brother over him. Now he has a chance for
vengeance, to take her young son and her new-found
freedom from her. Only he soon discovers that his long
dormant feelings for the beautiful widow can't be so
easily set aside.

Historical Romances by Jayne Castel

DARK AGES BRITAIN

The Kingdom of the East Angles series
Night Shadows (prequel novella)
Dark Under the Cover of Night (Book One)
Nightfall till Daybreak (Book Two)
The Deepening Night (Book Three)
The Kingdom of the East Angles: The Complete Series

The Kingdom of Mercia series
The Breaking Dawn (Book One)
Darkest before Dawn (Book Two)
Dawn of Wolves (Book Three)
The Kingdom of Mercia: The Complete Series

The Kingdom of Northumbria series
The Whispering Wind (Book One)
Wind Song (Book Two)
Lord of the North Wind (Book Three)
The Kingdom of Northumbria: The Complete Series

DARK AGES SCOTLAND

The Warrior Brothers of Skye series
Blood Feud (Book One)
Barbarian Slave (Book Two)
Battle Eagle (Book Three)
The Warrior Brothers of Skye: The Complete Series

The Pict Wars series
Warrior's Heart (Book One)
Warrior's Secret (Book Two)
Warrior's Wrath (Book Three)

The Pict Wars: The Complete Series

Novellas
Winter's Promise

MEDIEVAL SCOTLAND

The Brides of Skye series
The Beast's Bride (Book One)
The Outlaw's Bride (Book Two)
The Rogue's Bride (Book Three)
The Brides of Skye: The Complete Series

The Sisters of Kilbride series
Unforgotten (Book One)
Awoken (Book Two)
Fallen (Book Three)
Claimed (Epilogue novella)

The Immortal Highland Centurions series
Maximus (Book One)
Cassian (Book Two)
Draco (Book Three)
The Laird's Return (Epilogue festive novella)

Stolen Highland Hearts series
Highlander Deceived (Book One)
Highlander Entangled (Book Two)
Highlander Forbidden (Book Three)
Highlander Pledged (Book Four)

Guardians of Alba series
Nessa's Seduction (Book One)
Fyfa's Sacrifice (Book Two)
Breanna's Surrender (Book Three)

Epic Fantasy Romances
by Jayne Castel

Light and Darkness series
Ruled by Shadows (Book One)
The Lost Swallow (Book Two)
Path of the Dark (Book Three)
Light and Darkness: The Complete Series

***

For Timbo—you have been with me every step of the way.

***

Map

THE CLAN TERRITORIES
OF THE ISLE OF SKYE
IN THE 14th CENTURY
THE MINCH
SOUND OF RAASAY
INNER SOUND
MAINLAND
MACLEOD
MACDONALD
ISLE OF SKYE
ISLE OF RAASAY
FRASER
SCALPAY
MACKINNON
SEA OF THE HEBRIDES
MACDONALD OF SLEAT

Memories are dangerous things.
You turn them over and over,
until you know every touch and corner,
but still you'll find an edge to cut you.
—Mark Lawrence

Chapter One

The Missive

Duntulm Castle, Isle of Skye, Scotland

Winter, 1347 AD

"NOT POTTAGE ... AGAIN?"

Duntulm's cook, an elderly woman with white hair pulled back into a bun and a face as wrinkled as walnut, frowned. "It's a good, wholesome meal, milady."

Caitrin shook her head. "We've had pottage and dumplings thrice over the past week. The men are starting to complain. They want some meat."

Cook's mouth thinned. "We need to watch our stores, milady. Spring is still some way off."

Caitrin suppressed a sigh. "We had the best harvest in years ... and the men brought back many deer and boar from their hunting trips in the autumn. Ye don't need to worry about us running out of food."

Cook wrung her hands, clearly unconvinced. The two women stood in Duntulm's kitchen, a warm space dominated by a long scrubbed oaken table. The sulfurous odor of over-cooked onion, cabbage, and turnip surrounded them.

A huge cauldron of vegetable pottage simmered over the hearth at one end of the kitchen.

Caitrin did sigh then, irritation rising within her. Despite that she and cook planned Duntulm's meals together every week, the woman often took it upon herself to change things. Today was one such occasion.

Caitrin was just about to speak once more when the door to the kitchen opened and a small dark-haired woman entered. Her hand-maid, Sorcha's, cheeks were flushed, as if she'd just come in from the cold.

"Lady Caitrin, a message has arrived for ye." The young woman's eyes were bright; they rarely received missives at Duntulm. The fortress sat upon Skye's isolated northern tip. They had no news of the outside world for weeks on end here. The maid clutched a scroll in her hand, holding it out to Caitrin. "It bears the MacDonald seal," she said, her voice edged in excitement.

Caitrin's belly contracted.

Schooling her features into an expressionless mask, she took the scroll. "Thank ye, Sorcha."

Her hand-maid hovered, her gaze curious. "Do ye need anything, milady?"

"Aye, please check on Eoghan. I'll be up to feed him later."

Sorcha nodded before bobbing into a curtsy. "Aye, milady."

The girl bustled over to the door. Small and curvaceous, Sorcha MacQueen was the bastard daughter of a neighboring chieftain. Unable to keep her under his own roof, MacQueen had given her to the MacDonalds as a hand-maid to the chieftain's wife. Caitrin had expected the young woman to be bitter over it, for her father had essentially washed his hands of her, yet Sorcha seemed resolutely cheerful.

Maybe it was a front. Perhaps, underneath it all, Sorcha harbored sadness and resentment. Caitrin should know—for *she* was adept at holding up a shield to keep others at bay.

She did so even now as she stood with cook, the roll of parchment in her hand. She dared not let her true feelings show.

Instead, she turned to cook.

The elderly woman was watching her intently, a shrewd look in her dark eyes.

"No more pottage for the next week, Briana," Caitrin said, using a sharp tone she knew cook would heed. "And put out salted pork and cheese with the noon meal today."

Not giving cook an opportunity to argue, Caitrin left the kitchen, her ring of iron chatelaine keys rattling at her waist.

Outside, she crossed the snow-covered bailey, her boots sinking into the pristine crust. Then Caitrin navigated the slippery steps and entered the keep. Drawing her fur mantle close, she made her way up to her solar. Even indoors it was freezing today. Her breathing steamed before her. The snow had lain for days now. However, Caitrin's thoughts were not on the weather, but upon the rolled parchment she carried.

She held it gingerly, as if it were a venomous adder, coiled, ready to sink its fangs into her. And when she entered the solar, she had to quash the instinct to throw the missive directly on the fire without reading it.

Sinking down onto a high-backed chair before the hearth, she turned the parchment over, her gaze alighting upon the MacDonald crest. It showed an armored hand clutching a cross.

"Per Mare Per Terras," she whispered the MacDonald clan motto. *By sea and land*. The clan was one of Scotland's largest, stretching its influence down most of the kingdom's western coast.

This message could be from any of them, she told herself as nervousness tightened her throat. *It isn't from him.*

Yet her gut told her differently. None of the other MacDonalds had reason to contact her in the dead of winter. There was only one man who had any business here, and she'd thought him dead.

Had prayed that he'd died in that bloody battle against the English.

It was an uncharitable thought—for she'd never wished him ill previously—but she'd hoped for it nonetheless. She wanted the past buried.

With trembling fingers, Caitrin broke the seal and unfurled the parchment. Then she drew in a deep, steadying breath, and began to read. Like her sisters, she'd learned her letters as a girl. A nun from Kilbride Abbey had traveled to Dunvegan, where Caitrin had grown up, and had patiently taught them. It was something her mother had insisted upon, although after her death the lessons ceased.

Caitrin was grateful that she could read and write. The skills had proved useful for her role as chatelaine. Even so, she'd never been quick at it. She took her time over reading now. The letter was written in a bold, masculine script. It was brief and formal, with a chill undertone.

Dear Lady Caitrin MacDonald, widow of Baltair MacDonald,

News has reached me of my brother's death. I am currently in Inbhir Nis but will travel to the Isle of Skye presently. Upon my return, I will take up my rightful role as chieftain. Please make Duntulm ready for my arrival.

Yer humble servant,
Alasdair MacDonald.

Caitrin stared at the words so hard that her vision blurred.

Alasdair MacDonald was alive; it was there written in ink before her. She knew her father had sent word to the mainland in the hope of tracking down the MacDonald heir—and he'd found him.

Caitrin swallowed, cast the parchment aside, and stood up. Alasdair MacDonald's return put her life at Duntulm at risk.

After Baltair's death, she'd felt adrift, worried for her future. But then she'd returned to Duntulm and assumed the role of chatelaine. She now ran the fortress—and she'd discovered that she was good at it. She liked dealing with the servants, speaking to the villagers, ordering supplies, and making plans for the year ahead.

Would Alasdair allow her and Eoghan to remain living here?

Heart pounding, Caitrin left the fireside, crossed to the south-facing window, and ripped open the shutters. Snow fluttered in, tickling her face. Caitrin leaned on the stone ledge and looked out at the wintry morning. A blanket of white covered the world, making everything look clean and bright. However, dark clouds rolled in from the sea, bringing with them fresh snow. The flakes swirled as they fell upon Duntulm, frosting the battlements beneath her.

Caitrin's solar sat high and gave her a commanding view of the rest of the rectangular-shaped keep. In the bailey below she caught sight of a stocky figure crunching through the snow. Alban MacLean, steward of the castle. He would need to be told that Baltair's brother was alive and returning to take up his role as chieftain.

Over these past months Alban—a gruff but kind-hearted man—had willingly shared rule over Duntulm. Initially, she'd been nervous that he and Darron MacNichol, who captained the Duntulm Guard, might try to overrule her. She was, after all, a woman alone— left in charge of a castle and a great tract of land. But they hadn't.

Caitrin leaned against the ledge and closed her eyes, letting the icy wind and feathery touch of snowflakes caress her face.

These last seven months had been a blessing. She'd had a reprieve from the life her father had set out for her. As the eldest, she'd been the first of her sisters to wed. Two years of misery later, she'd become a widow. But

Baltair hadn't even been buried when her father—the MacLeod clan-chief—started talking of the need to find Caitrin a new husband once her mourning period passed.

Caitrin's breathing hitched. She couldn't bear the thought of being shackled to another man, of having to endure his touch, his demands. Being with Baltair had shattered all her illusions about what it meant to be a wife. Both her younger sisters, Rhona and Adaira, were wedded now, and happily so to men who loved them, but that wasn't to be her story.

Not all tales had a happy ending.

An ache grew in Caitrin's chest, and she reached up, rubbing at her breast bone with her knuckles. Opening her eyes, she stepped back from the window. She wished her sisters nothing but happiness, and yet thinking about them made her heart hurt from loneliness.

It was best not to dwell on such things.

"Good morning, Lady Caitrin." A tall warrior with silver-blond hair stepped forward to greet Caitrin as she made her way down the icy steps from the keep into the bailey. "Watch yer step."

Caitrin flashed Darron MacNichol, Captain of the Duntulm Guard, a tight smile. Darron could be a little over-protective at times, although she'd grown fond of him since coming to live here. Baltair had assigned Darron to escort her whenever she left the keep, and initially, Caitrin had worried the man would be as controlling as her husband. However, he wasn't. Darron merely shadowed her, letting her go where she willed.

He followed her now. Reaching the bailey, Caitrin's boots crunched on the fresh crust of snow, and she pulled the hood of her fur mantle up.

"Darron ... I've just received word that Alasdair MacDonald is alive," she said, leading the way toward the gates. "He'll return here soon to take Baltair's place."

Darron didn't reply immediately, and when Caitrin glanced his way, she saw his face was reflective. He was a handsome man, although somber. She rarely saw him smile.

"That is welcome news, milady," he finally replied, although his tone gave no clue as to how he really felt. Darron MacNichol could be infuriatingly inscrutable, like now.

"Aye." Caitrin looked away. "I shall go to the village now and let them know. The folk of Duntulm will be delighted."

She was aware of how flat her voice sounded, but she couldn't force joy into it.

They passed under the portcullis and crossed the drawbridge, taking the narrow road down to Duntulm village. The hamlet was a welcoming sight in the snow, a huddle of stacked-stone cottages with thatched roofs. The village kirk sat behind them, its peaked roof frosted with snow. To the north, the grey waters of The Minch, the stretch of sea that separated Duntulm from the isles beyond, appeared like a sheet of beaten iron against the leaden sky. It had stopped snowing at present, but one look at those ominous clouds warned Caitrin that the break in the weather wouldn't last long.

Caitrin swallowed a lump in her throat. She loved the folk here. She couldn't bear the thought of being sent away.

They were halfway down the hill when Darron spoke, his tone guarded. "Alasdair MacDonald isn't a harsh man, milady. He'll not turf ye out."

Caitrin huffed, keeping her gaze fixed upon the village below. Could the man read minds?

Darron was only trying to reassure her, but he'd just unwittingly made her feel worse. He didn't know of the history between her and the MacDonald heir.

Few besides her sisters did—and even they didn't know everything.

"I'm sure ye are right, Darron," she murmured. "Surely, Alasdair will treat Eoghan and me kindly."

Liar. She wasn't sure of that at all.

She wouldn't be surprised if Alasdair MacDonald now hated her.

Chapter Two

Too Much Ale

Kiltaraglen, Isle of Skye, Scotland

Two weeks later ...

"I'LL BET YE three silver pennies that I'll have that wench in my bed by midnight."

Alasdair MacDonald snorted, bringing the tankard to his lips and taking a deep pull of ale. "A bit overconfident, aren't ye? The lass hasn't looked yer way all evening."

Across the table, Boyd raised an eyebrow. "Ye think ye stand a better chance?"

Alasdair smiled back. "Aye."

"We'll see about that." Boyd leaned back in his chair, blue eyes narrowing. "Challenge accepted."

Alasdair huffed, his gaze traveling across the crowded common room. 'The Merchant's Rest', Kiltaraglen's only tavern, was packed tonight. Drunken male voices boomed around them. Situated upon Skye's northeastern coast, the port village was just a day's ride from their destination. Their journey back to Duntulm was almost over.

His attention settled upon a blonde and comely lass, with milky skin and a twinkle in her eye, who was carrying a tray of food over to a table in the far corner. She was the innkeeper's daughter, and Boyd had been leering at her since they'd stepped through the threshold of the inn.

A smile curved Alasdair's lips. Boyd was about to lighten his purse. His second cousin, who hailed from the MacDonalds of Glencoe, got bumptious whenever he was full of drink.

Shifting his gaze back to Boyd, Alasdair saw he was smirking at him. Tall and lanky with a shock of red-gold hair, his cousin had a look in his eye that Alasdair knew well. He liked to turn everything, even wooing women, into a contest.

"Very well," Alasdair drawled. "But ye are not to sulk like a bairn when I win."

Around them, the din increased as two men started having an argument near the fire. The inn had a low ceiling, trapping in the pall of smoke and the odor of roast mutton, unwashed bodies, and damp wool.

Boyd cast him a withering look and raised his hand, catching the serving wench's attention. "Lass!" he called out, beckoning her to their table. "More ale ... can't ye see we're thirsty?"

The young woman retrieved a jug and made her way across the sawdust strewn floor toward them. Reaching the table, she gave both men a bold smile and set the jug down.

"We can't have ye going thirsty, lads," she greeted them. Her gaze then went to the two empty plates that sat between Alasdair and Boyd. "Was the supper to yer liking?"

"Delicious," Boyd replied, his tone so lascivious that Alasdair swallowed a laugh. His cousin was a liar. The mutton had been greasy and tough, and the cabbage overcooked.

The girl eyed Boyd, her smile widening. "Will ye be wanting anything else?"

"Why don't ye pour yerself an ale and take a seat on my lap?" Boyd favored her with a toothy grin. "Take a well-earned rest."

The innkeeper's daughter laughed, not remotely cowed by Boyd's boldness. "Da would beat me for idleness if I did such a thing," she replied with a shake of her head. The girl's attention then shifted to Alasdair, where it halted. "Yer face is familiar … have I seen ye before?"

Alasdair held her gaze for a heartbeat before he allowed himself a slow smile. "I'm Alasdair MacDonald," he replied.

The young woman's eyes widened, her lips parting slightly. "Ye are Baltair MacDonald's brother?"

Alasdair's smile widened. He could feel Boyd's glare cutting into him. His cousin was a fool if he thought Alasdair wouldn't use his position to his advantage. Baltair had taught him how attractive women found a man with a title.

"Welcome home, milord," the lass said, her eyes gleaming with interest. "When ye didn't return after Baltair's death, we all thought ye lost … that ye had fallen against the English."

"Well, I'm alive, as ye can see," he replied, saluting her with his tankard.

Her smile widened. "I shall have our best chamber prepared for ye, milord."

"Thank ye," he replied, his gaze holding hers. "And what is *yer* name?"

"Catriona," she said, her voice lowering. "Will *ye* be needing anything else?"

Catriona. The name, so similar to that of the woman he'd once loved, caused Alasdair's breathing to still.

Caitrin. Baltair's widow, and the woman who'd once spurned him. She was only a day's journey away now, currently ruling as chatelaine of Duntulm. He'd sent a letter ahead of him; she would be awaiting his arrival, although he didn't imagine she'd be happy to see him. She probably wished he'd been gutted on an English sword.

Alasdair blinked, shoving thoughts of Caitrin aside. Instead, he leaned forward, his mouth curving. "Aye, bring another jug of ale up to my room, Catriona," he murmured. "And if it pleases ye, join me up there later as well."

The young woman's gaze grew sultry. "Aye, milord," she murmured, inclining her head. "It *would* please me."

She turned then and walked away, her hips swaying tantalizingly. Alasdair watched her go. She was indeed bonny, and not so different in looks from his sister-in-law. An image of Caitrin MacLeod, lithe and blonde, her sea-blue eyes twinkling with laughter, assaulted him then. The wellbeing that the warmth, a full belly, and copious amounts of ale had given him, ebbed.

Irritation surged. Alasdair would have to face Caitrin again soon enough—but he didn't want her ruining this evening for him.

He turned his attention back to Boyd. His cousin sat back in his chair, arms folded across his chest, scowling. "Cheating bastard," he growled. "I should have known ye wouldn't fight fair."

It was Alasdair's turn to smirk now. "Stop whining and hand over those pennies."

Alasdair's eyes flickered open. The light, even dim as it was inside the bed-chamber, assaulted him, and he squinted. It was early. The shutters were closed, and a fire still burned in the hearth, casting a golden veil over the inn's best room.

Rolling over, Alasdair stifled a groan. His mouth tasted rank, and his temples throbbed. Too much ale. Last night was little more than a blur of noise and fleeting images.

Alasdair's gaze slid to the back of the naked woman sleeping beside him, and he went still. More details of the night before flooded back. Their coupling had been rough and lusty. His wits addled with ale, Alasdair had almost forgotten to withdraw before the crucial moment, but somehow good sense had prevailed. The lass had seemed disappointed that he didn't spend his seed inside her, but Alasdair was relieved he hadn't.

He didn't want to father a bastard. Truth was, he didn't want to sire any bairns at all.

Catriona shifted, stretching as she awoke. She rolled over to face Alasdair, offering him a sleepy smile when she saw he was watching her. "Good morning, milord."

"Morning," Alasdair rasped. He sat up, wincing as pain thundered through his skull. What did they put in the ale in this place? He'd never awoken with such a sore head after a night of drinking.

Pushing aside the sheet, he rose to his feet and strode naked to where a pitcher of water sat on the sideboard. He picked it up and drank deeply, not even bothering to pour the water into a cup. He was parched and felt more than a little queasy.

As he lowered the pitcher, Alasdair noted that his hands trembled. He frowned. He'd hoped the tremors, which had begun shortly after the battle against the English months earlier, would stop.

It's just the ale, he assured himself. *I'll go easy on it in future.*

"It's still early," the girl crooned behind him. "Ye can have me again before the sun rises."

Her voice, although gentle, made Alasdair stifle a wince. He glanced over his shoulder, meeting her gaze. Sitting there amongst the tangled sheets, her blonde curls tumbling over her naked shoulders, Catriona was a bonny sight. Yet the desire to throw up the contents of his stomach was greater than that to spread her smooth thighs. His temples now throbbed as if someone had taken a hammer to them.

Swallowing down bile, Alasdair turned from her and grabbed hold of the clay washbowl. "Best ye leave me now, lass," he muttered. "I don't feel well."

Caitriona gave a soft huff of annoyance. A moment later he heard the slap of her bare feet on the flagstones. Then the door thudded as she departed the chamber.

The instant he was alone, Alasdair lurched forward and threw up into the bowl.

Chapter Three

Ye Are Looking Well

BOYD LET OUT a low whistle. "What a sight."

Alasdair followed his cousin's gaze west to where a mighty keep rose high against the pale sky. A smile stretched his face—for the first time all day. Last night's excesses had left him feeling wretched for the first half of the journey. Now, with his home in view, his head had finally stopped aching.

"Aye, welcome to Duntulm, cousin."

Boyd cut him a grin. "I used to think ye were exaggerating when ye told me the castle perched like an eagle's eyrie upon the edge of a cliff, but now I see ye weren't."

Alasdair's smile widened. "Aye ... no fortress in Skye is as well-defended as Duntulm. All sides of the keep save one are bounded by the cliff-face."

Urging his horse into a brisk canter, Alasdair led the way across a hump-backed stone bridge. He ran a critical eye over the structure as he went, noting the crumbling sides on the western edge. He frowned. Things had been let go in Baltair's absence.

A stretch of tilled fields greeted him on the opposite side of the bridge, followed by a sprawl of cottages. A crowd of eager-faced men, women, and children gathered at the roadside to greet him.

"Alasdair!" An elderly man called out. "The MacDonald heir returns!"

Alasdair slowed his horse to a trot, his gaze sweeping across the villagers' faces. He saw tears on their cheeks and joy in their eyes. His throat constricted. He hadn't expected such a warm welcome. It was humbling to see the folk of Dunvegan had missed him. There had been times over the past months when he'd told himself no one would mourn him if he failed to return. He was glad to see he'd been wrong.

His mood dimmed then, like a shadow passing across the face of the sun.

Caitrin awaited in Duntulm Castle.

He didn't wish to have any contact with his sister-in-law—and yet a part of him, a glimmer of that lovestruck lad he'd once been, longed to see her.

Alasdair frowned, crushing the longing that curled, unbidden, up within him. Such instincts were weakness—they had to be quashed.

Crossing the village, he led the way up the hill toward the castle. Duntulm's high basalt curtain wall loomed before him, the MacDonald pennant fluttering in the sea-breeze. Unslinging his hunting horn, Alasdair raised it to his lips. The sound echoed over the hillside, reverberating off the stone fortress.

Alasdair MacDonald had just announced his arrival home.

Caitrin watched the horses' approach, and a sensation of sick, cold dread seeped over her.

Finally ... he's here.

She supposed that she should be relieved in a way—for the waiting was over at last—but the stone in the pit of her belly weighed her down.

The moment she'd been dreading, ever since the arrival of the letter, had come.

Caitrin picked up her skirts and left the solar. Halfway down the stairs to the bottom level of the keep, she met Sorcha.

"Milady," her hand-maid gasped, out of breath from her hurried climb. "They're here."

"I know," Caitrin replied curtly. "I'm on my way."

Sorcha stepped aside to let her pass, her blue eyes clouded with worry. She was the only one Caitrin had confided in about how she dreaded this moment. Alasdair MacDonald loomed like a specter, about to destroy her peace.

Caitrin continued down the stairwell and hurried out into the bailey to find the newly arrived party there.

A tall, dark-haired man dressed in chain-mail, fur, and leather, stood talking to Darron and Alban.

All three ceased their conversation and looked her way as she approached.

The captain and steward forgotten, Caitrin's gaze remained upon the newcomer.

She barely recognized him.

The Alasdair MacDonald she remembered was tall and lanky with a mop of dark hair and a sallow complexion. Baltair had been favored when it came to looks; his brother had seemed gawky and shy in comparison.

The man before her was lean but strong. Alasdair's shoulders seemed broader, the bony angles and gaunt face had filled out, and his hair had grown long. It now spilled over the shoulders of his fur cloak.

Caitrin's step faltered when his gaze met hers.

Eyes the color of peat—dark-brown, almost black—tracked her path. Predatory. More like Baltair and not like the playful lad who had once brought her a bouquet of meadow flowers.

His features though would never have Baltair's chiseled perfection. They were slightly sharp, hawkish.

He didn't smile as Caitrin approached. Didn't move.

Caitrin forced herself to keep moving, even if her instincts told her to turn and flee.

She kept walking until she was but three yards from him, and there she halted.

"Lady Caitrin." Darron acknowledged her with a respectful nod of his chin. He then stepped aside so that she could welcome the returning MacDonald heir. Alban did the same.

Caitrin swallowed, her mouth suddenly dry. His gaze was so intense that she felt stripped naked under it. She resisted the urge to reach up and check that her hair was tidy; in her rush downstairs she hadn't even thought to take note of her appearance.

Foolish woman, she chided herself. *Alasdair won't care what ye look like.*

It was true. The chill in his eyes spoke volumes. As she'd feared, he wasn't pleased to see her.

"My Lord Alasdair." She dipped into a curtsy and forced a bright smile. "Welcome home. It's good to see ye again. Did ye have a pleasant journey?"

It was cold outdoors, a grey, sunless late afternoon with a damp that made her bones ache—yet suddenly, Caitrin felt flustered. Heat flared in her cheeks, flaming hotter still when Alasdair MacDonald didn't answer.

Caitrin nervously wet her lips. "Milord?"

Alasdair smiled then, although there was still no warmth in his eyes. There was definitely a hard edge to him these days. Two and a half years had changed him. It was like looking into the eyes of a stranger.

"Good morning, Lady Caitrin." When Alasdair spoke, she finally recognized him. He'd always had a different voice to his brother: low and slightly gruff. "Ye are looking well."

Caitrin stared at him, once again resisting the urge to smooth her skirts and touch her hair. She felt unbalanced, strange.

And then Alasdair stepped aside and walked past her without another word. A lanky warrior with long red-gold hair, who'd been standing behind Alasdair, sauntered past her an instant later. The man favored Caitrin with a wink and a roguish grin before he followed Alasdair MacDonald into the keep.

Ye are looking well.

Alasdair ground his teeth together and forced himself not to run up the steps. The huge keep reared up before him.

Dolt. What had possessed him to say something so inane?

Better to say nothing at all than to put himself at a disadvantage with this woman.

Caitrin had always been able to do that—just one look from her and he used to get tongue-tied. It galled him to see that little had changed.

Alasdair walked through the keep's entrance hall and past the wide stone steps leading upstairs. Every nook, every stretch of stone here was as familiar to him as the back of his own hand. Alasdair had expected to be relieved to be home, for he'd missed Duntulm in his time away.

Yet he was distracted.

Even dressed in mourning black, her pale-blonde hair twisted up into a severe style, Caitrin was lovely. He'd been rooted to the spot as she walked toward him.

She'd changed since he'd seen her last. There was a grave dignity to her face, a seriousness in those sea-blue eyes that had been absent in the lass he'd so foolishly courted. Her figure was lusher—motherhood suited her. Baltair had sent word after Eoghan's birth—just a few lines: "I have a son, an heir." The letter hadn't reached Alasdair until after the battle, by which time Baltair was dead.

"Is something amiss?" Boyd asked, appearing at Alasdair's shoulder as he strode toward the doors of the Great Hall. "Ye look grim for a man who's just come home."

"Nothing's wrong." Alasdair cut him an irritated look. "I'm just weary."

Boyd favored him with a sly smile. "Ye never told me that yer brother's widow was so bonny."

"Is she?" Alasdair replied lightly. "I thought she looked like a crow garbed all in black."

Boyd snorted. "That's not what ye told her though, is it? Ye looked like someone had struck ye over the head with a mallet when she walked out into the bailey."

"Enough," Alasdair growled, losing patience. "I tire of yer flapping tongue."

Boyd merely grinned in response, knowing his point had been made.

Seated upon the dais, farther down the table from Alasdair MacDonald, Caitrin took a sip of wine. She barely tasted it, for nerves made her belly clench.

Around them, servants, led by cook and her assistant, Galiene, were bringing out supper: venison stew, oaten bread, and braised kale. A wall of noise surrounded Caitrin, reminding her why she preferred to take most of her meals in her solar.

She found it difficult to relax, to enjoy food, in this cavernous, noisy space.

Five of them sat at the chieftain's table this evening: Alasdair and the warrior with red-gold hair he'd introduced as his kinsman, Boyd MacDonald, along with Caitrin, Darron, and Alban.

Cook favored the chieftain with a wide smile as she placed a bowl of stew before him. "It's good to have ye home, milord," she greeted him. "I've made yer favorite supper."

Alasdair leaned back in his chair, returning her smile. "Thank ye, Briana. It's good to be back."

A few feet away, the steward, Alban, rose to his feet, holding a goblet of wine aloft. Around him, the hall went quiet. The excited chatter of voices settled as all gazes swiveled to the steward.

"Today we've been blessed," Alban announced, his low, gruff voice echoing across the hall. "Today, the MacDonald heir has returned to Duntulm … raise yer cups. Let us welcome him home."

A chorus of "aye" and "welcome home" followed, thundering high into the rafters. Men and women rose to their feet, raising their cups. Those at the table followed suit, Caitrin included.

Alasdair inclined his head, his smile widening. For a moment, Caitrin glimpsed true warmth in his eyes. He might not be pleased to see her, but he was relieved to be home.

The toast ended, and the folk of Duntulm returned to their meals. Eating slowly, Caitrin found herself sneaking glances at Alasdair. He sat in the chieftain's chair, one arm resting casually upon the carven armrest as he swirled the wine in a goblet. Unlike the other men at the table, who all ate heartily, he'd barely touched his stew. Instead, his gaze had turned unfocused, as if he was suddenly leagues from here.

"Milord?" The steward leaned forward, trying to catch the chieftain's attention. "Alasdair?"

The chieftain blinked, his gaze snapping back to the present. "Aye, Alban?"

"I trust ye had a good trip home?"

"Aye … the weather was against us … but that's what happens when ye travel in winter." Alasdair took a sip of wine, fixing Alban with a level look. "How have things been in Duntulm since my brother's death?"

"Quiet, milord," the older man replied with a smile.

"And the harvest … was it good?"

The steward nodded. "Aye, last summer was the warmest in years. Our stores will see us and the village safely through into spring." Alban glanced at Caitrin then. "Lady Caitrin oversaw the harvest … she worked tirelessly and made sure every last ear of barley was reaped."

Alasdair's mouth quirked, his attention shifting to Caitrin for the first time since he'd taken his seat at the table. "Is that so?"

"Aye," Alban replied. "Lady Caitrin has managed Duntulm admirably as chatelaine in yer absence."

"That's good to hear."

Caitrin tensed. Was it only her who could hear the mocking edge to Alasdair's voice? She still had difficulty accepting that this swarthy, sharp-featured man was actually Baltair's younger brother. He had a rakish, careless edge that warned her to be wary of him.

Glancing around the table, she saw that Alban and Darron looked unperturbed, while Boyd MacDonald wore a slightly bored expression. Maybe she was imagining things.

"I noticed on the way in that the Cleatburn Bridge is in a poor state, Alban." Alasdair turned his attention back to the steward. "Why is that?"

Alban's brow furrowed. "We had heavy rains in late autumn, milord. It did some damage."

Alasdair met the steward's eye, and Caitrin saw his jaw firm, his dark gaze glint. "Then, we need to repair it."

Chapter Four

Trouble Sleeping

AN ICY WIND gusted in from the northeast, tugging at Alasdair's fur mantle and stinging his exposed cheeks. He hadn't forgotten how cold the wind got up here, on Skye's exposed northern tip. It could cut to the bone. Around him the last of the light was draining from the western sky, deepening the chill. He'd come straight here after supper, even though night had almost fallen.

Pulling up the collar of his mantle, Alasdair stepped forward, his gaze settling upon the headstone in the center of the windswept kirkyard.

All that remained of his elder brother.

Alasdair studied the grave. In the fading light, he could barely make out Baltair's name etched there. The stone had only been in the ground nearly eight moons, and already moss was starting to creep up its sides. After all that had happened, it felt as if his brother had been dead years, not months.

It had taken a while for news of Baltair's death to reach him on the mainland. Alasdair had been in Inbhir Nis when it arrived. He'd felt numb as he'd read the words sent from Malcolm MacLeod. Baltair had fallen in a skirmish against Clan-chief MacLeod's foes, the Frasers of Skye.

Once the shock faded, grief had surfaced. However, it was a sensation mixed with guilt. After his elder brother wed Caitrin, Alasdair had bitterly resented him. Everything fell into Baltair's arms. He'd been good-looking and charismatic—and he ruled northern Skye. Caitrin hadn't been the only woman upon the isle who'd wanted to wed him.

Alasdair's mouth thinned. Women were so predictable. They didn't see past the veneer. Unlike them, he wasn't blind to his brother's faults. Baltair could be insufferably arrogant and had a cruel edge that Alasdair, two years his junior, had often borne the brunt of when they'd been bairns.

But still, he was his brother. The only kin he'd had left.

Alasdair stood there for a while, letting the dark curtain of night settle over the world. He was alone in the kirkyard save a pair of ravens perched on a nearby gravestone. They watched him with cold beady eyes.

He ignored the birds, pulling his cloak tighter as a particularly hefty gust of wind ripped across the hillside.

It was time to go. He'd expected to feel something other than an odd emptiness upon visiting his brother's grave. But he shouldn't have been surprised really, for he wasn't himself these days.

Alasdair sighed, his breath steaming before him in the gelid air, turned from the grave, and strode out of the kirkyard.

At the entrance he found Boyd waiting for him.

His friend had accompanied him here but had then hung back while Alasdair visited his brother's grave.

Boyd nodded as Alasdair approached before falling into step with him. For once, his cousin didn't rib him or offer a flippant comment; something Alasdair felt grateful for. Wordlessly, the two men made their way through the village, down an unpaved street flanked with low stone cottages. The aroma of roasting fowl wafted out from one of the homes, and within another, a woman started singing.

"It's a nice place this," Boyd commented, breaking the silence. "I can see why ye were keen to come home."

Alasdair cast him a sidelong look. "Ye will stay on then?"

Boyd wasn't a close relative, but they'd struck up a friendship over the past few months. Boyd hadn't seemed in a hurry to return to Glencoe after the war, and so Alasdair had invited him back to Duntulm.

Boyd grinned. "Aye, if ye will let me."

"Ye can remain under my roof ... as long as ye earn yer keep."

Boyd rolled his eyes. "Ye are going to put me to work?"

"Aye ... the Duntulm Guard is looking a bit sparse. Talk to Captain MacNichol in the morning, and he'll get ye kitted out."

The two men left the village and took the path that wound up the hill toward the keep. Fires burned upon the walls, staining the pitted rock a deep gold.

"It's good to be here," Boyd said finally, his voice uncharacteristically serious. "Ye could almost think that disaster at Durham never happened ... that the English didn't whip our arses."

Alasdair stifled a wince. "Aye, but they did," he murmured.

Alasdair walked into the chieftain's solar and paused. Burning sconces threw long shadows across the stone walls, welcoming him, and yet he felt like he didn't belong here. It didn't feel right standing in the solar without either his father or brother present.

Shaking his head to rid himself of the sensation, Alasdair pushed the door shut behind him. This solar, and the adjoining bed-chamber, were now his. He'd get used to his new quarters soon enough.

A warm, masculine space surrounded him. Deerskin rugs covered a paved floor, and heavy tapestries depicting scenes of war hung from the walls. A great stag's head sat mounted above a huge hearth, where a lump of peat glowed, throwing out a considerable amount of heat. The stag had been his father's prize. Eoghan MacDonald had been a keen hunter, but, in the end, it was a stag hunt that claimed his life.

Crossing to the large oaken table that dominated the solar, Alasdair poured himself a goblet of wine. He took a sip, the flavor of rich spicy plum sliding down his throat and warming the pit of his belly. He still couldn't stomach the idea of ale, not after the excesses of the night before, but he enjoyed the wine. It took the edge off the tension that had plagued him all day.

This hadn't been an easy homecoming. Baltair was gone, and the woman Alasdair had once ached for was now chatelaine of Duntulm. Despite that he'd thought long and hard about how to deal with her, Caitrin's presence unsettled him.

He hadn't seen her since supper. When he returned from the kirkyard, she'd already retired for the evening. That was good, for even the sight of Caitrin made it difficult to concentrate. Boyd, the shrewd bastard, hadn't missed his reaction to her—which meant Caitrin had probably noticed it too.

Alasdair muttered a curse and downed the rest of his wine in a long gulp.

He needed to harden his heart, to cool his nerves and remind himself that he couldn't stand the woman now.

He had her exactly where he wanted her. Her position as chatelaine was vulnerable. One word from him and she'd have to pack her bags and return to Dunvegan, and her overbearing father. Alasdair remembered Malcolm MacLeod well, and he'd also noted the way Caitrin had stiffened when he'd questioned Alban at supper rather than her. She was proud of her role here. She wanted to stay.

He knew exactly where to start his campaign against her.

Setting the goblet down, Alasdair wandered through into his bed-chamber. Another, smaller, hearth burned there too. A huge four-poster bed dominated the room. Alasdair eyed it warily as he started to undress.

Baltair and Caitrin shared that bed.

The thought made him clench his jaw, a surge of vindictive fury rushing through his veins. The sensation galvanized him. He needed to keep reminding himself of what Caitrin had done to him, of what she'd taken from him.

Mist surrounded Alasdair, closing in on him. He stood ankle-deep in mud, his claidheamh mor impossibly heavy in his hand. Nearby, a man was screaming for mercy. Raw sobs followed, and then the dull, wet sounds of death being dealt.

Alasdair tried to rush to his countryman's side, his sword swinging. And yet he couldn't move. His legs and arms were paralyzed.

Terror pulsed through him. His heart felt as if it would leap from his chest, it was beating so hard.

Figures emerged from the mist. They were coming for him—but he couldn't fight back.

Alasdair sucked in a deep, ragged breath, his eyes flying open.

The mist receded, as did the cries of the dying. He was back in his own bed, in his bed-chamber lit by the fading glow of the hearth.

Chest heaving, Alasdair pushed himself up into a sitting position. It wasn't warm in the chamber, yet he dripped with sweat.

He dragged a shaking hand through his hair and forced himself to take deep, steadying breaths.

Satan's cods. He was sick of these nightmares. They plagued him. Ever since the battle, he'd had trouble sleeping, and whenever he did manage to fall into a deep slumber, his mind transported him back to the battlefield and that cool, misty October morning.

When the whole world had gone to hell.

Caitrin observed Alasdair over the rim of her mug of goat's milk.

He was pale, his eyes hollowed with fatigue.

"Milord," she spoke up, drawing his attention. "Are ye unwell?"

He cast her a look of thinly-veiled irritation. "No."

"It's just ..." Caitrin broke off here, aware that Boyd had glanced up from smearing honey over a wedge of bannock. Likewise, Alban and Darron both looked her way. "... ye look a bit peaky this morning."

"Maybe last night's supper didn't agree with him," Boyd quipped with a wink at Caitrin.

"The supper was fine," Alasdair growled, pouring himself a cup of milk from a pitcher in the center of the table. "I'm just tired."

"Ye have trouble sleeping?" Caitrin knew she shouldn't pry, for Alasdair was now viewing her with a jaundiced eye. Yet she'd fallen into the habit of helping those around her since becoming chatelaine—and she wanted to prove herself useful now.

"Aye ... sometimes," Alasdair replied, his gaze cautious.

"I can ask a servant to brew ye a drink with valerian root before bed," she suggested. "It helps with sleep."

Alasdair nodded, although his frown made it clear he wished her to drop the subject. Caitrin lowered her gaze to the buttered slice of bannock before her. Anxiety churned in her belly as she resumed eating. She'd awoken just before dawn, resolved to prove her worth to Alasdair MacDonald, but instead had succeeded only in annoying him.

"Who has been managing the accounts in my absence?" the chieftain broke the heavy silence that had settled over the table.

Caitrin glanced up to see that Alasdair was looking in Alban's direction. Irritation rose within her, dousing the nerves. Just like the evening before, he was deliberately favoring the steward, as if she had no responsibilities here.

Caitrin cleared her throat. "I have been ... although Alban often sits with me to ensure I have the numbers correct."

Alasdair's peat-dark eyes swiveled back to her, his mouth curving. It was his first smile since he'd sat down at the table, and it softened his face considerably. "Of course ... I'd forgotten that ye know yer letters."

Caitrin pursed her lips. "Aye, ye once teased me for it ... said that lasses were no good at such things."

Surprise flared on his face. Did he think she'd forgotten?

She and Alasdair were almost the same age—born in the same year just a month apart. Before that fateful day in Dunvegan's garden, when she'd rejected him, they'd been friends since childhood. Years earlier, when they were both around nine winters old, she'd told Alasdair that a nun from Kilbride Abbey was teaching Caitrin and her sisters to read and write. Alasdair had roared with laughter.

"Aye ... I did." Alasdair watched her for a long moment, his gaze pinning her to the spot. "Shall we see if I was right?"

Caitrin frowned. *Ye weren't.* The words boiled up inside her, but she choked them back. He was deliberately provoking her.

Alasdair smiled. "Meet me in my solar mid-morning," he said smoothly, "and we shall go over the accounts together." He paused here and reached for the last wedge of bannock on the tray before him. "Bring my nephew with ye ... I want to meet Eoghan."

Chapter Five

Taken Seriously

CAITRIN OPENED THE ledger and tried to ignore the
man who'd just pulled up a seat next to her.

Alasdair was sitting too close—it unnerved her. She
was keenly aware of the heat of his body and the scent of
his skin mixed with that of leather. In the past, his
presence hadn't affected her like this. She didn't
understand why it did now.

It was the last thing she needed.

They weren't alone in the solar. Alban wasn't present,
but Boyd had joined them instead. Dressed in the leather
armor of the Duntulm Guard, the warrior leaned against
the window sill, cup of ale in hand. Despite that it was a
chill day outdoors, Alasdair had opened the shutters to
the small window looking south. However, a few feet
away, a fire burned vigorously in the hearth. The warmth
enveloped Caitrin in a soft blanket, although it didn't
take the edge off her nerves.

She'd never liked the chieftain's solar, and after
Baltair's death had rarely set foot inside it, preferring to
keep to her own quarters instead. This chamber, with its
masculine aggression, reminded her of her husband.

They weren't pleasant memories.

Caitrin cast Alasdair a quick glance and found him watching her, a lazy smile curving his lips.

She wished he wouldn't look at her like that.

"What would ye like to see first?" she asked, all business.

"I'd like to see my nephew," he replied. "Where is he?"

"He'll be here shortly … my hand-maid has just gone to fetch him." Caitrin drew in a deep breath in an attempt to calm her rapidly beating heart. She didn't like that both men were now watching her. Why did Boyd have to be here at all? "In the meantime, let's get started."

"Very well," Alasdair drawled. "Turn to last year's expenses."

Caitrin reached out and leafed back through the pages, smoothing them open at the year's beginning. She then pushed the ledger toward Alasdair so that he wouldn't need to move any closer to her to read it.

She watched his hawkish profile as he leaned forward, his gaze tracking down the page. After a moment he paused. "Ye bought a lot of grain from MacLeod last autumn … oats especially. Why?"

"We didn't have a large harvest of oats," Caitrin replied without hesitation before she met Alasdair's eye. "Baltair had decided to use the lower fields for kale and cabbage instead."

Alasdair raised an eyebrow before shifting his attention back to the ledger. Caitrin watched him continue to read, although with each passing moment she could feel her spine growing more rigid. She hadn't missed the challenge in his voice.

"Ye have made a mistake here," he said after a pause, his finger tracing down one column to the sum at the bottom. "Twelve, eight, thirty-five, and twenty … does not equal seventy-eight."

"It's seventy-five," Boyd piped up with a laugh.

Caitrin's cheeks flamed. Alban had helped her do the calculations. Any errors belonged to them both. However, she wouldn't mention him here—it would only make her look as if she was making excuses for herself. Fury coiled up within her when she saw Alasdair flash Boyd a conspirator's grin. "Aye."

"It was an honest mistake," Caitrin said stiffly, forcing down her ire, "and one that I shall correct."

"See that ye do," Alasdair replied.

A knock at the door interrupted them, bringing Caitrin a reprieve.

"Enter," Alasdair called out, and an instant later Sorcha appeared, carrying Eoghan in her arms. The bairn was awake, clutching to Sorcha, his eyes wide as he surveyed the two strangers in the room.

Next to her, Caitrin sensed Alasdair grow still. She glanced his way to see that his gaze had fixed upon the lad. Eoghan stared back, equally fascinated.

"God's bones," Alasdair murmured. "He looks the image of Baltair."

Caitrin grew even tenser at this comment. She knew it to be the truth, yet hated that Eoghan's similarity to his father was the first thing folk noted when they set eyes on the lad.

"That's not surprising," she replied.

Alasdair cut her a glance, gaze widening at the sharpness of her tone. "Doesn't that please ye?" he asked, his dark brows knitting together. "At least ye have something to remember my brother by."

Caitrin didn't reply. She didn't trust herself to. However, she saw a shadow move in Alasdair MacDonald's eyes and realized that he'd drawn his own conclusions. "The grieving widow, eh?" he murmured.

Caitrin swallowed, dropping her gaze. She'd not engage him on this subject, not now with Boyd and Sorcha present. If he wanted to know about the state of her marriage to Baltair, he could show her some respect by bringing it up in private.

"Would ye like to hold the lad, milord?" Sorcha asked, favoring Alasdair with a warm smile.

Caitrin bit back the urge to say he wouldn't. Her hands clenched on her lap, her fingernails biting into her palms. Yet Alasdair pushed back his chair and rose to his feet. "Very well. Give the lad here."

"He's not used to strangers," Caitrin said tightly. Her body coiled as Sorcha handed Eoghan to Alasdair. Any moment now, Eoghan would start wailing.

"Aye ... but I'm kin," Alasdair replied, not bothering to glance her way.

Swaddled in lambswool, Eoghan stared up at his uncle, chubby fingers reaching forward to explore his leather vest. To Caitrin's surprise, the lad's face didn't crumple. Instead, he favored Alasdair with a beautiful, wide smile.

And in response, Alasdair MacDonald's own face transformed. For a few instants, he wore a soft expression, his dark eyes glowing with tenderness. "It's good to meet ye, Eoghan," he murmured. "Ye never met yer grandsire, but it's a fine name ye have inherited."

"The lad's taken a shine to ye, Alasdair," Boyd noted, grinning.

Alasdair snorted, never taking his gaze off the bairn. "Blood is blood ... the lad knows it too."

"I've never seen Master Eoghan so fascinated with someone, milord," Sorcha said. "Maybe he does sense ye are his uncle."

Alasdair smiled. "Aye ... I'm the closest thing ye have to a father now, wee Eoghan." He tickled the lad under the chin, and the bairn gave a gurgling laugh. "And one day ye will inherit all of this."

Caitrin drew in a deep breath, attempting to quell her irritation and failing. "I'm sure ye will have bairns of yer own, milord," she said, unable to hold her tongue any longer. "Ye won't need Eoghan to carry on the MacDonald line."

Alasdair tore his gaze from his nephew then, his attention fixing upon her. "I don't intend to wed," he said, his voice hardening, "and I won't be siring any bairns. Eoghan is the sole MacDonald heir."

A chill feathered down Caitrin's spine. Why wasn't he planning to take a wife? The proprietary edge to Alasdair's voice made her uneasy.

He handed Eoghan back to Sorcha. Meanwhile, Boyd caught the handmaid's eye and smiled. "We haven't been introduced ... Boyd MacDonald of Glencoe at yer service."

"My name is Sorcha MacQueen," she replied with a shy smile.

"Of the MacQueens of Skye?"

The girl's smile faltered. "Aye ... Chieftain MacQueen is my father."

Boyd inclined his head, his own smile widening "Pleased to make yer acquaintance, lass." His gaze held hers. "Since I'm new to Duntulm ... ye might want to give me a tour of the keep later."

"Captain MacNichol can do that," Caitrin cut in, her voice sharp.

Boyd shrugged, his gaze never leaving the hand-maid. "I'd prefer a prettier guide, milady."

"Thank ye, Sorcha," Alasdair cut in, drumming his fingers on the tabletop. His voice was edged with impatience. "Ye can take Eoghan back to his quarters now. We have work to do."

Sorcha nodded, dropped into a curtsy, and quit the solar. Caitrin noted that her hand-maid now wore a flustered expression, her cheeks pink. After her departure, Alasdair returned to the table and took his seat next to Caitrin once more.

Caitrin met his eye and, seeing the challenge there, tensed. This meeting thus far hadn't been pleasant—and she wagered the mood wasn't about to improve.

Alasdair favored her with a wintry smile. "Shall we return to the accounts?"

"Arrogant cur. He missed no opportunity to make me look small!" Caitrin knuckled away a tear that trickled down her cheek. The stress of the last two days was starting to take its toll.

Sorcha's blue eyes widened. "Milady," she gasped. "I'm sure the chieftain meant no offense."

"Oh, he did."

Caitrin snatched up the woolen tunic she'd been knitting for Eoghan and viciously started to unravel her last session's work. There were imperfections in the knit, a few small holes that annoyed her. She took vindictive pleasure in undoing her hours of labor. *Good*—she preferred anger to tears.

"He went through those accounts, line by line, and picked on the slightest things." She paused in her unraveling and fixed her hand-maid with a look of fury. "He even questioned the amount of produce we've set aside to pay this year's cáin."

Sorcha's brow furrowed, setting down the embroidery she'd just started. "Isn't it enough?"

"Of course it is," Caitrin huffed. "I'm a clan-chief's daughter ... I know exactly how much yearly tribute the king requires of his vassals. The cáin is sufficient."

"But the chieftain doesn't think so?" Sorcha appeared genuinely concerned. Caitrin clenched her jaw. She knew that her handmaid's loyalty would always go first to her master, but even so, it grated upon Caitrin.

A woman was never taken seriously in a man's world, even by other women.

"It doesn't matter what he thinks," Caitrin muttered. Yet as she said those words, a weight settled in the pit of her belly. Unfortunately, Alasdair MacDonald's opinion did matter—and she needed to try harder if she wanted to stay on as chatelaine.

Chapter Six

Too Far

CAITRIN FROWNED, PEERING into the bubbling cauldron of sulfurous, over-cooked vegetables. "I thought we already planned out all the meals for the week?"

"Aye, milady ... we did."

Caitrin glanced over her shoulder, at where cook and her two assistants were busy kneading bread dough on the large table that dominated the kitchen. "Pottage wasn't on the list."

Cook gave her a wary look. "No, but I decided we should have it for today's noon meal. We had old vegetables that needed using up."

Caitrin inhaled deeply. She wasn't in the mood for this. Tired and on edge, Caitrin had gotten up well before dawn over the past week to redouble her efforts as chatelaine. She didn't want to give Alasdair MacDonald any excuse to criticize her.

But now, Briana wanted to cross swords with her—again.

After their last confrontation, she'd thought she and cook had reached an understanding: they made a plan of the week's noon meals and suppers, and then cook followed it. But, clearly, Briana wasn't ready to do as she was told.

"Ye need to start heeding me, Briana," she said finally, careful to keep her tone low, even though she was inwardly seething. "I don't plan the keep's meals with ye because I have nothing better to do with my time. I've made an inventory of the stores and know exactly what needs using up and what doesn't. Those vegetables would have easily kept another few days."

Cook stared back at Caitrin, a mutinous expression settling upon her face. An older woman named Galiene, and a red-headed lass who worked alongside Briana, now exchanged nervous glances. Cook then drew herself up, holding Caitrin's eye boldly. "Ye don't have to plan the meals with me anymore, milady."

Caitrin's gaze narrowed. "Excuse me?"

"I don't need yer help."

Anger curled up like wreathing smoke within Caitrin. Her patience was nearing its limits now. "I care not what ye think ye need," she growled. "As chatelaine, the running of the household is my responsibility ... and that includes this kitchen. Ye take orders from me."

"No, I don't." Cook blurted, the words tumbling out of her now she'd worked up the courage. "The chieftain rules here, milady ... and he says I can prepare whatever meals I choose."

Caitrin went still. "Ye have spoken to Alasdair about this?"

Cook pursed her lips before nodding. "Aye, and he agrees that ye have no need to meddle in my affairs." The victorious gleam in cook's eyes made Caitrin want to slap her face.

Wordlessly, for rage had momentarily rendered her speechless, Caitrin walked to the kitchen door, aware of the three pairs of eyes tracking her path. At the threshold, she halted, swiveled around, and pinned cook under a hard stare. "We'll see about that."

How dare he?

Caitrin stormed across the bailey toward the archway leading out of the castle. It was a chill windy day outdoors, but she was so incensed that she hadn't even gone back inside to fetch her cloak. Instead, she marched over the drawbridge and down the hill toward the village, ignoring the cold that bit into her flesh through her kirtle and léine.

She knew where to find Alasdair MacDonald. He and a group of men had spent the last day beginning work on shoring up the Cleatburn Bridge.

Reaching the bottom of the hill, she strode through the village, attracting curious looks from folk she passed. It was an odd thing to see the Lady of Duntulm out on such a chill day without a winter mantle—or an escort. Darron usually shadowed her whenever she left the keep.

Caitrin, who often liked to wave and stop to chat with the villagers, ignored them this morning. She was too upset to focus on anyone right now—other than the man who'd taken vindictive pleasure in thwarting her ever since his return.

The bridge loomed up ahead, and Caitrin spied the outlines of men working on it. She recognized Darron first, for his pale-blond hair gleamed even in the winter's dull light. He'd just picked up a stone from the back of a wagon, and was about to turn and carry it into the waters of the Cleatburn, when he spied Caitrin approach.

Darron's brow furrowed. "Good morn, Lady Caitrin." His gaze shifted behind her, his eyes narrowing when he realized she was alone. "Ye should have asked one of the guards to escort ye down here."

Irritation surged within Caitrin. She didn't need MacNichol or one of his men following her about.

"Morning, Captain MacNichol," she replied curtly, deliberately ignoring his comment. "Where is the chieftain?"

Darron's frown deepened. "Is something amiss, milady?"

"Just answer me, please."

Darron jerked his head to the left, indicating that the man she wanted was behind him. He then stepped to one side.

Caitrin's gaze shifted to the water, to where Alasdair and Boyd worked, clearing debris from around the bridge's stacked-stone pillars. Both men were shirtless, their braies sodden. Mud splattered their torsos and arms as they wielded heavy shovels.

Without realizing she was doing so, Caitrin found herself inspecting Alasdair's half-naked body. He was lean and strong, the light dusting of hair across his muscular chest tapering down to a hard, flat stomach. Even through her fury, she acknowledged that he was an attractive, virile sight.

Angrily, she shoved the thought aside.

Sensing the weight of her stare, Alasdair looked up, and their gazes fused. An instant later, he smiled. "Lady Caitrin. Have ye come down to oversee the repairs?"

Boyd laughed at this. "Keeping an eye on ye, is she?"

Caitrin clenched her hands by her sides. Their mockery hardened her temper into something dangerous. "I've come from the kitchen." She bit out the words, aware that the surrounding men had all stopped work and were watching her. She didn't care. Let them gawk. "It appears ye have told cook that I have no right to oversee the meals that are prepared for the keep?"

Alasdair's mouth curved. "Aye, and what of it? Briana's been around since my father was a lad. She doesn't take kindly to having another woman oversee her."

"We were getting along fine before ye returned home ... milord."

"Really?" He gave her an arch look. "That's not what she said."

"We'd made a truce," Caitrin snarled. "Briana's a fine cook but manages the supplies poorly. She'd have the keep eating boiled turnip and stale bannocks while she let fresh meat rot in the stores."

This comment brought a scattering of laughter from the surrounding men. Even Darron raised a smile. They all knew it was the truth. Cook was stingy with supplies, as if she'd paid for them out of her own purse.

"My father and Baltair never found fault with her," Alasdair replied. His tone was mild although his gaze had hardened. "Maybe ye are too overbearing."

Overbearing.

Caitrin drew in a shuddering breath. "I'm merely doing my duty as chatelaine," she finally managed, her voice trembling with the force of the rage that caused a red mist to cloud her vision. "Why don't ye let me?"

A heavy silence settled, broken only by the gurgle and chatter of water running over stones and the whistle of the wind. However, Caitrin barely heard those noises, for she could discern little over the thundering of her pulse in her ears. She was so angry that she felt sick.

Alasdair watched her for a long moment before pushing strands of hair from his face with his forearm. "Go back to the keep, Caitrin," he said, his voice low and firm. "We'll discuss this later."

Caitrin swallowed hard. "No, I—"

"Didn't my brother teach ye any manners?" he growled. "Go back ... *now.*"

They stared at each other, before fear flickered up within Caitrin, penetrating the anger that had shielded her till now. The mention of his brother turned her blood cold. Baltair wouldn't have stood for such defiance. He'd have waded out of the burn and backhanded her across the face for arguing with him.

Tears of frustration and rage blurred Caitrin's vision. She wondered then how she'd ever once called Alasdair MacDonald a friend. The past years had altered him, turned him callous and cruel.

He'd been wanting to anger her, and in coming down to the bridge, she'd played straight into his hands. She knew though that continuing to rage at him out here would only end badly for her.

Swallowing a sob, Caitrin spun on her heel, picked up her skirts, and fled.

Alasdair watched Caitrin's eyes glisten, her jaw tighten, and wondered if she'd obey him. To his surprise, his breathing quickened. He almost wished she wouldn't. It would give him the excuse to throw her over his shoulder and carry her back up to the keep—an excuse to touch her.

She was beautiful this morning, her sea-blue eyes gleaming with ire, her supple body encased in flowing black. He itched to feel her softness against him.

But a heartbeat later, she turned and hurried away. He could see, from the stiffness of her posture and her uneven gait, that she was upset. Her long blonde hair, braided in a long plait down her back, bounced between her shoulder blades as she walked.

Watching her go, a sensation of loss washed over Alasdair.

He'd enjoyed that altercation—far more than he should have.

"That's quite a temper the lass has on her," Boyd observed.

Alasdair snorted. "Aye ... I'm surprised Baltair didn't whip her for her adder's tongue."

Silence followed this comment.

Alasdair glanced around him to see that only Boyd was grinning. Most of the surrounding men wore hard expressions, while one or two looked horrified. Darron MacNichol was actually glowering at him.

Alasdair went still. Those words had only been said in jest—but he'd misread his audience it seemed.

After a hard morning's work, the men made their way back up to the keep for the noon meal. Captain MacNichol fell in step with Alasdair as they walked up the hill.

Glancing across at him, Alasdair saw that the captain was watching him, his expression shuttered.

Alasdair frowned. "What is it, MacNichol?"

Darron's own gaze narrowed. "Ye should know that Lady Caitrin would never to have spoken to Baltair like that," he said quietly.

"Really?" Alasdair didn't bother to temper the scorn in his voice.

"Aye ... she was afraid of yer brother."

A pause followed. "Did he beat her?"

"If he did, it was behind closed doors."

"But it wasn't a happy union?"

Darron pursed his mouth.

"Answer me, MacNichol."

"They didn't speak much, milord ... it seemed to me that Baltair ignored Lady Caitrin for the most part."

Alasdair digested this news. It didn't overly surprise him. Baltair had never had much use for women beyond swiving them.

Loosing a sigh, Alasdair cast a glance up at where the castle loomed before them. He'd enjoyed putting Caitrin in her place, humiliating her in front of his men, but an uneasiness had settled over him in the aftermath.

Vengeance didn't taste as sweet as he'd expected. He felt strangely empty, disappointed.

Maybe he'd taken things too far.

Chapter Seven

Taking Instruction

ALASDAIR SWALLOWED A mouthful of pottage and stifled a grimace. It was awful: overcooked with a faintly acrid taste as if the bottom of the pot had burned. Alasdair frowned. How was this possible? Cook usually served up delicious meals.

Next to him Boyd also tasted the pottage, his face screwing up. Mumbling a curse, he reached for his goblet of wine to wash it down. "Foul," he muttered. Likewise, the others at the table looked similarly unimpressed with the fare before them.

"I thought cook agreed not to serve up this slop anymore," Alban grumbled. The steward cast Caitrin a questioning look, but she didn't meet his eye. Instead, the chatelaine appeared fascinated with the piece of bread she was buttering.

Caitrin hadn't made eye contact with any of them since taking a seat at the table for the noon meal.

"Lady Caitrin?" Alban, who hadn't been down at the bridge earlier that morning, spoke up once more. "Didn't ye have a word with cook?"

Caitrin did glance up then. "Aye," she replied, her tone clipped, "but it appears I'm to have no say in what meals are prepared in future." Her attention shifted to where Boyd was looking down at his bowl with a look of disgust. "I hope ye like pottage ... because Briana likes to serve it at least four times a week."

Boyd's gaze snapped up, his mouth thinning.

Watching Caitrin, Alasdair noted that her expression was shuttered. He let out a long exhale and pushed his bowl away, reaching instead for some bread. "I don't remember Briana's cooking being this bad," he said mildly. He then pulled a wheel of cheese toward him and cut off a large wedge.

"She's not usually," Darron replied. "Except for when she makes pottage. It's the dish she cooks when she wants to use up old vegetables and grain."

Caitrin glanced Darron's way, gaze narrowed, yet didn't reply.

"Maybe ye should let Lady Caitrin plan the meals, milord?" Alban ventured, frowning. "She knows how to utilize the stores. Cook needs a firm hand."

Irritation flared within Alasdair. He didn't appreciate the steward speaking up on Caitrin's behalf. Of course, the man had no idea what had happened earlier. Alban had served both Alasdair's brother and father. He was a good, solid man who'd always been staunchly loyal to the family he served. Yet it appeared he was also protective of Caitrin.

"Briana knows what she's doing," he growled.

Boyd snorted. "Really?"

Alasdair ignored him, his attention shifting to Caitrin. This time she met his eye. "I shall talk to cook," he said.

Caitrin's mouth thinned. She gave a barely perceptible nod before dropping her gaze.

The noon meal continued, the atmosphere strained. Around them, the rumble of voices in the Great Hall rose and fell along with the clunk of tankards and the clatter of wooden spoons. Servants circled with pots of pottage, offering a second serving.

Alasdair noted that no one partook.

The vegetable stew was barely edible. Cook had chosen a fine time to disgrace herself, especially just after his confrontation with Caitrin.

Alasdair glanced the chatelaine's way once more. At least she wasn't smirking over being proved right. He remembered that Caitrin had never been that kind of lass. Years earlier, when they'd been friends, she'd beaten him once or twice at the board game 'Ard-ri'. His young ego had taken a battering, but she'd been a graceful victor. It was after one such game that he'd realized he was in love with her. It had been a rainy spring afternoon, and they'd been seated near the hearth in her father's Great Hall. He'd visited Dunvegan with his father. Caitrin had taken his king before glancing up at him, a smile of disbelief stretching her face.

The impact of that moment had been like a punch to the guts. Alasdair had been unable to breathe. She'd won more than just a game of Ard-ri that day—she'd won his heart.

Alasdair tore his gaze from Caitrin and took a bite of bread and cheese. What a gullible idiot he'd been.

A short while later, the noon meal ended. Men and women rose to their feet and began filing from the hall, returning to their chores.

"Back to the bridge, milord?" Darron MacNichol asked, getting up.

"Aye," Alasdair replied. "I want to make sure the pillars are shored up by nightfall."

Boyd pulled a face, but Darron slapped him heartily on the back. "Come on, MacDonald. Not afraid of hard graft, are ye?"

Muttering under his breath, Boyd cast Darron a jaundiced look. The men moved off, and Caitrin rose to her feet. She was about to turn from the table when Alasdair spoke.

"Lady Caitrin ... wait a moment."

She paused, although her body had gone rigid. He watched a nerve feather in her cheek; she was uncomfortable in his presence.

"Join me for supper in my solar this eve," he murmured. "I think it's time we spoke privately."

Caitrin's gaze flicked up, her sea-blue eyes alarmed. Her throat bobbed. "My lord," she began, her voice low and hesitant. "I don't think that's necessary."

A lazy smile stretched Alasdair's mouth. "On the contrary, it is," he replied. "If ye are to stay on as chatelaine at Duntulm, ye and I must talk."

Their gazes fused for a long moment, and then, reluctantly, she nodded.

Caitrin stopped before the door to the chieftain's solar and drew in a sharp breath. She'd been dreading this meeting all afternoon. Unable to concentrate on her chores, she'd been unusually snappish with the servants. Even Eoghan's company hadn't relaxed her.

She wished there could be some way to avoid this supper. But there wasn't.

Alasdair MacDonald had been insistent.

Releasing the breath she was holding, Caitrin raised her clenched fist and knocked.

"Enter." Alasdair's voice greeted her.

Tensing her jaw, Caitrin pushed open the door and stepped inside the solar.

Alasdair stood before the fire warming his back. "Good evening, Lady Caitrin," he greeted her with a smile. "Shut the door ... ye are letting a draft in."

Caitrin did as bid, pulling the door closed behind her.

They were now completely alone—for the first time since his arrival at Duntulm.

For the first time since he proposed to her on that balmy summer's day.

Caitrin clenched her jaw. She didn't want to be in this man's presence. Ever since he'd gotten back, he'd taken pains to torment her. He might be smiling at her now, but she didn't trust him. She'd seen the glint in his eyes as he'd humiliated her earlier that day.

And she wasn't about to forgive him for it.

"Don't look so worried, Caitrin," Alasdair said, raising an eyebrow. "I'd just like a word." He motioned to the huge oaken table that dominated the center of the solar, where two places had been set. "Take a seat. The servants will bring the food up shortly."

Caitrin turned, moving woodenly to the table. The sight of it reminded her of how unpleasant he'd been when they'd gone over the accounts together. She wasn't about to forgive him for that either.

Anger coiled within her, overcoming her nervousness. It occurred to her then that she wasn't afraid of Alasdair, not like she had been of Baltair. The few times she'd stood up for herself with her husband, he'd been brutal with her. She'd never have spoken to him as she had to Alasdair today.

But she wasn't going to apologize for it.

Caitrin sat down at the table, and a moment later Alasdair joined her, lowering himself into a seat opposite. He was watching her, an intent expression on his face.

"Ye are annoyed," he noted.

Caitrin started. "No, milord," she said quickly. "I—"

"Yer eyes turn dark blue when ye are riled," he cut her off. "I remember that from when we were bairns."

Caitrin dropped her gaze to the polished wood surface before her. His comment made her feel uncomfortable, exposed.

"Would ye like a cup of wine?" he asked, a smile in his voice.

Caitrin nodded. She glanced up to see Alasdair pour two goblets of bramble wine. He handed one to her.

Their fingers accidentally brushed when she took the goblet, and a shiver went up Caitrin's arm. Unnerved by the reaction, she pulled her hand back and sloshed wine on the table.

"Sorry," she gasped. She went to rise, "I'll find something to wipe that up."

"Please, sit down." Alasdair waved her away. "The servants can clean it when they bring the food."

At that moment there came a knock at the door. "Supper, milord?"

"Bring it in," Alasdair called back.

Fingers still tingling, Caitrin glanced up at the chieftain's face. His smile had gone. His brown eyes were now hooded.

Three servants, led by Galiene, entered the solar. They carried trays of food: a tureen of what smelled like pork and bean soup, fresh bread, and an array of aged cheeses.

Caitrin felt queasy at the sight of it. She hadn't eaten much at the noon meal—for that pottage had been virtually inedible—yet Alasdair's presence robbed her of appetite.

The pair of them sat in silence while the servants placed the platters on the table. Galiene spotted the spilled wine, whipped a cloth from her apron, and mopped it up. She then turned to Alasdair, favoring him with a smile.

"Will ye be needing anything else, milord?"

Alasdair met Galiene's eye, his mouth curving. Galiene, who was nearing her fiftieth winter, had lived at Duntulm all her life. Caitrin sensed the affection between them. "No, that will be all, Galiene … thank ye."

The servants departed, and Alasdair leaned forward, ladling the thick soup into two bowls. He handed one to Caitrin, and she noted he made sure to keep his fingers far from hers.

Caitrin helped herself to some bread and ripped a piece off it. Despite that she wasn't hungry, eating would keep her busy, give her something to focus on.

Silence stretched between them.

Caitrin feigned a deep fascination for her supper, which she forced down with gulps of strong bramble wine.

She was cutting herself a piece of cheese when Alasdair spoke.

"I've spoken to cook … she will take instruction from ye in future."

Caitrin glanced up. "She will?"

He shrugged, leaning back in his chair and taking a sip from his goblet. "The men will riot if she serves up any more of that pottage."

Caitrin's gaze narrowed. "Why then, did ye tell her she wasn't to heed me?"

Alasdair stared back at Caitrin, his gaze searing hers. His expression turned serious as a long pause drew out between them. When he answered, his tone was cool. "Because I knew it would hurt ye."

Chapter Eight

Friends Again

CAITRIN STARED BACK at Alasdair. His reply shouldn't have surprised her, and yet it did. When she finally spoke, her voice held a rasp. "So … this is revenge?"

Alasdair crossed his arms over his chest. "Did ye think I'd forgotten?"

Caitrin swallowed. Her fingers tightened around the stem of her goblet. "Ye are still bitter because I chose yer brother over ye?"

There it was—the unspoken had finally been uttered. His mouth twisted.

A brittle silence stretched between them, and eventually, it was Caitrin who broke it. "I'm truly sorry for that day, Alasdair … for hurting ye."

His face hardened. "I don't need yer apology."

"Clearly, ye do," she replied, holding his gaze. "If ye are bent on exacting some kind of petty revenge upon me."

He snorted. "Petty?"

Caitrin drew in a deep breath, forcing down her ire. Even now he was deliberately baiting her. "I thought we were friends," she said after a pause. "When ye proposed, ye took me by surprise."

Heat flooded across her chest at the memory of that afternoon. They'd been walking in the gardens south of Dunvegan, laughing and teasing one another, when Alasdair suddenly halted and turned to her. Then he'd gone down on one knee and proposed—just like that. Caitrin had been so shocked, she'd laughed. Her reaction had been one borne of surprise and nervousness, but the look of hurt on Alasdair's face had haunted her for days afterward.

"Aye," he replied, his voice bitter. "Ye wanted a proposal from my dashing brother instead."

Caitrin swallowed. "I couldn't help how I felt." She paused here, looking into his eyes. "Ye didn't have to run away."

He barked a humorless laugh. "Is that what ye think I did?"

She held his gaze. "Didn't ye? Ye had never shown any interest in joining the king's army before ... and then once my betrothal to Baltair was announced, ye couldn't leave Skye fast enough."

Caitrin finished speaking and dropped her gaze, heart pounding. She hated confrontation—and this one was fast spiraling out of control. Soon one of them would say something there would be no coming back from.

Alasdair didn't reply, and when she looked up, she saw that he was staring into the fire. The ruddy light played across his lean face and the clenched line of his jaw. It reflected off his dark eyes.

Caitrin's belly clenched. He looked furious.

He turned his gaze from the fire then and reached for his goblet of wine.

To her surprise, Caitrin saw that his hand trembled.

"Alasdair ... what's wrong?"

He glanced down at his hand, and his mouth thinned. He then set the goblet down. "Nothing."

"I know I've upset ye but—"

"It's nothing," he snapped.

She frowned. Alasdair met her eye a moment before he muttered a curse and leaned back in his chair, raking a hand through his long dark hair. After a long pause, he finally spoke. "It happens ... sometimes. Ever since the battle, I've been on edge."

Caitrin's frown deepened, and she lowered her gaze to where his hand now rested upon the table. She'd heard of men being scarred by war, not just physically but on the inside, in places where no soul could ever see. "Is that all?" she asked.

He shook his head, his attention shifting back to the fire. "I don't sleep well anymore."

Caitrin nodded, remembering that she'd suggested a brew of valerian root a few days earlier. "It was bad then ... the war?"

Alasdair nodded. He shifted his attention back to Caitrin, pinning her under his stare. "I see I'm not the only one who has changed ... ye have too. Ye are so stern these days, and ye hardly ever smile."

Caitrin tensed. She didn't like how easily he had shifted the focus to her. "It's a while since we saw each other last," she said stiffly. "Of course I'm not the same lass."

"I hear ye weren't happily wed to my brother."

Caitrin sucked in a breath. She should have realized tongues would wag.

"I'm surprised," Alasdair continued. "He was yer choice after all."

Heat rose to Caitrin's cheeks, and she dropped her gaze to the goblet of wine before her. "He was."

"Handsome, charming, and powerful. My brother had women vying for his hand."

Caitrin wet her lips before glancing up. "Ye knew what he was?"

He held her gaze. "Aye ... and I thought ye did too."

She shook her head. "I was infatuated with him."

"And how long did that last?" Alasdair asked, his gaze boring into her.

Heart racing now, Caitrin looked away once more. "Until the wedding night."

Silence fell between them, the hush broken only by the crackle of the hearth. When Alasdair finally shattered it, his voice was tired. "Neither of us is the same person we were, Caitrin. I'll admit that when I arrived home, my first thought was to make ye suffer … but I see now that it'll only cause disruption in the castle if things continue in this way."

Surprised by his frankness, Caitrin glanced back at Alasdair. His fingers were curled around the stem of his goblet, but he made no move to lift it to his lips.

"Can't we be friends again?" she asked softly. "Like we once were?"

He watched her, his expression softening. Then his mouth curved into a smile. "Aye," he said after a pause. "Perhaps we can."

Caitrin walked back to her quarters with a light step.

She'd never had such a strange conversation. The words that had passed between them had ranged from confrontational and accusing, to conciliatory—and strangely honest.

But in the end, they'd managed to clear the air. They now had a chance to start over. Maybe the atmosphere at Duntulm would finally start to thaw.

On the way to her quarters, she stopped by Eoghan's chamber to check on him. The bairn lay on his side, sleeping peacefully. Caitrin had fed him before joining Alasdair for supper. With any luck, the lad would sleep through into the early hours of the morning.

Leaning on the edge of the cot, Caitrin stared down at Eoghan's face. During her pregnancy, she'd been worried she'd find it hard to love Baltair's child. Yet the moment she'd set eyes on her newborn son, she'd been lost. It was impossible not to love this sweet boy.

She enjoyed her responsibilities as chatelaine here at Duntulm, but she was a mother first. Caitrin's chest constricted as love welled within her. Baltair had given her very little worth keeping—except for this bairn.

Caitrin left her son and slipped silently back into the hallway. Reaching her bed-chamber, she found Sorcha awaiting her. The hand-maid sat by the fire, mending clothing by the light of a cresset that burned on the wall above her. Sorcha glanced up. "Good eve, milady."

"I'm tired, Sorcha," Caitrin informed her with a weary smile. "I think I'll go to bed early tonight."

Her hand-maid nodded, although she looked a little disappointed. It was their nightly routine to sit by the fire and talk awhile before bed.

"Do ye wish me to fetch ye some warmed milk?"

Caitrin shook her head and sank into a chair next to the bed. "No ... not tonight."

Sorcha set her sewing aside and rose to her feet. She crossed to Caitrin and, standing behind her, started to unpin her hair. It was a nightly ritual, one that relaxed Caitrin.

"Is something amiss, milady?" Sorcha asked as she unwound the heavy braid and reached for a hog-bristle brush. "Ye don't usually retire at this hour?"

"I'm just feeling a bit drained."

Sorcha didn't reply immediately. Of course, she knew where Caitrin had been—and would be wondering how the supper had gone. "Are ye still at war with the chieftain, milady?"

Caitrin twisted her head around, smiling as she met Sorcha's eye. "No ... I think we've managed to mend things."

"That's welcome news indeed." Relief flowered across the handmaid's face before her blue eyes narrowed. "Galiene told me about cook. The old woman's a trouble-maker."

"She's never liked having another woman oversee her," Caitrin agreed, turning back so Sorcha could finish unpinning her hair. "Alasdair's return was just the opportunity she needed. Unfortunately, the chieftain was looking for a reason to obstruct me."

"Why would he do that?"

Caitrin hesitated, wondering if she should confide in Sorcha or not. She trusted her hand-maid. Sorcha didn't have a loose tongue. Even so, it was a personal thing to divulge.

"Alasdair proposed to me once," she said finally. "I rejected him in favor of his brother."

Sorcha paused her brushing. "He wanted to wed ye?"

"Aye ... but ye aren't to breathe a word to anyone about this. The chieftain won't want folk knowing."

"I won't tell a soul," Sorcha assured her. She resumed the long slow strokes of the brush. "Why *did* ye choose Baltair over Alasdair, milady?"

Caitrin went still.

"Because Baltair was chieftain?" Sorcha pressed.

Caitrin sucked in a breath. "He was handsome and gallant," she replied after a pause, "the kind of man who dominates any room he walks into. I was mesmerized."

The two women fell silent. Sorcha knew more than anyone in this keep just how unhappy Caitrin had been with Baltair. Sorcha had found her sitting in her solar alone weeping into her hands more than once. He'd treated his wife's hand-maid with thinly-veiled contempt as well. Sorcha liked most folk, but she'd never warmed to Baltair.

"Alasdair MacDonald seems a different man to his brother," Sorcha said finally. "He's proud ... determined ... but I'm glad to see he lacks Baltair's cruel edge." She set the brush aside and went to fetch her mistress's night-rail. "I'm glad he's returned home."

Caitrin smiled. For the first time since seeing Alasdair again, she dared feel the same way.

Chapter Nine

Planting Barley

"WHAT SAY YE, Lady Caitrin?" Alasdair turned, meeting Caitrin's eye. "Shall we plant out the lower fields in oats this year?"

Caitrin hesitated before answering him. She'd been wary when he'd asked her to join him and Alban that morning. They were meeting the villagers to discuss the spring plantings. But, looking into his eyes, he seemed sincere.

"Aye," she replied, casting a look in Alban's direction. She and the steward had already discussed the coming season's plantings at length. Baltair had made a mistake, one that they'd planned to rectify. "We use more oats than any other grain ... it makes sense to plant more of it." She paused here, shifting her attention back to Alasdair. "We'll need to set aside at least twenty bags for the cáin."

Alasdair nodded before turning from her. "Go ahead and plant out those fields," he told the men.

"And what of the summer barley," an elderly farmer called out. "It grows badly on the hillside ... the land is too dry there. We should move it down to the meadow next to the burn."

"Let's go up to the hill now and take a look at the soil in the barley field," Alasdair replied. "Lead the way."

They followed the knot of farmers down the path amidst rows of kale and cabbages. A light rain fell in a chill mist over the fields. Grey clouds hung low; it was a grim day to be outdoors, yet Caitrin enjoyed the kiss of the misty rain on her face and the fresh air. Winter days inside the keep could start to feel restrictive, the air stale and heavy with the odor of peat smoke.

After a few strides down the path, Alasdair slowed his pace, allowing Alban to draw ahead with the others, and deliberately fell in step with Caitrin.

"Baltair never had much interest in farming," Alasdair said with a rueful smile. "I'm pleased to see that his widow does."

Caitrin compressed her lips. Baltair had been a warrior to the core. He loved hunting and fighting—everything else bored him. "Da always told me that fallow fields and bad harvests are signs of a poor leader," she replied. "Folk are always happier with full bellies."

Alasdair's smile widened. "Wise man, MacLeod." He paused here, his gaze narrowing slightly. "How's he doing these days?"

Caitrin huffed. "Well enough."

"That sounds ominous."

"Da hasn't been that impressed with his daughters of late," she said with a grimace. "Both my younger sisters have had trouble with him over the past year ... and I'm likely to soon."

Alasdair inclined his head. "What happened with yer sisters?"

"He tried to force Rhona to choose a husband ... and when she refused, he organized games where she was to wed the winner."

Alasdair gave a soft laugh. "That would have been ill news for yer sister. Did she not rebel?"

"She did ... Rhona ran away but failed in her attempt to flee the isle. In the end, she wed Taran MacKinnon."

Alasdair's gaze widened. "That scarred brute ... yer father's right-hand?"

"Aye, the same. He won the games." Caitrin paused here, her mouth quirking. "She wasn't pleased ... but fate turned in her favor. They're now in love."

Alasdair shook his head in disbelief. "And wee Adaira. What happened to her?"

"Da tried to wed her to Aonghus Budge."

"Lord ... he didn't?"

Caitrin grimaced. "Luckily, that never came to pass, for Adaira freed a prisoner from Dunvegan dungeon and escaped with him. They're now wed and live in Argyle."

Reaching out, Alasdair placed a hand on her arm, forcing her to stop walking. "God's bones, Caitrin. Ye must be spinning me a tale?"

Caitrin shook her head. Strangely, she was enjoying this conversation. It reminded her of years past when she and Alasdair had swapped stories of the goings-on in their respective castles. It seemed a lifetime ago. "The man she freed was Lachlann Fraser, the Fraser chieftain's eldest," she replied. "Da nearly went mad when he learned of it, but he has given them his blessing now."

Alasdair gave a low whistle, his gaze searching her face. "And what of ye, Caitrin? Surely the old dog has let ye off the leash?"

Caitrin pulled a face. "Ye would think so, yet now I'm a widow, he's already scheming. He wishes to find me another husband."

Alasdair's face tensed. "He does?"

"Aye ... I imagine ye will receive a missive from him soon enough, asking ye to send me home."

Alasdair nodded, his gaze shuttering. They resumed walking, following the party up the hillside now to the fallow barley field.

"And what do *ye* wish?" Alasdair asked finally. "Do ye want to wed again?"

Caitrin shook her head. "I'd prefer to remain at Duntulm as chatelaine," she murmured. "I have a son and a life here."

She glanced away then, aware that she'd possibly said too much. It was bold for a woman to make such statements. However, Alasdair had just given her the opportunity to make her wishes for the future clear. He might help her keep her father at bay.

Caitrin met his eye once more and smiled. "I'm glad we are friends again, Alasdair."

He held her gaze for a moment before glancing away. His voice, when he answered, was soft and reflective. "So am I."

They reached the barley field then, a wide gently sloping stretch that crowned the top of a hill behind the lower fields.

The farmers were waiting for them, gathered in a huddle as they bickered together over the best spot to plant the barley.

Caitrin moved past them, walking across the fallow earth a few paces. She then crouched down and scooped up a handful of soil and examined it.

"What say ye, milady?" The elderly farmer approached her, his brow furrowed. "It's too dry, isn't it?"

Caitrin sighed, brushing off her hands and rising to her feet. "Perhaps ... but I'm not sure the meadow next to the burn is the right spot to plant barley either. It gets waterlogged in heavy rain."

"The lady has a point." Alasdair stepped up next to the farmer. "Barley doesn't thrive in wet soil. It needs a well-drained field."

"Aye," Caitrin replied with a smile. "If I may make a suggestion, milord ... I think ye would be best to plant out this year's barley in the field behind the kirk."

The mist had lowered when they made their way back down the hill. The rain shrouded the winter landscape in a heavy veil. Picking her way down the slippery, pebble-strewn path, Caitrin cast Alasdair a quick look. "Ye love this land, don't ye?"

He glanced up, smiling. "Is it so obvious?"

"Aye."

He huffed a breath. "I once found it too small, too isolated ... but after some time away I have a new appreciation of Duntulm."

"I like the folk here," Caitrin replied with a smile of her own. "They've been good to me."

Alasdair met her eye. "I take it, my brother never took ye with him to speak to the cottars?"

Caitrin shook her head, her smile fading. "He sent Alban to do such tasks. I wasn't consulted." She was surprised by the bitter edge she heard in her own voice.

Alasdair raised an eyebrow. He'd noted it too. "Why does it matter that much to ye?"

Caitrin's mouth compressed. "Ye wouldn't understand."

"Wouldn't I?"

Caitrin shook her head, once again taken aback by her own vehemence. "I'm as clever as any man ... yet because I'm a woman I've been patronized and dismissed all my life." She couldn't believe she was voicing such thoughts to Alasdair. But as the words poured out, relief settled over her. It felt good to be able to be honest with him. "I only ever once made a suggestion to Baltair about the running of the keep," she said softly, "and he humiliated me in front of his men for it."

Alasdair's gaze clouded. "Like I did by the bridge."

Caitrin looked away. "No ... ye didn't go as far as he did."

Silence fell between them as they reached the bottom of the hill and took the muddy path through the fields toward the village. The way was narrow here, forcing them to walk in single file. Caitrin went ahead with Alasdair following a few paces behind. However, when they reached the hamlet, Alasdair increased his pace and fell into step beside her once more.

"Ye *are* a clever woman, Caitrin," he said, favoring her with a boyish smile that reminded her of the old Alasdair. "I can see why ye have been frustrated."

"Aye ... better that I was born dull-witted and content with my lot."

He threw back his head and laughed. The sound, warm and rich, filtered through the wet air. "I'd almost forgotten how sharp ye are," he said, grinning. "How I used to enjoy sparring with ye."

Caitrin cast him a sidelong glance. "Ye liked it?"

His mouth lifted at the corners. "Aye ... I still do."

Chapter Ten

Deer Stalking

CAITRIN STEPPED OUT into the bailey and raised her face to the sky. The sun had finally appeared after days of grey. It barely warmed her skin but was a welcome sight all the same.

"It's a fine morning to be alive, Lady Caitrin!"

Lowering her face, Caitrin spied Boyd MacDonald emerging from the stables, leading his horse.

"Aye, it is," she replied with a smile. Her gaze drifted over to where Alasdair also appeared, leading his stallion. "Where are ye all off to?"

"To stalk some deer." Boyd flashed her a grin.

Alasdair approached her. Dressed in hunting leathers and a dark-green woolen cloak, he was an attractive, distracting sight. "I remember MacLeod used to take ye and yer sisters deer stalking," he greeted her. "Do ye still hunt?"

Caitrin's mouth curved at the unexpected question. "I haven't been since I wed. Baltair wouldn't let me ride out with him ... said a stag hunt was no place for a woman."

Alasdair held her gaze, a smile spreading across his face. The expression made Caitrin's breathing catch.

She shoved the sensation aside. Attraction had no place between a chieftain and his chatelaine. She needed to watch herself around him.

"We're leaving shortly," he said. "Will ye join us?"

Caitrin nodded. Excitement arrowed through her, making her forget her discomfort. "Just give me a few moments," she said, pivoting on her heel. "I need to get changed."

A grin stretched across Caitrin's face. The thunder of hooves crossing soft turf, the sting of the wind on her skin, and the feel of the horse's body under her, made her feel truly alive.

It had been too long since she'd done this.

Alasdair MacDonald rode up ahead, flanked by Boyd and Darron, while a cluster of men from the guard brought up the rear. They'd left Duntulm as soon as Caitrin had gotten ready, and headed south over bare hills. Caitrin rode astride, like the men, having changed into leggings and a plain kirtle that was split at the sides so she didn't need to perch side-saddle.

Up ahead, Caitrin spied the shadowed boughs of woodland approaching. This was where they'd begin the hunt. Reaching the edge of the trees, the party drew up their coursers and swung down from the saddle. Here, they tethered the horses, retrieved their weapons, and continued onward on foot. A small herd of red deer had been spotted in a valley just south of here—they would stalk them.

Alasdair carried a longbow over one shoulder and a quiver of arrows on his back, as did the other men. Only Caitrin didn't bear a weapon. It had been a long while since she'd used a bow, and she feared she'd be a useless shot. Instead, she followed quietly behind Alasdair, Boyd, and Darron.

Caitrin inhaled the damp, pine-scented air, glad of the woolen cloak she wore. Despite that the sun was out today, there was little warmth in it. Winter still held the world in its grip. Pale sunlight filtered in amongst the trees, pooling on the mattress of pine needles below. It allowed the hunting party to move stealthily toward their destination. None of the men spoke, and Caitrin found herself enjoying the peace. Apart from the sanctuary of her solar, the keep was a hive of activity and distraction.

Alasdair led the way through the trees, soft-footed and keen-eyed. He paused now and then, gaze shifting ahead, before he turned, communicating with Boyd and Darron with a nod or hand gesture.

Eventually, they reached the edge of the valley.

Creeping up to the top of the ridge, the hunters fanned out in a line. Caitrin approached Alasdair, crouching down next to him. He was peering through a gap in the foliage. Caitrin craned her neck forward, moving closer to him to get a clear view.

"There they are," Alasdair murmured.

"I can't see anything," she whispered back, her gaze scanning the bottom of the valley. The pines fell back, revealing a swathe of green intersected by a creek.

Alasdair shifted his weight, angling his head toward her. "Shift yer gaze left," he whispered, his breath feathering against her ear.

Caitrin swallowed. His nearness distracted her. She could feel the heat of his body just inches from her. Stiffening, Caitrin forced herself to ignore the sensation.

Tracking her gaze left as he'd suggested, she caught sight of three deer cropping grass at the tree line. They were too far away at present. Alasdair and his men would need to draw closer before any of them would get a clear shot.

Alasdair shifted again, his knee accidentally brushing hers as he twisted right and motioned to Boyd and Darron. He then inclined his head to Caitrin once more.

"The fewer of us who approach them the better," he said softly. "Stay here with the others."

Caitrin nodded. She remained in a crouching position and watched as the three men crept over the edge of the ridge, moving like wraiths through the tall trees. However, her gaze remained upon Alasdair.

He moved with a hunter's grace. Unlike Baltair, who'd looked most at ease when dressed for battle,

Alasdair seemed at home here in the midst of the woods. His green cloak made him blend in with his surroundings. His long dark hair was tied back at his nape, accentuating the sharp, lean angles of his face.

He led the way down the hill, winding his way through the trees. The other two men followed him. Up ahead, the deer continued to graze, unaware of the danger that stalked them.

Caitrin watched Alasdair halt between two spruce saplings and motion to his companions. Then he unslung his bow, nocked an arrow, and raised it. Caitrin heaved in a deep breath and went still.

Alasdair sighted one of the deer, a large doe that now cropped grass at the edge of the creek. It was a long shot, one only an experienced bowman would dare make. Nearby, Boyd and Darron had sighted the other two deer. They were all ready.

A heartbeat later, the arrows flew, the whistle of their passage shattering the valley's peace. The doe near the edge of the creek leaped into the air—and then fell, an arrow piercing its neck.

Boyd's curse echoed through the trees as his and Darron's deer bounded away, unhurt.

Alasdair moved, running swiftly through the trees. He emerged at the bottom of the valley and reached his quarry in half a dozen long strides. Steel flashed when he dropped to his knees next to the fallen deer and brought its suffering to an end.

Only then did Caitrin release the breath she'd been holding.

"Good shot!" Boyd slapped Alasdair on the shoulder, "although ye chose the hind closest."

Alasdair grinned back at him. "Ye can never concede defeat gracefully, can ye?"

Boyd snorted. "MacNichol got in the way of my shot, or I'd have brought a deer down too."

A few feet away, Darron looked up from where he had just hog-tied the fallen doe and bound its fetlocks to a pole. "I'm surprised ye didn't scare the hinds off with yer heavy breathing."

"Come on." Alasdair jabbed Boyd in the ribs with his elbow. "Make yerself useful and help MacNichol carry the deer."

Boyd muttered something rude under his breath, but did as bid, stepping forward and taking hold of one end of the pole. He and Darron heaved it into the air, resting it on their shoulders. Then, the party turned and traveled north back through the pine woods, toward where they'd tethered their horses.

Unlike the journey south, the men talked and laughed as they walked, their voices drifting through the trees. The hunting was done. They no longer needed to keep silent.

Alasdair followed at the rear, deliberately slowing his pace so that Caitrin drew up alongside him.

He cast her a smile, admiring her in the pale winter light. She was still clad in black, although he liked her attire, and how she'd donned leather leggings and long hunting boots under her kirtle. He caught a glimpse of her shapely legs with each stride. Her long pale hair hung between her shoulder blades in a thick braid.

"Did ye enjoy that?" he asked.

Caitrin met his gaze, her mouth curving. "Aye ... ye look like ye were born knowing how to wield a bow and arrow?"

His smile widened. "Da used to take me out hunting with him before I could walk. I could fire a longbow before my fourth winter."

Caitrin arched her finely drawn eyebrows. "Now ye are exaggerating."

"No ... although I'll admit he had a special bow made for me, to fit my size."

Caitrin laughed, a soft melodious sound that made Alasdair's breathing quicken. "I remember seeing ye compete at archery once at the summer games at Dunvegan," she replied. "Ye even bested yer brother."

"Aye." Alasdair's smile turned rueful. "Baltair wasn't pleased about that. He waited till he got me alone before he punched me in the belly."

Chapter Eleven

Before the Beltane Fire

Four months later ...

CAITRIN WALKED DOWN the hill, following the line of revelers. Pulling her woolen shawl closer, she glanced up at the sky. It was clear, although the air held a bite as if the ghost of winter still lingered. It had been a cold, wet last few months.

She, like most folk, had been looking forward to Beltane—the night that symbolized the transition from spring to summer. No more huddling around hearths. No more chilled fingers and toes, and having to wear layers of woolen clothing to keep warm.

Halfway down the hill, the Beltane Fire blazed, a beacon that illuminated the night. The heat kissed Caitrin's face as she stopped around ten yards back from it.

"Would ye like me to get ye some ale, milady?"

Caitrin glanced over her shoulder at where Darron stood. She'd almost forgotten he was there, that he'd followed her down from the keep. The man had mastered the art of becoming invisible it seemed.

Caitrin's mouth curved. "Aye, thank ye, Darron."

With a nod, he went off to fetch her a drink. Folk had dragged down barrels of ale and wine from Duntulm's cellar. Cook had spent the last week preparing for this night. Huge rounds of 'Beltane Bannock' sat upon a table and were being sliced up and handed out. Nearby, a row of lamb carcasses finished roasting over a spit.

Boom. Boom. Boom.

Caitrin's attention shifted to where two young men sat beating calf-skin drums. The sound, slow and steady like the beating of a heart, called folk from miles around to join the revelry.

"Here ye are, milady." Darron had returned. He held out a wooden cup of ale to her and a wedge of cake. "I got ye some bannock too."

Caitrin took the bannock in one hand and the cup of ale in the other. Then, with a smile, she bit into the cake. Crumbly and enriched with milk and honey, it was delicious.

Taking a sip of ale to wash down her mouthful of cake, Caitrin's gaze traveled across the milling crowd. She watched as folk from the village approached the fire with unlit torches. They had doused their hearths at home and would light them afresh with the Beltane fire. Folk believed that the fire had protective qualities.

Bleating drifted across the hillside. A woman had brought up two goats to be blessed by the fire. The woman, who wore a harassed expression, led the skittish beasts around the fire, letting the smoke drift over them, before she dragged them off home.

Darron had taken his place next to Caitrin, his fingers curled around a cup of ale. Caitrin studied his profile in the firelight. He wore a pensive expression this evening, and when Caitrin followed the direction of his gaze, she saw it was focused upon Sorcha MacQueen.

Caitrin had given her hand-maid the evening off and left one of the older servants with Eoghan. Sorcha stood at the edge of a group of servants from the keep. She was nibbling at a piece of bannock.

The intensity of Darron's stare took Caitrin aback.

Could it be that the inscrutable Captain MacNichol had gone soft on her hand-maid?

At that moment, as they both watched Sorcha, Boyd MacDonald sauntered up to the lass. The warrior greeted her with a roguish smile. Boyd was a good-looking man and pleasant enough, yet Caitrin found his arrogance grated upon her. However, judging from the blush his greeting brought to Sorcha's cheeks, the lass didn't share her mistress's opinion of him.

Caitrin shifted her attention back to Darron and saw that he'd stiffened, his jaw tightening.

Clearing her throat, Caitrin broke the silence. "There's no need to stay with me," she said with a smile. "I'm happy here watching the fire."

Darron tore his gaze away from where Boyd and Sorcha now laughed together. "I should remain with ye, milady."

Caitrin clicked her tongue, irritated. "I'm perfectly safe, as ye well know, MacNichol. Now stop fussing and go enjoy yerself."

Darron frowned. "Very well, milady. But please, come and find me when ye wish to return to the keep."

"I will."

Caitrin watched Darron wander off, although she noted he didn't head in the direction of Sorcha and Boyd.

Caitrin took another bite of Beltane Bannock and chewed slowly.

In the midst of the crowd, she spotted Alasdair MacDonald.

He was surrounded by a few of his men as they drank and laughed. Alasdair appeared to be telling a story. His hands moved expressively and his dark eyes gleamed. One of his men then said something and Alasdair laughed.

The firelight bathed his face and shone upon his long dark hair, which he wore loose this evening. He'd matured into a striking-looking man, Caitrin had to admit.

She wasn't sure what she thought about the MacDonald chieftain these days.

There were moments when Caitrin could believe they were friends again, as they once had been, while at other times she found herself wary of him. A reserve existed between them now. And yet they'd settled into a comfortable working relationship over the last four months. Caitrin saw Alasdair a few times daily, although never alone. She hadn't joined him for supper in his solar again, and when they did speak, it was usually about factual matters.

Lost in thought, Caitrin continued to observe Alasdair. Another of his men asked him something, and he shook his head. He raised a cup to his lips—and then his gaze lifted, meeting hers.

Caitrin froze.

Mother Mary, he'd caught her staring.

Resisting the urge to tear her gaze away, Caitrin took a deep breath and casually shifted her attention to the fire, as if he was just part of the scene she'd been observing. However, she felt her cheeks warming under the weight of his answering stare.

Raising her cup of ale to her lips, Caitrin took a sip. Nearby, a lass laughed as a young man approached her for a dance.

Seizing the opportunity to look elsewhere, Caitrin focused on the young couple.

The girl was blushing furiously and laughing to cover up her embarrassment. She was small and blonde with a lush figure. The lad who'd approached her stared into her eyes with a look of such naked longing that Caitrin felt heat flush across her chest.

Beltane was a life-affirming evening, a night when the hard-working folk of this isle could cast aside their cares and give themselves up to revelry. Not surprisingly, it was said that many bairns were conceived on this night.

"Enjoying yerself, Lady Caitrin?"

Caitrin yanked her gaze from the couple to see that Alasdair MacDonald now towered over her. She hadn't even seen him leave his place with the other men and approach her.

Caitrin lifted her chin, angling her face up. She wished she was taller; she felt at a disadvantage every time she had to crane her neck to meet a man's eye.

"Aye, thank ye," she murmured. "It's a fair night."

"Ye should have brought Eoghan down here."

Caitrin huffed. "I will when he's a little older. He's getting too big to carry." It was true, the lad was growing like a weed, and now that he could crawl everywhere and had started to pull himself up onto furniture, he was into everything. "Old Lachina is with Eoghan tonight. I hope he behaves himself."

They stood in silence for a few moments, laughter and excited chatter eddying around them. A farmer was ushering his small herd of long-haired cattle past the fire. The beasts were mooing loudly and trying to run back down the hill, much to the entertainment of a cluster of lads nearby, who hooted at the farmer's attempts to herd the cows.

But Alasdair paid none of the chaos any mind. He watched Caitrin steadily. "Do ye remember that one Beltane our clans spent together?" he asked finally.

Caitrin nodded before smiling. "How could I forget? Yer father tanned yer hide after ye tried to set fire to my hair."

Alasdair snorted. "It was windy ... yer hair blew into my torch." He grinned then. "One of yer uncles got caught swiving a woman behind the bonfire ... do ye remember?"

Caitrin looked away, focusing her attention on the dancing flames before her. "Of course," she replied, her mouth curving. "We were the ones who caught him. I had nightmares about Dughall's hairy arse for months afterward."

Alasdair laughed, and Caitrin glanced back at him to see his dark eyes gleamed with mirth. "We used to take delight in observing the goings-on in our households."

Caitrin snorted. "Aye, we were like two gossiping crones, always speculating on which servants would end up wedded ... or bedded."

"And what of those three?" Alasdair jerked his head to the left. Caitrin shifted her attention and saw that Sorcha now had Boyd and Darron standing with her. The captain of the guard was asking Sorcha something. He gazed down at her as he spoke, his gaze intense. Next to him, Boyd wore a slightly irritated expression.

"Which man do ye think yer maid will choose?"

Caitrin raised an eyebrow. "She may pick neither."

Chapter Twelve

Looking for a Wife

"IT LOOKS AS if a storm is brewing."

Caitrin glanced up from where she was picking herbs to find her hand-maid looking up at the sky. Following her gaze, Caitrin frowned. The dark grey and purple clouds to the south certainly looked ominous. Four days had passed since Beltane, and the weather had warmed considerably, but it seemed the warmth was about to come to an abrupt end. "Aye, ye could be right," she murmured.

It was a relief to venture outdoors without a cloak or woolen shawl. The afternoon was humid, the air heavy and close. As such the scents of the herbs in the courtyard garden were heady. She breathed in the perfume of the lavender she'd been cutting. This was her favorite place in the keep: a tiny walled courtyard that sat against the western edge of the curtain wall. A riot of flowering and culinary herbs surrounded her.

Both Sorcha and Eoghan had joined Caitrin this afternoon. Her hand-maid kept an eye on Eoghan as he crawled over the lichen-encrusted cobbles. The poor lass had been forever wresting objects from Eoghan's fingers and confiscating them before he stuffed them into his mouth.

Caitrin turned to watch her son now. He was sitting up, his pink cheeks flushed, as he examined the sage leaf Sorcha had just given him. Her chest tightened at the sight of him. His dark hair grew thick now, so much like his father's.

Turning back to the lavender she'd been collecting, Caitrin resumed her work, cutting off the tips. She regularly made lavender tonic and lotion. It was good for the hair and skin, and she always made enough to share with other women in the keep.

She'd only been working a few moments when a large splash of water hit her in the face. Another swiftly followed, and then thunder rumbled over them.

Behind her, Eoghan let out a loud squawk.

Caitrin huffed a curse and turned from the lavender bush once more. Thunder boomed again, much louder this time. Eoghan's face crumpled, and he drew in a deep breath before letting out a frightened wail.

"Oh, laddie." Sorcha put down the trowel she'd been using to weed a herb bed. "All will be well … it's just a wee bit of thunder."

Eoghan ignored her, his crying explosive now. Face bright red, he reached out his hands to Caitrin.

"I'll take him, milady," Sorcha offered, but Caitrin shook her head. She handed her hand-maid the basket of lavender. "Please take this up, I'll carry Eoghan."

Scooping up her son, she murmured soothing words as the bairn hiccoughed against her shoulder.

Meanwhile, the rain was starting in earnest; large wet drops soaked into her charcoal kirtle.

The women made their way out of the courtyard garden into the bailey beyond. Thunder crashed overhead once more and Eoghan's wails turned into panicked screeches. His cries echoed over the bailey, ricocheting off the high surrounding walls.

Men turned their gazes to the hysterical child.

Alasdair MacDonald was one of them. He was leading his horse toward the stables, having just returned from a patrol. Handing the reins to one of his men, he strode toward Caitrin, intercepting her as she headed toward the steps leading up into the keep.

"What's wrong with the lad?" he asked, frowning. "Is he unwell?"

Caitrin shook her head, struggling to keep Eoghan still. He was writhing in her arms. "He's never heard thunder before ... it frightens him."

Their gazes met then, and Caitrin suddenly struggled to draw breath.

Ever since Beltane she'd been aware of Alasdair in a way she hadn't before. She'd found herself stealing glances at him at mealtimes. And just the day before, she'd watched Alasdair from her solar window. He'd been shoeing a horse, and she'd been unable to look away, admiring the play of muscles in his shoulders and upper-arms under the thin material of his léine.

He wore a loose léine this afternoon, stuck to his torso in places from the rain that now swept across the bailey.

Caitrin's breathlessness increased. A strange weakness went through her. She forgot the struggling bairn in her arms, the rumbling thunder, and the rain that was soaking her hair and clothing. Meanwhile, his gaze seared her.

Alasdair broke the spell first, looking away. "Ye had better get the lad inside," he said, a slight rasp to his voice. "Ye don't want him to catch a chill."

Caitrin nodded, gripped Eoghan tightly to her, and was about to flee into the keep when the ground shook beneath her feet. For a moment, she thought it was more thunder, but then movement behind Alasdair caught her eye.

Horses entered the bailey, ridden by men clad in wet leathers and sodden woolen cloaks. The riders out front carried a standard bearing a plaid of red, threaded with green and blue: MacNichol clan colors.

Caitrin's brow furrowed. Such an arrival was unexpected. They weren't due a visit from their neighbors.

The company of riders filled the bailey, and a big man with dark-blond hair swung down from his horse. He strode over to Alasdair, a grin stretching his face. "Good day, MacDonald!"

"MacNichol!" Alasdair greeted him with an equally wide smile. "What are ye doing here?"

The two men embraced before the MacNichol chieftain slapped Alasdair hard on the back. "I thought it time I paid the new MacDonald chieftain a long overdue visit." He pushed wet hair out his face, his gaze sweeping over the bailey courtyard.

"Uncle!" Darron MacNichol strode out of the stables, grinning.

Oblivious to the rain that now hammered down, the two men hugged.

Chieftain MacNichol's eyes were gleaming when he pulled back. "It's been too long." He saw Caitrin then, and he inclined his head, smiling. "Lady Caitrin."

"Good day, milord," she greeted him. The rain had drenched her and Eoghan now. The bairn still squawked loud enough to bring down the heavens. She then favored Gavin with an apologetic smile. "Excuse me, but I must get my son inside."

"Aye," Alasdair replied with a grimace, just as more thunder boomed overhead. An instant later, lightning lit up the sky. "None of us should linger out here."

"How long has it been since we saw each other last?" Gavin MacNichol regarded Alasdair over the rim of his goblet.

"A while," Alasdair replied with a wry smile. "At least four years, I'd wager."

The MacNichol chieftain snorted. "I remember now." He cut a glance to where Darron sat a few yards away. "It was when I accompanied my nephew here. The pair of ye could barely grow half a beard between ye ... and now look at ye both. One's a guard captain and the other is a chieftain." He shook his head. "Makes me feel old."

Darron laughed. "That's because ye *are*, uncle."

"Not too old to whip yer arse," the chieftain rumbled.

Observing the MacNichol chieftain, Caitrin noted that his face bore lines that hadn't been there the last time she'd seen him. During her marriage to Baltair, he'd visited Duntulm twice—the first time with his wife, the second alone, for his wife had been ill. Gavin MacNichol now neared his fortieth winter, but he was still an attractive man: blond and broad-shouldered with warm blue eyes. Yet recent events had left their mark upon his face. He looked tired.

"Milord," Caitrin spoke up, meeting his eye. "I was so sorry to hear about Lady Innis."

The MacNichol chieftain's gaze shadowed, and the light went out of his usually affable face. "Aye ... thank ye, Lady Caitrin. I can't believe it has been nearly a year since she died." He raised his goblet to his lips and drank deeply. "With her gone, and losing many of my men to the war, my broch feels empty these days."

"I'm sorry, Gavin," Alasdair spoke up, frowning. "I didn't know about yer wife."

MacNichol waved him away. "No offense taken. Ye were off fighting for Scottish freedom. Ye weren't to know."

An awkward silence fell across the table then. They were seated in the Great Hall. Outside, the storm still raged, battering the thick stone walls, while indoors the air was humid and heavy with the odor of wet wool and leather.

Gavin MacNichol reached for more wine. "In the meantime, life goes on ... as it must," he said quietly. His attention returned to Caitrin. "I received word from yer father two days ago, milady."

"Ye did?" Something in the man's tone made Caitrin tense, as did his change of expression.

"Aye ... he tells me that ye are in search of a new husband?"

Caitrin's fingers tightened around the stem of her goblet. She'd known her father would start meddling sooner or later. He'd gone suspiciously quiet of late, which could only mean he was planning something.

"*He* is in search of a husband for me, milord," she said after a pause. "However, I am content to remain as chatelaine here."

"So ye don't wish to remarry?"

Caitrin swallowed, suddenly uncomfortable. She was aware that all the men at the table—Alasdair, Darron, Boyd, and Alban—were watching her.

"No," she murmured. "I don't."

The chieftain held her eye for a long moment before his mouth curved. He shifted his attention to Alasdair then, his expression curious. "I take it that Lady Caitrin has proved herself invaluable to Duntulm?"

"Aye," Alasdair replied. His expression had turned serious, his gaze shuttered. "She ran things well after Baltair's death ... and continues to do so."

"So ye will let her remain here? A good chatelaine is hard to find."

Alasdair nodded, although his face had tensed, warning Gavin MacNichol to cease his line of questioning.

Heeding him, his guest took a sip from his goblet and glanced back at Caitrin. "It's a pity ye aren't interested in wedding again, milady," MacNichol said, favoring her with a warm smile. "For I am looking for a wife."

Chapter Thirteen

A Waste of a Good Woman

EOGHAN'S WAILS ECHOED down the hallway.

Caitrin picked up her skirts and hurried toward his bed-chamber. She'd just left her solar, and was about to descend the stairs, when she heard his cries. Eoghan usually had a nap mid-morning, but it appeared he'd awoken early.

Inside the warm, dimly-lit chamber, she found Eoghan red-faced and gripping the sides of his cot.

"What is it, my wee laddie?" She scooped him into her arms. "Worry not ... Ma's here."

Caitrin carried Eoghan across to a chair and sat down. Her son was growing heavy to hold now. She'd recently weaned him, and he'd taken to solid food with relish. As she settled Eoghan on her knee, her hand brushed his face.

Caitrin frowned. It was warm in the chamber, as Sorcha made sure the hearth was well stoked, but Eoghan's brow was hot to touch. His cheeks were flushed, not from crying, but fever. He hadn't been outdoors long in the rain the afternoon before—but he appeared to have caught a chill.

The bairn wriggled on her knee, his flushed face scrunched up as he cried. Murmuring to him, Caitrin cradled him against her breast. After a few moments, Eoghan quieted. Caitrin closed her eyes, enjoying the peace. Gavin MacNichol's visit had thrown the keep into chaos. They hadn't been expecting him, so there had been chambers to ready for him and his men, and extra food to be prepared.

Caitrin had just come up from the kitchens, where cook had been in a temper about having no time to plan for the visitors. Caitrin had left her with instructions to put out an extra haunch of mutton with the noon meal. Briana had muttered under her breath about this but had acquiesced in the end.

She'd been much more compliant of late since Alasdair had spoken with her.

Once Eoghan had calmed, Caitrin lay him back into his cot. She needed to find Sorcha. Slipping out of the bed-chamber, she had almost reached the stairs when she met her hand-maid.

"I was coming up to fetch ye, milady," Sorcha greeted her with a smile. "The supplies have just arrived."

This was good news, for Caitrin had been waiting for a delivery of goods from the mainland for days now: cloth, spices, and other items that were difficult to buy on the isle. She wanted to make an inventory of the items before they were put away.

"Thank ye, Sorcha," Caitrin replied. "I've just seen Eoghan. He has the beginnings of a fever. Can ye please stay with him while I see to the supplies? I hate to leave him when he's upset."

Sorcha's brow furrowed, worry lighting in her blue eyes. "Of course."

Leaving her hand-maid to look after Eoghan, Caitrin fetched her wooden board and a stub of charcoal from her solar. She then continued down to the bailey. Picking her way across the muddy ground, doing her best to avoid the puddles left by yesterday's storm, she approached a large wagon. A young man had just pulled back the hide tarpaulin, revealing tightly stacked wooden barrels and crates.

"Good day, Tory," she greeted the servant.

"Good morning, milady," Tory returned the greeting with a grin. "Shall we take these into the stores?"

"Open them up first, please," Caitrin instructed. "I want to make sure we've gotten what we ordered."

He obeyed, using a knife to pry the lid off a small barrel. A sweet, woody scent drifted into the damp air, and Caitrin peered inside, a smile curving her lips. "Cinnamon," she breathed. She'd forgotten that she'd ordered some all those months ago—the scent reminded her of mulled wine at Yuletide.

Scratching a note on her board, Caitrin nodded to Tory.

"Open that one next to it."

The young man pried the lid off another small barrel, which was filled with black peppercorns. Another costly spice, and one which would hopefully last them a while.

"Make sure ye close those barrels well," Caitrin ordered, "and put them on the top shelf in the stores."

"Aye, milady." Tory carried the barrels of precious spice away, leaving Caitrin alone. She was just scratching another note when a male voice behind her made her start. "Good day, Lady Caitrin."

She glanced over her shoulder to see that Gavin MacNichol had approached. Her heart sank at the sight of him. After the words they'd shared the day before, she felt a little uncomfortable around the chieftain. She'd always liked Gavin, but during that meal, she'd seen the glint of interest in his eyes. Her father hadn't helped matters either, but she didn't want to encourage him further. She also didn't want to linger out here in the bailey any longer than necessary. With Eoghan so restless, she needed to return to her son as soon as possible.

"Good day, Chieftain MacNichol."

"Busy, I see," he observed. The corners of his eyes crinkled as he smiled. "Alasdair is lucky to have yer help here."

"These are long-awaited supplies," she replied, favoring him with a smile of her own. "The first since the war."

He gave her a long, searching look. "It's good to see ye happy again, lass." Caitrin tensed, and when she didn't answer, he continued. "Innis told me how unhappy ye were … but the last time I visited, I didn't need anyone to point it out to me. I've never seen a woman with such sad eyes."

Caitrin dropped her gaze to the muddy ground, aware that Tory would return soon. MacNichol had been so direct she didn't know how to respond.

"Baltair could be a brute, and he wasn't easy to like," the chieftain said after a pause. "I'm just sorry he put ye off wedding again."

Caitrin glanced up, meeting his gaze. Gavin MacNichol was watching her with a soft look that made her feel wretched.

"Not every woman is meant to be a wife," she replied, her tone brittle.

He inclined his head. "No … but it's a waste of a good woman such as yerself."

"How is he?" Caitrin let herself into her son's bedchamber to find Sorcha seated by the fire, sewing in hand. Eoghan lay asleep in his crib.

As soon as the supplies had been dealt with, she'd made her way back upstairs.

Sorcha cast aside her sewing and rose to her feet, her face tense with concern. "His cheeks are very red … but he has been sleeping since ye left."

Caitrin crossed to the crib and gazed down at her son's sleeping face. Sorcha was right. His cheeks were deeply flushed now, and when she pressed a hand to his forehead, she drew in a sharp breath. He was burning up. "Go and fetch a healer, Sorcha," she ordered. "Quickly, please."

Sorcha nodded. Without another word, she left the chamber.

Alone, Caitrin let out a deep sigh. Massaging a tense muscle in her shoulder, she continued to watch Eoghan, calmed by the steady rise and fall of his chest.

It's only a fever, she reassured herself.

Why then did cold dread curl in the pit of her belly?

"Where are ye off to in such a hurry?"

Sorcha was looping a woolen shawl over her shoulders as she crossed the keep's entrance hall, when a familiar voice hailed her. She glanced over her shoulder to see Darron MacNichol approach.

"Wee Master Eoghan has a fever," she replied briskly, "I'm off to the village to fetch the healer."

Darron stepped close to her. "I'll come with ye."

Sorcha clicked her tongue. "There's no need for that, MacNichol. Ye don't have to escort a hand-maid."

He favored her with a stubborn look. "Ye serve Lady Caitrin, Sorcha. That makes ye my responsibility as well."

Sorcha huffed. "Suit yerself."

They made their way outside and crossed the bailey under an overcast sky, their boots splashing through the mud. Crossing the drawbridge, Sorcha avoided looking down at the deep ditch that surrounded the curtain wall on three sides. If she ever slipped and fell into it, she'd break her neck for sure.

Striding down the hill toward the village, Sorcha stole a glance at Darron. The captain of the guard was an enigma. Upon her arrival at Duntulm, she'd suffered something of an infatuation for him. But after realizing he barely noticed her existence, she'd promptly put him out of her head.

These days though, he'd altered in his manner toward her. It seemed that everywhere she went, Darron MacNichol appeared. He wasn't a garrulous man, yet he'd approached her at Beltane—much to Boyd's irritation.

Boyd MacDonald. She wasn't sure she trusted him. He often went out of his way to speak to her—and when he did his charm was breathtaking—but just yesterday she'd heard two of the scullery maids gossiping about how he'd stolen a kiss from one of them. Sorcha had gone cold. Suddenly, his compliments and melting looks took on a different meaning.

Pushing thoughts of Boyd aside, Sorcha broke the silence between her and Darron. "Is yer uncle still at Duntulm?"

Darron glanced her way. "Aye ... Gavin leaves tomorrow. Why?"

"I heard he's looking for a wife."

Darron raised an eyebrow. "Are ye interested?"

"Of course not." Sorcha cast Darron an irritated look. As the bastard daughter of the MacQueen chieftain, men like Gavin MacNichol were far beyond her reach. "Galiene told me that he was showing an interest in Lady Caitrin."

Darron snorted. "Galiene has the loosest tongue in the keep."

"Is she wrong?"

"Ye shouldn't gossip, Sorcha. It's unbecoming."

"Oh, stop being such an old woman, MacNichol, and answer me."

He cast her a censorious look. "My uncle is a widower. If he's considering taking another wife, there's nothing strange in that."

"He's wasting his time on Lady Caitrin ... she doesn't wish to wed again."

"I know," he replied with a shake of his head. "And she's not the only one. Alasdair MacDonald doesn't want to wed either it seems."

Sorcha nodded, remembering the chieftain's words that day in his solar months earlier when she'd brought Eoghan in to see him.

When Darron spoke once more, his tone was introspective. "Ye didn't meet Alasdair before he went away, did ye?"

"No ... I arrived at Duntulm the same time as Lady Caitrin. He'd already joined the king's cause."

"The war changed him," Darron said, glancing her way once more. They'd almost reached the bottom of the hill now. "There's an edge to Alasdair that wasn't there before … like he's expecting someone to sneak up behind him and sink a knife into his back."

Sorcha nodded. "I've seen him staring off into the distance sometimes," she murmured. "He's tries to hide it … but he's troubled."

Silence stretched out between them for a few moments before Darron broke it. "Do ye ever give some thought to yer own future, Sorcha?"

Surprised, Sorcha cut him a sharp glance. "Not really … why?"

His gaze met hers. "Do ye wish to one day wed?"

Embarrassment flushed through Sorcha at the direct question. "I … don't know," she stammered, trying to tamp down the heat that was now rising up her neck. "I've not thought about it."

Chapter Fourteen

A Trifling Thing

"DARRON ... WHERE'S LADY Caitrin this evening?" Alasdair put down his goblet, his gaze settling upon Captain MacNichol. "She usually takes her supper with us."

Darron glanced up from his bowl of stew. "Hasn't Lady Caitrin spoken to ye, milord?"

"Not since this morning ... why?"

Darron frowned. "I thought she would have told ye."

Alasdair went still. "Told me what?"

"Her son's ill ... she'll be upstairs with him."

Silence fell at the table. After a long moment, Gavin MacNichol broke it. "Poor lad. Is he—"

"What's wrong with him?" Alasdair cut in.

"A fever."

Alasdair tensed. Why hadn't Caitrin sent word? If his heir was ill, he had the right to know. Pushing down his irritation, he met Darron's eye once more. "Has the healer been fetched?"

"Aye."

Alasdair pushed himself back from the table and rose to his feet. "I'd better check on the lad."

"Can't it wait till after supper?" Boyd spoke up. He'd just finished setting up a board with stone markers. "I thought we were going to have a game of Ard-ri?"

"Later," Alasdair snapped.

Without another word, he turned on his heel and left the Great Hall.

"Lady Caitrin," Sorcha slipped into the bed-chamber closing the door behind her, "the chieftain is here ... he wants to see Master Eoghan."

Caitrin, who'd been rocking Eoghan in her arms, tensed. "Let him in," she murmured.

Sorcha nodded before disappearing into the hallway beyond.

A moment later a tall figure stepped into the dimly-lit room. Dressed in plaid braies, a léine, and a leather vest, Alasdair wore an unusually severe expression.

"Good eve, milord," she greeted him.

"How is my nephew?" he asked. "I hear he has a fever?"

His brusque manner made Caitrin frown. "He does, milord."

"Where's the healer?"

"I sent him away. He's visiting again in the morning." Caitrin rose to her feet, cradling the hot body against her. Her arms ached from holding him, yet she didn't want to put him back in his crib, not yet.

Alasdair walked forward so that he loomed over her. However, it wasn't Caitrin he was focused on at that moment, but the bairn. His brow furrowed further when he reached down and touched the lad's flushed face. "He's on fire."

"Aye ... he must have caught a chill yesterday."

Alasdair glanced up, his gaze spearing hers. "Why didn't ye call for me?" he asked softly.

Guilt wreathed up within Caitrin. "I didn't want to bother ye," she murmured. "I thought it was a trifling thing."

It was a lie. She'd deliberately kept Eoghan's fever from Alasdair. A fierce protective instinct had come over her when she'd realized Eoghan was unwell. She'd hoped that it would break during the night, and Alasdair wouldn't have been any wiser.

His expression hardened. "He's the MacDonald heir. I have the right to know if he's ill."

Annoyance surged within her, pushing aside the guilt. This was why she'd not told him. She didn't like how Alasdair claimed ownership over Eoghan. He was her son, not his property.

Alasdair straightened up, his dark brows knitting together. "The healer is to stay with him until the fever abates," he announced, stepping back from her. "I don't want him leaving Eoghan's side."

Caitrin's lips compressed. "But he has other patients to attend."

"None more important than Eoghan MacDonald. Send a servant to fetch him back. Tell him I shall pay him for his time."

With that Alasdair turned and strode from the bed-chamber.

Alasdair stepped into the hallway to find the hand-maid Sorcha waiting there.

His sudden appearance made her start. "Milord?"

He nodded curtly before stepping past her to the stairwell. Behind him, he heard the hand-maid re-enter the bed-chamber. Frowning, he climbed the stairs to the next level of the keep, to his solar.

He'd almost reached the door when a voice hailed him. "Milord!"

Alasdair turned to see Alban hurry up the last of the steps behind him, puffing like an old plow horse. The steward grasped something in his right hand, which he thrust at Alasdair when he reached the landing.

"A rider just arrived from Dunvegan," he announced, red in the face from his climb. "He brought this for ye."

Alasdair looked down at the rolled parchment, sealed with wax. It bore a stamp he recognized instantly: a bull's head between two flags. *The MacLeod crest.*

The steward hovered, his face expectant, but Alasdair turned from him.

"Thank ye, Alban. I'll read it in my solar."

Letting himself into his quarters, Alasdair carried the message over to the fire. With an irritated sigh, he broke the seal and unfurled the parchment. Then he read it.

Dear Chieftain Alasdair MacDonald,

It is now nearly a year since my daughter was widowed. I understand Caitrin has proved herself useful as chatelaine at Duntulm, but I feel the time has come for her to wed once more.

I have made inquiries and have three suitors who wish to meet with her. Please make arrangements for her to return to Dunvegan at yer earliest convenience.

Yer humble servant,
Clan-chief Malcolm MacLeod.

Alasdair lowered the parchment, a frown creasing his brow. He'd expected such a letter to arrive sooner or later. Gavin MacNichol had warned them that MacLeod was growing restless.

Caitrin had no wish to wed, or to leave Duntulm, but her father had other ideas.

Malcolm MacLeod wasn't a man to be crossed.

Alasdair's already sour mood darkened further as he realized he didn't want Caitrin to leave.

He'd returned home intent on making her suffer for the hurt she'd caused him—but after a while, his quest for revenge had felt childish, pointless. Instead, they'd slowly built up a companionship that he'd grown to enjoy.

Certainly, he was annoyed that she'd deliberately tried to hide Eoghan's fever from him—it really was unacceptable behavior—but such things could be overcome.

Alasdair loosed a breath and placed MacLeod's letter on the mantelpiece. He wouldn't think about Caitrin's fate tonight, not with Eoghan burning with fever. He'd discuss this with her once her son had recovered.

Caitrin gently lay the back of her hand on Eoghan's brow—and let out a sigh of relief.

His skin was warm, not burning hot as it had been. After two long days and nights, the fever had broken.

The healer had informed her that her son was over the worst, before he departed the keep, face gaunt with fatigue, his purse heavy with silver pennies.

Leaning against the edge of the cot, Caitrin closed her eyes. That was the second fever that Eoghan had suffered since his birth, although it was much worse than the first. Even the healer had started to look worried as the second night wore on.

But now the worst was over.

Caitrin felt wrung out. Her eyes were gritty from lack of sleep, her head heavy. She needed to rest.

As if reading her mistress's thoughts, Sorcha spoke up. "I'll watch over the lad, Lady Caitrin. Why don't ye go and lie down awhile?"

Opening her eyes, Caitrin cast a grateful smile over her shoulder at her hand-maid. "I don't know what I'd do without ye, Sorcha."

The young woman smiled back, her cheeks dimpling. She looked tired in the grey light that filtered in from the open window. It was a sunless day outdoors. Sorcha's face was strained, her eyes hollowed.

Caitrin was sure *she* looked far worse.

"Ye are a good mother, milady," Sorcha replied. "Ye couldn't have done more for Eoghan."

Caitrin heaved a sigh. "I keep blaming myself. I shouldn't have had him outdoors … if he caught a chill because—"

"Ye don't know that, milady," Sorcha cut her off, her voice firm. "Ye aren't to blame."

Caitrin pushed herself away from the edge of the crib. "I just thank the Lord it's over," she murmured.

Eoghan was all she had. She couldn't bear to lose him.

Leaving Sorcha with her son, Caitrin made her way back to her own quarters. She entered her solar: a small, yet comfortable space, warmed by a glowing hearth. A servant had been in here, she noted. They'd left a tray of food—bannocks with butter and honey—for her.

Caitrin had thought she'd be too exhausted to eat, but the sight of the food made her belly growl, reminding her that she'd missed supper the night before. Seating herself at the table, she poured out a cup of milk and started to butter a wedge of bannock.

She was halfway through her meal when a knock sounded at the door. "Come in," she called, expecting to see a servant.

Instead, Alasdair MacDonald appeared. Leaning against the doorframe, he folded his arms across his chest and favored her with a tired smile. "I saw the healer leave earlier. He tells me Eoghan is on the mend?"

Caitrin put down the bannock she'd been about to bite into. She had not spoken to Alasdair since their brief conversation two days earlier. "Aye," she replied, her manner guarded. "His fever broke just before dawn."

"I'm relieved to hear that."

Not knowing what to say to him, Caitrin fell silent.

"Are ye angry with me?" he asked after a moment.

"No," Caitrin replied warily.

Pushing himself off the doorframe, Alasdair took a step into the solar. "I haven't been inside this chamber for years," he said, his gaze shifting around the solar. "Not since my mother was alive. It was Ma's favorite spot … but I see ye have made it yer own."

His words eased the tension between them, and Caitrin nodded. Indeed, since her arrival at Duntulm, she'd imbued the solar with her own character. There were baskets of dried herbs and flowers dotted around the space. Colorful hangings, which she and Sorcha had spent the last three winters laboring over, covered the damp stone walls.

Alasdair met her eye then. "I'm sorry about how I spoke to ye last. I was worried about Eoghan ... it made me harsher than I intended."

"I was worried about him too," she reminded him quietly, "but I also owe ye an apology ... I should have told ye he was unwell."

Alasdair's gaze clouded. "Why didn't ye?"

Caitrin looked away. "I don't know."

He'd take offense if she told him the truth. Despite that they'd gotten along well over the past few months, when it came to Eoghan, she still didn't trust him.

She glanced back to see Alasdair watching her. "Are we still friends, Caitrin?" he asked softly. The way he said her name made a shiver of pleasure run down her spine.

Doing her best to ignore the distracting sensation, Caitrin frowned. "Of course."

He gave her a lopsided smile. "Then would ye have supper with me this evening in my solar?"

Caitrin heaved in a deep breath. The air between them was suddenly charged. She wasn't sure she wanted to spend an evening alone with him. It was best they kept their relationship well-defined. He was the chieftain, and she was his chatelaine. They spoke daily about what needed to be done to keep Duntulm running, but they didn't need to take things further than that.

Yet she couldn't refuse without giving offense. The boyish smile he gave her then, unraveled the last of her reserve toward him. He looked so hopeful she couldn't deny him.

"Very well," she huffed before favoring him with a smile. "Now, please go away and let me finish my bannocks in peace."

Chapter Fifteen

I Don't Want This

CAITRIN TOOK A sip of wine. The deep, spicy flavor exploded on her tongue, and she glanced up, eyes widening. "This is delicious ... what is it?"

"Spiced black plum," Alasdair replied with a smile. "The last of the wine laid down by my father."

Caitrin lowered her gaze to the deep red wine in her goblet, before she took another sip. "I thought we didn't have any of that left?"

His smile widened. "Aye ... that's because ye don't know of Da's secret store."

Caitrin inclined her head. "Clearly not."

The evening was drawing out. They had long since finished their supper of pork and kale pie. The servants had cleared away the dishes before Alasdair suggested they shared a goblet of wine together. Caitrin had now taken a seat before the window while Alasdair leaned up against the stone ledge opposite.

Alasdair drank from his goblet, his expression turning wistful. "No one could make wine like my father. We haven't had a decent drop here since he died."

Caitrin watched him, noting Alasdair's relaxed posture as he leaned against the sill, legs crossed at the ankles before him. She'd been tense upon first entering the solar—for she couldn't set foot in this chamber without remembering Baltair—but after a good meal, she was starting to unwind.

The tension and worry of the past days slowly unraveled, and she found that she was enjoying the evening. The shutters were open, giving her a view of the deep indigo sky, where the stars were just twinkling into existence. The air filtering in was cool and laced with the scent of the sea.

"The seeds are sown for the summer now," she said finally. "All we need is a few months of sunshine."

He huffed a laugh. "Ye are never guaranteed that on this isle."

"I saw the new grain store yesterday."

"Aye." He met her eye, his mouth curving. "What do ye think of it?"

"It's a very clever design … I never thought of raising it so high off the ground."

Alasdair smiled. "It keeps rodents out. I saw one similar in Inbhir Nis … ye needed a ladder to get up to it. We're going to build three more before summer ends."

Caitrin inclined her head, studying him. "Ye make a fine chieftain, Alasdair MacDonald. The folk of this land are fortunate to have ye."

Alasdair held her gaze. "Are they?"

The atmosphere suddenly altered between them, a tension rising that had been absent earlier. Suddenly, Caitrin felt nervous. She looked away and took a large gulp of wine to fortify herself.

"I know Eoghan is important to ye," she said finally, "but why not find yerself a wife and father children of yer own?" She raised her chin, forcing herself to meet his eye once more. "The MacDonalds of Duntulm risk dying out."

His gaze guttered, and yet he didn't reply. Instead, he looked away, focusing upon the dark sky outdoors.

Caitrin's breathing quickened. She probably shouldn't have spoken of something so personal, and yet this issue had been bothering her. "Alasdair?"

He shifted his gaze back to her, and the look on his face made Caitrin swallow hard. She curled both hands around the goblet as if anchoring herself to it.

"After ye wed Baltair, I made a decision." His voice held a rasp. "If I couldn't have ye, I would have no one."

The words fell heavily in the solar.

For a long moment, Caitrin merely stared at Alasdair, and then her chest constricted as guilt tore into her. She knew she'd hurt him—but the wounds went deeper than she'd thought. "Ye shouldn't throw yer life away like that," she whispered. "It's a waste. Ye would make a fine husband and father."

He set his goblet down on the window ledge with a thump. "I'm not sure I would."

Caitrin heaved in a deep breath. Suddenly, it felt airless inside the solar, even though she sat next to the open window. Caitrin put down her goblet and rose from the seat, taking a step away from him. "I should go," she said quietly, her heart racing now. "It's late."

Alasdair moved.

One moment, he'd been standing there, watching her with eyes aflame, the next he stepped forward, covering the distance between them. He reached out, grasped Caitrin's shoulders, and pulled her toward him.

Then he bent his head and kissed her.

It was a searing, hard kiss—and it scattered Caitrin's thoughts like autumn leaves caught by the wind.

At first, she was shocked and stood there rigid as his mouth slanted over hers. And then the feel of his lips on hers ignited something deep in Caitrin's belly. His touch made her body quiver.

Still gripping her shoulders, Alasdair pushed Caitrin back against the wall. His lips parted hers, his tongue sliding into her mouth as he deepened the kiss. The hard length of his body pressed up against hers. The spicy male scent of him filled her senses. He kissed her as if he was starved.

Caitrin gave in to the heat of Alasdair's embrace for a moment, before a chill washed over her.

What am I doing?

If she submitted to this, she'd risk losing everything she'd worked so hard to achieve here at Duntulm. Independence. Respect. She wouldn't let another man control her. Caitrin's hands went up to Alasdair's chest.

Never again.

She braced herself against him, pushing hard.

Alasdair pulled back, surprise filtering over his face. "Caitrin?"

"I can't," Caitrin gasped. She slid along the wall, away from him. "We can't."

Alasdair frowned, his eyes shadowing with concern. "What's wrong?"

He took a step toward her, but Caitrin held out a hand, warning him not to come any closer. "No … Alasdair. Please don't."

He stopped short, his face going taut. "I'd never hurt ye."

Caitrin shook her head. She should have seen this moment coming. Tension had been building between them for a while now; it had only been a matter of time.

"This was a mistake," she whispered.

His features hardened. "We haven't done anything wrong, Caitrin. All I did was kiss ye."

"No." The word ripped from her. "I don't want this."

She backed up from him, knocking into the edge of the oaken table that dominated the center of the solar. Then she turned and fled from the chamber.

Alasdair watched Caitrin run from him.

He took two swift steps to follow her and then brought himself up short.

No.

His heart slammed painfully against his ribs as the door to the solar thudded shut, and he heard her footfalls receding quickly down the hallway beyond.

I don't want this.

The words had struck him like physical blows. They still stung in the aftermath.

Alasdair dragged a hand through his hair and spat out a curse.

He hadn't meant to kiss her. The conversation had spiraled out of control, and then he'd forgotten himself. Alasdair hadn't thought about the consequences of his actions. He'd reached for her on instinct, and when she was in his arms, her mouth under his, he'd been unable to stop kissing her.

Caitrin had tasted even better than in his dreams.

But then she'd pushed him away. She didn't want him.

Alasdair strode back to the window and threw himself down on the window seat, where Caitrin had been sitting until a few moments earlier. He reached for his goblet of wine and stopped. His hand trembled badly as if he were an old man struck by palsy.

Jaw clenched, Alasdair fisted his hand and lowered it to the window-sill.

He couldn't believe he'd made an utter fool of himself for the second time—kicked in the guts twice by the same woman.

It had taken everything he had to reach for Caitrin. And she'd rejected him—again. Only this time it felt worse. This time he'd been kissing her, and she'd recoiled from him.

There was no coming back from such an act. Caitrin had made her feelings clear.

Alasdair squeezed his eyes closed. The pain that constricted his chest made it hard to breathe. Disappointment and hurt churned within him, making his bile rise.

Enough.

Alasdair opened his eyes, his gaze shifting to the mantelpiece, where the rolled missive from Malcolm MacLeod still sat. He'd been meaning to discuss it with Caitrin during supper but had forgotten.

Truthfully, he'd been reluctant to, for he'd wanted her to remain in Duntulm.

But that was before he'd kissed her, before she'd shoved him away from her as if his very touch made her skin crawl.

I don't want this.

No—she couldn't stay here. Caitrin needed to go home.

Chapter Sixteen

He Will Want for Nothing

CAITRIN STABBED HER finger with the needle before letting out a curse.

Shocked, Sorcha glanced up from her own sewing. "Milady?"

Caitrin cast the hand-maid a baleful look but didn't reply. Instead, she sucked on her injured finger, which now throbbed. She wasn't in the best frame of mind for embroidery. Her nerves felt stretched tight as a drawn bow-string this morning.

"Is something amiss, Lady Caitrin?" Sorcha asked gently.

Caitrin shook her head. "I'm just tired," she replied. "After so much worry over Eoghan." She cast a glance left at where the lad sat upon a rug, playing with blocks of wood. He was building a tower, which he then knocked over with a squeal of laughter. Caitrin's expression softened as she watched him. The sight of her son was like a balm, soothing her anxiety.

As long as she had Eoghan, life was manageable.

"I'm so relieved he's better," Caitrin murmured.

"Aye, milady. We've all been worried about him."

Caitrin glanced up, smiling. Sorcha's words soothed her. "I'm sorry I've been snappish this morning."

The hand-maid held her gaze. "Ye are more than just tired, milady," she observed. "Ye have been jumping at shadows since dawn."

Caitrin sighed, considering whether to confide in Sorcha about what had happened between her and Alasdair the evening before. She sometimes felt so alone, and at moments like this missed her sisters terribly. Rhona and Adaira had always been there for her, but they couldn't listen to her now.

"I—" she began, but a knock on the door to the solar prevented her from continuing.

"Come in," she called, irritation rising. No doubt one of the servants wanted her help with something, only this morning she didn't have the patience it. She just wanted to be left in peace for a while.

The door opened and a tall, dark-haired figure stepped inside.

Caitrin went cold, dread curling in the pit of her belly. Alasdair was the last person she wanted to see this morning. She'd deliberately broken her fast in here, avoiding the chaos of the Great Hall—and hiding from this man.

Sorcha hurriedly put aside her sewing and rose to her feet, smoothing her skirts. "Milord," she greeted him with a curtsy.

"Morning, Sorcha." Alasdair favored the hand-maid with a smooth smile. "Could ye give Lady Caitrin and me a few moments alone, please?"

"Of course." Sorcha stepped away from the fireside, scooped up Eoghan, and left the chamber.

Silence followed her departure.

Caitrin had thought that Alasdair's smile might fade once Sorcha was no longer present, yet it did not. He sauntered over to the hearth and took the seat that the hand-maid had just vacated, crossing one ankle at the knee with loose-limbed grace. Then he leaned back and viewed Caitrin with a shuttered gaze.

"Good morning, Caitrin."

Swallowing, in an attempt to ease the tightness in her throat, Caitrin met his eye. "Milord."

"I hope ye are no longer upset?" he drawled. "I assure ye I won't touch ye again."

Caitrin stared back at Alasdair. She couldn't believe the change in him. Last night he'd been vulnerable before her. The naked want on his face, the hunger in his eyes had haunted her later as she'd lain in bed, trying in vain to fall asleep. Yet now, he was utterly composed and wore a lazy half-smile as if she amused him.

He was treating her like he had upon his arrival at Duntulm months ago—and she knew why.

He was trying to cover up the fact she'd offended him, wounded his pride.

Caitrin's breathing quickened as panic curled up within her. She'd pushed him away to preserve her status here, to protect herself and Eoghan—and yet angering him wouldn't help them either.

Afterward, when she'd been safely back in her bed-chamber, Caitrin had felt wretched over how violently she'd pushed him away. He hadn't hurt her—in fact, the brief kiss had consumed her—yet she'd shrunk from him. She didn't blame him for taking offense. She felt the need to explain.

"Alasdair," she said hoarsely. "About last night ... I must—"

"Please, Caitrin," he cut her off with a lazy wave of the hand. "We don't need to ever mention it again. Ye made yer feelings clear, and I'll respect them ... I'm not here to talk about that." He reached under the neckline of the leather vest he wore and withdrew a rolled parchment. "This came from yer father two days ago. I was waiting till Eoghan was better before giving it to ye."

Caitrin took the letter from him and unfurled it. Then she silently read the missive, going cold as she did so.

Finally, her father had run out of patience.

"I imagine ye knew this day would come," he observed. The dry tone to his voice made Caitrin glance up, her gaze spearing his. He was still smiling, and it was starting to make her angry. "Ye had better start packing yer bags."

Caitrin drew herself up, her fingers clenching around the letter. "What if I wish to remain here?"

He arched a dark eyebrow. "Yer father wishes otherwise."

"And ye?"

The easy smile faltered then and his gaze hooded. "I think it's best if ye leave Duntulm."

There it was, the anger that simmered just beneath the surface, hidden by an urbane smile and a devil-may-care veneer.

Caitrin quelled the urge to cry, blinking furiously. She loved living at Duntulm. She hated the thought of returning to Dunvegan, of being paraded in front of suitors—of being put back inside a cage.

"When?" she finally managed, the question coming out in a croak.

"Tomorrow. We'll set off just after dawn." Alasdair paused here, his gaze boring into her. "But Eoghan will be remaining here."

Caitrin jerked as if he'd just struck her. Then she lurched to her feet, her embroidery falling to the floor. "No!"

Alasdair slowly pushed himself up off the chair, as if he had all the time in the world, and rose to his full height. He towered over her, but Caitrin lifted her chin, fists clenching at her sides. "Ye will not take my son!"

His mouth quirked. "Eoghan is my heir."

"So ye keep saying. But he's not yer property. He's half MacLeod, and he's not staying here."

"Aye ... he is. Eoghan is weaned now. He doesn't need ye anymore. I will teach him everything he needs to know—so that one day he can take over from me ... he will want for nothing."

"I'm his mother," Caitrin countered, "and I'll go nowhere without him."

Alasdair snorted. "Ye will ... even if I have to throw ye over the back of yer horse and tie ye down."

Caitrin stared up at him, trembling now. "This is monstrous," she rasped, heart pounding. "What kind of man would separate a mother from her bairn?"

"One who wishes to ensure the MacDonald bloodline endures."

"That's all ye care about, isn't it?" Caitrin snarled. "Having an heir. Ye are a cold-blooded, heartless rogue, Alasdair MacDonald!"

Alasdair stepped closer to her, his gaze never leaving hers. The smile had faded, and a nerve flickered in his cheek, revealing that her words had managed to wound him. "Aye, I am," he murmured. "But very soon I will be the least of yer concerns."

"I can't believe it, milady," Sorcha whispered, aghast. "The chieftain wouldn't do such a thing."

Caitrin straightened up from where she'd been laying out her clothes on the bed ready for packing. The look of abject horror on her handmaid's face, the disbelief in her eyes, made Caitrin's anger bubble to the surface once more. "Well, ye should believe it," she snapped. "For it's true."

Sorcha's dark-blue eyes now glittered with tears. "But why?"

"Because he's been looking for a way to hurt me ... and he's found it."

"But ye seemed to get on well of late." The lass knuckled away a tear that now trickled down her cheek. "I thought ye might—"

"Well ye thought wrong," Caitrin cut her off. "Now stop looking at me with cow eyes and help me pack my things."

Sorcha heaved in a deep, shuddering breath and nodded. A large wicker chest sat on the floor at the foot of the bed ready to be filled with Caitrin's belongings.

Caitrin got to work, rolling, folding, and packing with ruthless efficiency. Her movements were jerky as anger roiled within her. She'd been harsh with Sorcha, and didn't mean to be—but when the lass had tried to tell her that Alasdair MacDonald wasn't capable of such cruelty, something within her had snapped.

I should never have let my guard down with him.

It was too late now for such regrets, too late to change things. She'd almost begged him earlier—only pride had prevented her—but she knew that wouldn't help her. He'd only despise her all the more.

"I'm sorry, milady." Sorcha's broken whisper pulled her out of her seething thoughts. Caitrin glanced up from her packing to see that her hand-maid now stood, head buried in her hands. Her shoulders were shaking. "I can't bear the thought of ye going away," she gasped, "of ye leaving Eoghan behind."

Grief bubbled up within Caitrin. She hated to see Sorcha so upset; she could deal with her own suffering, yet she hated to see it in others.

Wordlessly, she pulled Sorcha into her arms. However, this only made the girl start to sob. Tears stung Caitrin's eyelids then, scalding her cheeks. She'd told herself she wouldn't weep until she was alone, but it was impossible not to, not with Sorcha inconsolable. They clung together for a few moments before Sorcha drew back, her face distraught.

"Surely yer father will oppose this?" she choked out. "He won't let MacDonald keep ye from yer son."

Caitrin loosed a heavy sigh and shook her head, wiping at her wet cheeks with the back of her hand. "My father is a calculating man ... political alliances have always meant more to him than the happiness of his daughters. Why do ye think he's so keen to see me wed again?"

"But surely he wouldn't want ye separated from yer bairn?"

Caitrin favored Sorcha with a sad, watery smile. "No ... but if it keeps his neighbor appeased, I doubt he'll oppose it."

Chapter Seventeen

Out for Vengeance

A COOL WIND fanned Caitrin's face.

Her throat was raw from weeping, her eyes swollen. She was barely aware of those who escorted her: Alasdair up front and Darron behind, with a handful of the Duntulm Guard bringing up the rear.

All she could think about was Eoghan, and how it had ripped out her heart to leave him.

Sorcha had been heartbroken that morning. She'd helped her mistress finish packing, all the while weeping. Now that Eoghan was weaned, Sorcha would bring the lad up within the walls of Duntulm. Caitrin trusted Sorcha and knew Eoghan was in good hands. Yet that didn't make her feel any better. *She* was the lad's mother. She needed to be with him.

Tears flowed silently down Caitrin's cheeks. She didn't bother to wipe them away. Casting a glance over her shoulder, she looked upon the high basalt curtain wall of the fortress. Sorcha would be watching from her solar window, Eoghan in her arms.

Pain gripped Caitrin's ribs in a vise, and she turned away from Duntulm.

Instead, her gaze settled upon the man who rode ahead of her, leading the way out of Duntulm village. Alasdair sat tall and proud in the saddle, his long dark hair tied back. He appeared completely unmoved by what he was doing to her.

She'd grown to hate her husband during their marriage and to fear him. But the loathing she now felt for his younger brother made those emotions seem gentle.

If she had a dirk, she'd throw it at him, and enjoy seeing the blade sink between his shoulder blades.

Since their confrontation in her solar, she hadn't seen him—not until this morning when she'd been escorted downstairs to the bailey, where her saddled horse awaited.

Even then, he'd barely acknowledged her. Impatience bristled off his body while she mounted and servants loaded her belongings onto a cart that would accompany them south.

He was out for vengeance; she'd seen it in his eyes the day before.

She didn't think anyone could be so cruel. It shocked her to the core—but at the same time, a defiance rose within her.

He won't win. Caitrin clenched her jaw, pushing against the despair that threatened to smother her. *I'll get my son back. I'll fight this ....*

Night settled over the world, and the last of the rosy sunset faded from the western sky.

Caitrin sat upon a boulder, staring sightlessly at the hearth the men had just lit. It wasn't a cold evening, yet the fire provided a focal point for the small camp. They'd erected a tent a few yards back, where Caitrin would rest tonight. The men, Alasdair included, would sleep around the fire and take turns keeping watch.

"Here's yer supper, milady." Darron hunkered down before Caitrin and handed her a wooden platter with bread, cheese, and salted pork upon it. Caitrin took it without a word. "There's a skin of ale as well," he added, placing the leather bladder at her feet.

Caitrin nodded. She wouldn't touch the food; her stomach was clenched in a tight knot. She was too angry to eat.

Darron went to rise to his feet but hesitated. She saw the sympathy in his eyes. "I wish things were different, milady," he murmured, keeping his voice low so that none of the others heard him. "Ye shouldn't be separated from yer son."

Caitrin swallowed a sudden lump in her throat. She'd spent the day in brooding silence, rage seething inside her. Anger made her feel better as it forced down the grief and despair of losing Eoghan. But with just a few kind words Captain MacNichol threatened her composure. Her vision now blurred. "Thank ye, Darron," she said softly. "Ye have been a good friend to me over the last few years ... I'll not forget it."

Darron's mouth curved into a rare smile although his gaze remained solemn. "If there's anything I can do, milady ... just ask."

Caitrin blinked rapidly and heaved in a deep breath. She needed to save her tears till later, for when she was alone. "Just keep an eye out for Eoghan, will ye?" She favored him with a brittle smile.

"Of course," he promised. "Ye have my word."

Darron moved away, returning to the fireside, where one of the men had started singing a bawdy drinking song about a lonely traveler, lusty wenches, and a tavern in the midst of winter. Boyd was grinning at the singer, raising his cup of ale at the end of each lewd verse.

Alasdair sat amongst his men, eating his salted pork and bread. He raised his gaze and smiled when the warrior finished his song and the others cheered. Boyd slapped the singer hard on the back and demanded another.

Not once did Alasdair look her way.

Caitrin set the tray aside and reached for the skin of ale instead. She took a large gulp of the sweet, warm liquid. She wasn't the least bit hungry, but the ale would blunt the world's sharp edges, for a short while at least.

The last of the light faded and night cloaked the campsite. There was no moon so Caitrin found herself watching the stars instead. They were particularly bright tonight. The sight steadied her, as did the knowledge she'd soon see her sister Rhona.

They would reach Dunvegan tomorrow morning, and she would be in a familiar place at least. Once she'd been delivered, Alasdair would leave, and she would be spared having to look upon him.

Caitrin took another deep pull of ale. The drink relaxed her, although her fury continued to simmer. He'd had his vengeance on her—how she wished she could revenge herself upon him.

Around the fire, the singing eventually ceased. The men spoke now in low voices punctuated by the odd burst of laughter. After a while, the world around their campsite grew quiet. They'd made camp at the edge of woodland, and the wind that had buffeted them on the journey south had died.

Weary, Caitrin rose to her feet and, without a word to any of the men, retired to her tent. Inside she found a small brazier burning and a thick fur spread out upon the ground, where she would sleep.

Stretching out, Caitrin rolled onto her back and listened to the rumble of the men's voices beyond.

Eoghan.

Caitrin wrapped her arms around her torso, squeezing her eyes shut as a wave of loss crashed into her.

Her son would be wondering where she was, why she never came into his bed-chamber to tuck him in and sing him a lullaby.

I'll find my way back to ye, my darling.

Tears leaked from her eyes, trickling down her cheeks, where they soaked into her hair. Despair pressed down upon her like a great boulder upon her chest, but she wouldn't give into it.

She wouldn't give up. She owed it to Eoghan to be strong.

I promise.

Alasdair leaned forward and poked the glowing embers with a stick, ignoring Darron. He'd deliberately sat apart from the others, while Boyd took the first shift of the night watch.

But the captain had sought him out.

Darron lowered himself onto the edge of the large flat stone where Alasdair sat. Neither man spoke, yet Alasdair could feel the weight of the captain's stare.

Moments passed, and eventually, Alasdair turned to him with a scowl. "For God's sake, MacNichol ... out with it."

Darron's mouth thinned. "Taking Lady Caitrin's bairn from her seems ... harsh."

Alasdair snorted, although his ire rose at Darron's impertinence. "It *is* harsh—but necessary. Eoghan is the last of my family's bloodline. He must stay at Duntulm."

Darron fell silent, his attention shifting to the glowing embers of the fire pit before them. "Lady Caitrin did a fine job as chatelaine," he said finally. "I don't understand why ye would send her away."

Alasdair frowned. "Ye know why ... her father wants her to remarry."

Darron glanced his way. "But *ye* could wed her?"

Alasdair threw back his head and laughed. "I'd be the last man in Scotland that Lady Caitrin would deign to wed."

"Why?" Darron looked confused now, and Alasdair wished the man would cease his incessant questioning. "Ye seem well suited."

"Appearances deceive, MacNichol," Alasdair replied, his tone making it clear that the conversation was over.

The night was still, the darkness smothering. Alasdair found he couldn't settle.

Rising from the fireside, he walked to the edge of the camp, stepping up next to where Boyd stood watch.

"I'll take over," he said quietly. "Ye get some rest."

Boyd glanced over at him. "Are ye sure? I can keep watch for a while yet."

"I can't sleep anyway. There's no point in both of us being awake."

Boyd nodded, although his face, illuminated by the faint glow of the torch behind him, was thoughtful. "Still not sleeping?"

Alasdair shrugged. "Some nights are better than others." He cast an eye over Boyd. Unlike him, his cousin appeared to have emerged from the war unscathed. "Ye sleep easy these days then?"

Boyd gave a jaw-cracking yawn and stretched. "Aye ... like a bairn." He clapped Alasdair on the back and stepped away from him. "My bedroll beckons. I'll leave ye to it."

His cousin walked off, returning to the camp and leaving Alasdair alone.

Somewhere in the undergrowth, an animal rustled, and then an owl softly hooted. Alasdair drew in a deep breath, listening to the slumbering land around him. The night sounds were gentle, calming, yet they did little to relax him.

He felt as if he stood upon a knife's edge. Every nerve in his body was taut, ready to fight. It was as if danger lurked behind each surrounding shadow. He'd get little rest tonight.

His encounter with Caitrin in the solar had thrown his world back into chaos. It had been a slap in the face, a brutal reminder of why he should have never let his guard down with her.

He had no one to blame but himself.

He'd been a gullible fool twice now. The first time he could have claimed ignorance, but this time he'd known full well the risk he'd been taking.

Alasdair stared out at the darkness, his gaze unfocused. He'd hurt Caitrin deeply by taking Eoghan. There was no worse revenge he could have exacted upon her. MacLeod's demand had been the perfect excuse to send her away while keeping his nephew.

Vengeance.

It had once been his constant companion, especially after he learned of Baltair's death. Yet, for a brief few months, it had released him from its claws, allowing him to hope that one day he might know happiness again. That was—until two days ago.

Now the beast had seized him once more. It perched upon his shoulder and whispered to him. It told him that Caitrin deserved his wrath—that she deserved to suffer as he had. As he did now.

Alasdair drew in a deep breath. Aye, this was what he'd wanted, what he'd planned for on the journey back to Duntulm all those months ago. He should feel jubilant, vindicated that he'd finally achieved his goal.

Why then did he simply feel hollow?

Chapter Eighteen

Return to Dunvegan

"LORD, HOW I'VE missed ye!" Rhona MacKinnon flew across the bailey and threw her arms around Caitrin. She drew back from her sister, storm-grey eyes gleaming. Tall and statuesque with a mane of auburn hair, Rhona looked as vibrant as ever. "Ye don't write often enough!"

Caitrin swallowed a lump in her throat and forced a smile. She was aware that she and Rhona had an audience. Alasdair MacDonald and the rest of her escort were approaching the keep just a few strides behind her. The dove-grey bulk of Dunvegan keep towered above them. Much bigger than Duntulm, Malcolm MacLeod's fortress faced west. It perched on the edge of a loch surrounded by lush green, with rugged hills at its back.

Usually, Caitrin was happy to come home, but this morning the sight of Dunvegan brought her no solace. It was just a reminder of what lay in store: a forced marriage.

"I'm sorry I'm so terrible at keeping in touch," she replied. "The days pass and then, before I know it, a month has gone by and the letter I promised to send ye is still sitting on my desk half-written."

Rhona gave an unladylike snort. "It sounds as if ye are much busier than me." Her gaze shifted from Caitrin then, moving past her to the rest of the company. "Where's Eoghan?"

Caitrin stiffened, struggling to keep the smile plastered to her face. She didn't want to tell Rhona about Eoghan now, not with Alasdair MacDonald just a few feet behind her. "He's remained in Duntulm."

Rhona frowned. "But ye usually travel with him?"

"Not this time … he's in good hands. Sorcha is minding him while I get this over with."

Rhona nodded, her gaze shadowing. "That makes sense I suppose. Da's got the bit between his teeth. He has three suitors lined up already … they'll keep ye busy enough. Ye will be able to send for Eoghan once all this is done." She looped her arm through Caitrin's, and together they walked toward the set of steps leading up to the keep. "I bet the lad has grown."

"Aye." Caitrin's face was starting to ache from the effort it was taking her to keep the smile frozen to her face. "He'll be walking soon." Caitrin paused here, desperate to change the subject. "Have ye heard from Adaira? The last letter I had was two moons ago."

"I heard from her last around then too," Rhona replied. "It sounds as if Gylen Castle suits her and Lachlann very well. Ma's family welcomed them without hesitation. The descriptions of her new life there made me quite jealous."

Caitrin huffed a laugh. "Then we shall have to organize a visit to see her … I have to admit I'm curious about Ma's kin. I'd love to visit Gylen." Even to her own ears Caitrin's voice sounded forced. Of course she wanted to visit Adaira, but right now her priority was Eoghan.

They entered the keep and made their way through a wide entrance hall with stairs leading off it to the left and right. Straight ahead were the heavy oaken doors leading to the Great Hall.

"The noon meal is still being prepared," Rhona said, steering her toward the left stairwell. "Come on, let's go to the women's solar. There's so much I've got to tell ye."

Caitrin set down the goblet of wine she'd just taken a sip from and tried to focus on her sister's happy news. "Congratulations ... I'm so pleased for ye both."

Rhona beamed back at her. "I've been throwing up my bannocks in the mornings for over a week now ... the healer confirmed it this morning. I'm with child."

Caitrin smiled. "Taran must be overjoyed."

"That's an understatement. He hasn't stopped grinning since I told him." Rhona paused here, her gaze searching. She set aside her own goblet of wine. "There is something up with ye, Caitrin. I sensed it from the moment I set eyes on ye downstairs."

Caitrin swallowed. She'd always been adept at masking her feelings from others—even her sisters—but not today it seemed. Her vision misted then; she was so tired of being strong, of having to keep up a wall. Now that she was alone with Rhona her defenses crumbled.

Bowing her head, she covered her face with her hands and began to weep.

Rhona was at her side in an instant, her arm circling Caitrin's shoulders. "Caitrin ... what's wrong?"

"It wasn't my choice to leave Eoghan behind," Caitrin finally gasped. "Alasdair MacDonald is keeping him ... as his heir."

She raised her face, turning to her sister. Rhona's face had gone ashen. "But he can't keep ye from yer son," she whispered.

Tears streamed down Caitrin's face. "He can ... and he has."

Rhona's features tightened. "Only the worst kind of rogue would do such a thing!"

"Aye ... I didn't think him capable of such an act, but I was wrong."

"Why would he be so cruel?"

Caitrin loosed a breath. "He's never forgiven me for spurning him."

She deliberately didn't mention the incident of a few days prior. She wasn't sure how to articulate it. Rhona knew about the proposal Alasdair had once made though.

Rhona stared at her for a moment, before her expression hardened. It was a look Caitrin knew well—the look of a woman steeling herself for a fight. "MacDonald will not get his way. Da will learn about this. He'll put things right."

"No, Rhona," Caitrin replied firmly. She sniffed, wiping her wet cheeks with her sleeve. "Da will only make things worse ... if he helps at all."

"How can ye say that?" Rhona scowled. "Eoghan is a MacLeod as much as he's a MacDonald. Da will tell that bastard to send yer son to ye."

Caitrin shook her head. She'd already had this discussion with Sorcha; it wearied her to have to explain it to her sister as well. "Ye have a short memory, Rhona. Da's alliances mean more to him than we do. Ye would be wasting yer breath."

"But after what happened with Adaira he might—"

"That was different," Caitrin cut her off. "Adaira forced Da's hand that day. If I want Eoghan back, I need to be the one to fight for him."

Rhona's gaze narrowed, and she folded her arms across her breasts. "But how will ye do that. We live in a man's world."

Caitrin's expression hardened. "And that's why we must fight using our own weapons."

"Ye should have brought Eoghan with ye," MacLeod grumbled. "I haven't glimpsed my grandson in months."

"Ye shall see him on my next visit to Dunvegan," Alasdair assured MacLeod with a smile. "I thought it best

Lady Caitrin wasn't distracted ... ye want her to focus on finding a husband, do ye not?"

Across the table, Caitrin tensed. She glared at Alasdair, but he ignored her. Instead, he sipped from his goblet with a nonchalance that made her temper flare.

The MacLeod clan-chief's brow smoothed. Tall, broad, and heavy-set with greying auburn hair, he had eyes the color of a stormy sky. He was a portly man and had gotten so fat of late that it was difficult to see where his chin ended and his neck began. "Aye ... maybe ye are right."

"We can travel to Duntulm together, Da," Caitrin spoke up, forcing a lightness of tone she didn't feel. "Once I've chosen a suitor."

"There will be no time for that," Alasdair replied before MacLeod had a chance to answer. "I imagine ye will be wed as soon as ye choose a suitor. Yer new husband won't want ye disappearing to Duntulm."

"Aye," MacLeod said, eyeing the MacDonald chieftain in surprise. He then shifted his attention to Caitrin. "He's right again, lass. I've sent word. Yer suitors are due to arrive tomorrow. One of them is traveling from the mainland."

Caitrin clenched her jaw, dropping her gaze to the plate of boiled mutton, turnips, and oaten bread before her. Around her, the table went quiet. They sat in Dunvegan's Great Hall, a massive space dominated by two hearths. The noon meal had just been served, and the greasy odor of mutton hung in the air.

Steeling herself, Caitrin glanced up, her gaze traveling to where Rhona and her husband, Taran, sat watching her. Rhona wore a pinched expression, while Taran, whose scarred face gave him a frightening look at the best of times, was scowling. Rhona must have told him about Eoghan, for her brother-in-law then favored Alasdair MacDonald with a dark look.

"Ye are fortunate indeed, Caitrin," Una, her stepmother, spoke up. Small and dark, Una favored Caitrin with a smug smile. "One of yer suitors is my brother, Ross. A fine warrior he is too—any woman would be lucky to have him.”

MacLeod huffed, holding his goblet up for a passing servant to fill. “Gavin MacNichol and Fergus MacKay are both worthy too. We’ll see whom Caitrin prefers.”

Caitrin went still. Chieftain MacNichol was one of her suitors? She remembered then her brief conversations with him during his visit to Duntulm—and the interest she’d glimpsed in his eyes.

Across the table, Caitrin saw Alasdair MacDonald stiffen. While Gavin had indicated an interest in Caitrin during his visit to Duntulm, Alasdair obviously hadn’t imagined he’d take it further.

“What if she doesn’t like any of them?” Caitrin’s younger brother, Iain, asked. A sallow-faced lad with sharp features and a mop of auburn hair, he was watching his father, a gleam in his grey eyes.

Caitrin frowned. She didn’t like the evident pleasure Iain took in asking this. She’d had little to do with the lad over the past few years, but Rhona had warned her about his vindictive streak.

“My daughter will do her duty.” MacLeod rumbled before turning his attention to Caitrin. She stiffened at the hard look in his grey eyes. The events of the past year hadn’t softened him it seemed; he still saw his daughters as his pawns. “If she refuses to make a choice, I shall do it for her.”

MacLeod raised his goblet to his lips and took a large gulp. He then shifted his attention to Alasdair, his expression lightening. “Will ye stay on in Dunvegan awhile, MacDonald?”

Caitrin froze. *No ... Da. Please don’t.*

Alasdair inclined his head. “I should really return to Duntulm.”

MacLeod snorted. “What’s the hurry? Stay on for a few days and enjoy some fine MacLeod hospitality. I’ve got a boar hunt organized for tomorrow.”

Silence fell at the table. Caitrin held her breath. She stared down at her meal, willing Alasdair to refuse. However, when the hush drew out, she raised her gaze and looked at Alasdair. He met her eye briefly before he shifted his attention to MacLeod and smiled, raising his goblet to the clan-chief. "Why not? I like a good hunt."

Caitrin caught up with Alasdair in the entranceway outside the Great Hall once the noon meal had ended. Hurrying ahead of him she stepped into his path, forcing him to stop.

Alasdair halted, while Darron and Boyd continued on.

"Why are ye staying?" she demanded, rounding on him.

He cast her an infuriating smile. "Yer father insisted."

"Ye could have refused."

"It seemed rude."

Caitrin drew in a sharp breath, fighting the anger that made her want to slap his face. "Twisted bastard—ye are remaining here to spite me," she accused. "To gloat when I am forced to wed."

He barked out a laugh. "Ye give yerself too high an importance, Caitrin. I'm staying to appease yer father, and for no other reason."

She stepped close to him, drawing herself up as tall as she could. Even then, she still had to angle her head back to meet his gaze. Alasdair stared back at her, a challenge in his eyes. He was goading her, and she hated him for it.

"Ye are an unwelcome guest, MacDonald," she snarled. "Ye might fool my father with yer smiles and flattery, but I know what ye are. Keep out of my way."

Chapter Nineteen

First Impressions

CAITRIN STOOD IN her bed-chamber, nervously smoothing the skirts of her sky-blue kirtle. It was the first time since Baltair's death that she'd worn any color besides black. She felt naked without her somber clothes.

Heaving in a deep breath, she glanced over her shoulder at her sister's hand-maid, Liosa. "So, they're all waiting for me in the Great Hall, are they?"

The maid paused in brushing Caitrin's hair. "They are, milady."

Caitrin swallowed, nervousness rising in her breast. She wasn't ready for this. "Have ye seen them?" Although Caitrin had already met Gavin MacNichol, she had no idea what her other two suitors looked like.

"Aye ... I was in the bailey when they rode in."

"And?"

Liosa's green eyes grew round. "Ye are fortunate, milady. They're three fine warriors." She sighed then. "I can't decide which of them is the most handsome."

Caitrin cast a look over her shoulder at where Rhona perched upon a seat near the window.

Her sister met her eye with a wry look. "At least Da isn't trying to wed ye off to the likes of Aonghus Budge."

Caitrin pulled a face. "I'd rather he wasn't trying to wed me off at all."

Rhona studied her a moment, her expression turning thoughtful. "Ye are taking all of this better than I would," she murmured. "I take it ye have a plan of some kind?"

"Perhaps." Caitrin looked away, allowing Liosa to finish brushing her hair. She had piled half of it on the top of Caitrin's head while allowing the rest to tumble free down her back. It was the first time she'd worn her hair loose in a long while.

"That sounds mysterious," Rhona replied. "Are ye going to keep it to yerself?"

Caitrin glanced back at her. "For the moment."

Rhona's gaze narrowed. "Ye didn't use to be this secretive."

Caitrin didn't reply, despite that she could sense her sister's frustration.

"Well?" Rhona pressed.

Caitrin sighed. "All I care about is getting Eoghan back," she admitted. "There's no point appealing to MacDonald, or Da … but if I choose a husband wisely, he might be able to help me."

When Rhona didn't answer, Caitrin turned to face her. Liosa gave a huff of frustration and stepped back, giving up on her finishing touches to Caitrin's hair. "Do ye think that's calculating of me?"

Their gazes met before Rhona's full-mouth curved. "No … I think it's clever."

The soaring strains of a harp greeted Caitrin when she stepped inside the Great Hall, Rhona following close behind her. It was early evening, and supper would be served soon. Her father's retainers hadn't yet entered the hall. However, a small group sat upon the raised dais at the far end.

Caitrin's heart raced, and she surreptitiously wiped her damp palms upon the skirt of her kirtle. She hadn't been looking forward to this—but now the moment had come to greet her suitors, she wished she could turn and flee back to her bower.

She had no wish to sit and simper before these men, not when her son was in her enemy's keeping. And yet, if she wanted Eoghan back, she had no choice.

Her father and Una sat at the head of the table, with the three suitors flanking them. They weren't alone though. Taran, Alasdair, Boyd, and Darron sat at the opposite end of the table.

Caitrin stiffened at the sight of Alasdair. She'd hoped he wouldn't be present for this meeting. Yet she should have known he'd make a point of attending—if only to watch her suffer.

The moment she stepped inside the hall, she felt Alasdair's attention swivel to her. The weight of his gaze unsettled her, but she ignored him. Instead, Caitrin shifted her attention to the three men who had come to woo her.

Breathe, she counseled herself. *Don't let any of them see ye are nervous.*

Gavin MacNichol met her eye, a warm smile stretching his ruggedly handsome features. Next to him was a dark-haired warrior with swarthy good looks and bright blue eyes. Instinctively, Caitrin knew this must be Ross Campbell. The family resemblance to Una was striking. The third suitor, Fergus MacKay, was a broad-shouldered man with a mane of thick brown hair and green eyes. An appreciative smile stretched his comely face as he watched Caitrin approach.

Drawing in a deep, steadying breath, Caitrin favored them with a warm smile and stepped up onto the dais. "Good eve, milords ... thank ye all for coming."

Alasdair's fingers tightened around the stem of his goblet.

All conversation had ceased when Caitrin entered the hall. Alasdair's gaze hadn't been the only one to track her path toward them.

It was a surprise to see her not wearing black. The sky-blue kirtle clung to her lithe form, accentuating the high curve of her bust, the womanly flare of her hips. It brought out the color of her eyes, the creamy texture of her skin. Her hair, which she usually wore up in prim braids, tumbled down her back.

Alasdair had forgotten to breathe as she'd walked toward the dais—forgotten about anything except the beauty gliding toward him.

And then, he'd watched her attention focus upon the three men seated near MacLeod.

When she'd smiled, his gut had twisted.

That smile wasn't for him—it would never be for him. Especially now.

The three suitors rose to their feet. MacNichol, the oldest of them, stepped forward first to greet Caitrin. "It's a pleasure to see ye again, milady," he said with a smile. He took her hand and raised it to his lips for a brief kiss.

Jealousy knifed through Alasdair, causing him to suck in his breath.

His reaction caught him off guard. When MacLeod had invited him and his men to join them for a goblet of wine and a light supper, he'd been happy to accept. He was curious to see Caitrin's suitors and her reaction to them. He wanted to see her struggle, possibly even disgrace herself.

But he hadn't expected this—this stomach-wrenching surge of possessiveness.

As if Caitrin belonged to him. As if he had any claim on her.

Alasdair stared down at his wine and struggled to master his reaction. When he glanced up, the tall, raven-haired man with midnight blue eyes had stepped forward to greet Caitrin. He too took her hand and kissed the back of it. "Ross Campbell at yer service, milady."

The third suitor approached her then, dropping to one knee before Caitrin. "Such a vision of loveliness," he boomed in a deep baritone. "A fairy queen stands before me."

"Daughter, meet Fergus MacKay, son to the chieftain of Strathnaver," MacLeod spoke up with a grin. "He has traveled a long way to meet ye."

Caitrin inclined her head, favoring MacKay with a gentle smile. "I am honored, milord."

Alasdair raised his goblet to his lips and took a deep draft.

Jealousy writhed in his gut like an eel. He tried to quell it, but the beast would not be calmed. It had been a mistake to accept this eve's invitation. But now it was too late. He would have to sit through torture.

Caitrin took a seat at the long table. Gavin MacNichol sat to her left while Ross Campbell and Fergus MacKay faced her.

When Liosa had claimed her suitors were all fine-looking men, she'd thought her to be exaggerating. The hand-maid tended to go a bit silly over such things and couldn't be trusted to give an accurate view. However, this time, the lass was right.

It didn't help ease Caitrin's nervousness though. It had been a while since she'd been the center of attention like this.

Courage. Ye need to do this ... for Eoghan.

Squaring her shoulders, Caitrin's gaze swept over the faces of her three suitors. "I'm flattered ye have come all this way," she addressed them with another smile. "I look forward to getting to know each of ye a little better."

She glanced over then, at the man seated next to her. Gavin MacNichol smiled back. Despite that he was around eighteen years her elder, the MacNichol chieftain was still a virile man. He wore his long blond hair unbound this eve. He looked less weary than the last time she'd seen him. His blue eyes were warm as he poured her a goblet of wine.

Opposite her, Ross Campbell was dangerously attractive. The warrior, who appeared to be in his late twenties, had a magnetic gaze and chiseled features. The sensual edge to his gaze as he briefly met her eye made Caitrin uneasy. She imagined he was used to women fawning over him.

Fergus MacKay was of a similar age to Campbell, although his looks were less brooding. He was built like an ox; his leather jerkin strained against his muscles. MacKay stared at her, his fern-green eyes gleaming with frank admiration.

Caitrin surveyed her suitors under lowered lashes. She needed to think. Which one would get her closer to Eoghan? Which one might even defy MacDonald for her?

She decided then that she would make her position clear.

"I should start this eve by telling ye what I'm looking for in a husband," she declared, her voice carrying across the table.

Silence fell. No one here—visitors or kin alike—had expected Caitrin to be so direct. A lady didn't speak so. But Caitrin didn't care. Her time as chatelaine had taught her the value of taking control of situations before others did.

"My future husband will be honest and loyal," she continued. "A fair-minded man who would never seek to undermine or mistreat me in any way."

She shifted her attention down the table then, past Rhona and Taran's shocked faces, to where Alasdair MacDonald sat. His face was pale and strained, his gaze hooded. He didn't look happy at all, and Caitrin felt a surge of vindictive pleasure.

Good.

Caitrin looked back at her father to see that Malcolm MacDonald was frowning, his gaze perplexed. He was probably wondering what had come over her. Caitrin had never spoken out of turn like this.

An awkward pause followed while Caitrin waited for her suitors' responses.

Ross Campbell met her eye and inclined his head slightly, his expression amused. Next to him, Fergus MacKay favored her with a wide grin, whereas Gavin MacNichol merely smiled, his blue eyes twinkling.

Then, unexpectedly, MacNichol raised his goblet into the air. "Shall we toast to that then?"

At the head of the table, MacLeod struggled to his feet. "Aye ... a toast." He too held his goblet high, although he now wore a slightly stunned expression.

The suitors raised their goblets, smiles stretching their faces.

"To the lovely Lady Caitrin," Fergus MacKay boomed, with a wink to his two competitors. "May she find a man among us worthy of her beauty ... and failing that ... may the best man win!"

MacNichol threw his head back and laughed at this, while Campbell smirked.

Raising the goblet to her lips, Caitrin took a sip of sloe wine. The liquid warmed her belly, soothing the last of her nerves. The courtship she was about to endure was a game, she might as well try to enjoy it.

"I'm taking MacDonald out boar hunting tomorrow." Her father's hearty voice jerked Caitrin's attention back to the head of the table. "Ye three must join us." He then picked up the MacLeod drinking horn—taken from a massive ox. "When we return, there will be feasting and dancing ... and the mightiest hunter among ye will have to drain this."

"There will also be wooing," Una reminded her husband, casting him an exasperated look. "Maybe ye shouldn't encourage heavy drinking, my love. Caitrin's suitors must keep their wits about them."

"Of course, wife." MacLeod dismissed Una's comment with a wave of his hand. "Although a real man should be able to hold his drink *and* win my daughter's heart."

Chapter Twenty

Competition

ALASDAIR THRUST THE spear deep into the boar's chest.

Man and beast were so close that he could smell its pungent odor: oily and slightly sweet. Staring into the beast's eyes, Alisdair watched them glaze over. Then it fell to its knees and collapsed with an agonized wheeze.

A cheer went up in the clearing.

"Well met, MacDonald!" Malcolm MacLeod limped toward him, a grin splitting his face. "I've never seen anyone bring down a boar with such style."

Breathing hard, Alasdair straightened up and pulled his spear free of the boar's chest. It had been a clean kill. He'd rammed the spear into its heart.

MacLeod slapped him on the back. "Nothing like a good boar hunt, eh?"

Alasdair nodded, still out of breath from the dance the boar had led him on. In the end, he'd closed in on it, flanked by Taran MacKinnon on one side and Gavin MacNichol on the other. All three men wielded boar spears, but it was only Alasdair who'd managed to get close enough to strike.

"Impressive," MacNichol congratulated him with a wide smile, while MacKinnon merely gave a reluctant nod. Ever since his arrival at Dunvegan, Caitrin's brother-in-law had viewed Alasdair with a jaundiced eye.

"I thought ye were about to get yerself gored," Fergus MacKay called out. He still sat astride his courser.

Ross Campbell had pulled his horse up next to MacKay's, his dark-blue eyes narrowing as he viewed the massive dead boar at Alasdair's feet. Campbell then cast Alasdair an incredulous look. "Ye are either lucky or extremely skilled."

Alasdair tossed both men a careless smile. "I knew what I was doing ... ye need to get close enough to look yer opponent in the eye before ye end him."

"Aye," Clan-chief MacLeod agreed with a snort. "Yer Da always did that ... every time we went out hunting I expected him to be speared in the guts by an enraged boar."

He didn't add that Eoghan MacDonald had actually died while out hunting, although it had been during a stag hunt. He'd fallen from his horse and snapped his neck.

Nearby, a whimper punctuated the clearing. One of the dogs that accompanied them was bleeding, caught by the boar's sharp tusk on its shoulder. Turning his attention from MacLeod, Alasdair crossed to the hound, hunkering down before it. The dog whined again and tried to lick his hand. It was a young, rangy beast with a wiry grey coat and soulful dark eyes.

"How deep is it?"

Alasdair glanced up to see Taran MacKinnon looming over him. He'd forgotten that the scar-faced warrior was master of MacLeod's hounds.

"Deep enough to need some stitching," Alasdair replied, stroking the dog's ears.

MacKinnon knelt next to him, and the dog nuzzled his arm, delighted to be the center of attention. "Does it need binding for the trip back?"

Alasdair shook his head. "The tip of the tusk sliced across the bone, but not deep. It should stop bleeding shortly."

"Good." MacKinnon gave a tight smile. "Lady Adaira would never forgive me for letting her hound bleed to death out on a hunt."

Alasdair glanced up at him. "This is her dog?"

"Aye. His name's Dùnglas. He's barely a year old. She picked him out of a litter when he was a pup."

Alasdair smiled. Grey Fort: a noble name for a wolfhound.

The dog gave another whine before nudging Alasdair's arm once more.

"Go on," Alasdair murmured, giving his ears another rub. "Ye will live, lad."

He rose to his feet, leaving MacKinnon with Dùnglas, and turned back to where the other men had dismounted from their horses and gone to inspect the boar he'd taken down.

It really was a prize. The beast had been in its prime. It had a coarse ebony coat, long deadly tusks, and a mane of spiky bristles that stretched from the crown of its head to the end of its spine.

Alasdair was still gazing at it when raindrops, cool and wet, splashed onto his face. He glanced up to see that the sky had gone a deep, ominous grey.

Nearby, MacLeod also looked up, his heavy brow furrowing. "That's us done for the morning," he announced. "Let's get this beast over the back of one of the horses and make for home."

The rain swept over the woodland northeast of Dunvegan in blinding sheets. The hunting party had turned back, but the decision had come too late—the rain had arrived, soaking them all within moments.

Initially, Alasdair resisted, bowing his head and pulling up the hood of his woolen cloak. But after a while, there didn't seem any point. The rain kept coming, even heavier than before.

Finally, he just surrendered to it, pushing down his hood and letting the rain run down his neck in a river. The rain was cool, but not cold. This storm brought the smell of warm earth and lush vegetation: the scents of summer.

At some point on the journey back to Dunvegan, Alasdair found himself riding next to Gavin MacNichol. The chieftain had been traveling alongside his nephew, but then Darron moved ahead to join Taran MacKinnon, leaving Alasdair and Gavin alone.

Like Alasdair, Gavin hadn't bothered resisting the rain. He hadn't even pulled his hood up, and his dark blond hair was slicked back from his wet face. He cast Alasdair a wry smile. "Looks like I won't need to bathe before this afternoon's feast."

Alasdair huffed in response. He'd intended to avoid the feast, but since he'd brought that boar down, the clan-chief intended to make a fuss of him. MacNichol, Campbell, and MacKay would compete for Caitrin's attention like stags during rutting season. He didn't want to see Caitrin smile at them and flirt with them.

His belly twisted. One of them would become her husband. *One of them will bed her.*

Alasdair hadn't considered this outcome when he'd decided to heed MacLeod's letter. He'd thought only about distancing himself from Caitrin, about making her suffer. Maybe this was his punishment for keeping Caitrin's son from her?

Perhaps he deserved it.

Silence stretched between them before Gavin spoke once more. He had to raise his voice to be heard over the thrumming of the rain.

"How are things in Duntulm these days?"

Alasdair glanced over at him. "Well enough ... I'm kept busy."

"The life of a chieftain isn't as exciting as some think, is it?" MacNichol replied. "There are walls to be built, crops to be planted, and an estate to be managed ... not to mention all the petty disputes ye have to deal with."

Alasdair's mouth curved. "Aye ... I had two farmers visit me last week. They were bickering over a goat."

MacNichol laughed. "Have ye missed the warrior's life ... fighting for king and country?"

Alasdair's expression sobered. "No, I haven't."

Gavin MacNichol studied him for a long moment before he spoke once more. "Three of my men returned home from the mainland a few days ago. They tell me the battle near Durham is to be named after the English commander."

Alasdair raised an eyebrow. "Lord Neville?"

"Aye, they're calling it the Battle of Neville's Cross."

Alasdair snorted. "The victor always gets to write history."

Gavin's brow furrowed then. "Ye would have seen a lot of yer countrymen die. That never leaves ye."

Alasdair drew in a deep breath. He wasn't about to admit to MacNichol that it hadn't. "We should have won that day," he growled. "Our force was much bigger than theirs."

"So, what happened?"

"We were poorly positioned," Alasdair replied looking away, his gaze focusing on the rain-swept woodland path before him. "The mist lay heavily as we readied ourselves for battle, and when it lifted, we saw that we stood upon rough ground. Our movement was made difficult by ditches and walls. We started the battle on the defensive ... and it only got worse from there."

MacNichol's frown deepened. Alasdair didn't blame him; the whole thing was a sorry, humiliating affair.

"I hear they've taken King David prisoner," Gavin said finally.

"Aye, he was badly injured, but I think he still lives. They took him back to England with them. I doubt he'll ever set foot on Scottish soil again."

The two men fell silent then, each brooding over the loss that had cost all of them dearly. After a lengthy pause, Alasdair spoke, deliberately changing the subject. "I was surprised to see ye here," he said casually. "I didn't realize ye wanted to pursue Lady Caitrin?"

MacNichol's mouth quirked. "Who wouldn't? She's a lovely lass … and she's proven that she can run a castle too."

Alasdair forced down a surge of irritational jealousy. He liked Gavin MacNichol, but at that moment he wanted to choke the life out of him. "And what say ye to yer competition? Both Campbell and MacKay are younger than ye."

Gavin laughed, not remotely offended by this observation. When he'd sobered, he winked at Alasdair. "Many women appreciate an older man. We make better lovers."

Chapter Twenty-one

Ye Want to Choose Wisely

CAITRIN CLOSED THE shutters against the rain and began to pace the solar. The chamber—filled with embroidered cushions, dried flowers, and pieces of weaving and sewing in progress—was a warm, comfortable space that would forever remind Caitrin of her mother. She'd always liked this room, but this morning she couldn't relax here.

Just two days back in Dunvegan, and she already felt bored and restless. She was used to moving about Duntulm, her chatelaine's keys rattling at her waist, overseeing servants and making decisions about the running of the keep.

Here, she felt useless.

"For the love of God, sit down," Rhona chided her. "My belly's already churning. Watching ye circle this chamber is making it worse."

Caitrin huffed, stopping and turning to face her sister.

Rhona's face was pale this morning, her expression strained. She sat rubbing her lower sternum. "How long will this go on?" she muttered.

"I felt ill most mornings until I was around three months in with Eoghan," Caitrin replied with a sympathetic smile. "But I hear it differs with each woman."

Rhona sighed, her hand shifting to her belly. She wasn't showing signs of carrying a bairn yet as it was still early. "I wish Taran could share some of this," she grumbled. "Men have the easy part."

Caitrin gave a soft, humorless laugh. "They do indeed."

Rhona's grey eyes clouded. "I'm sorry, Caitrin. That was insensitive of me … ye must be missing Eoghan terribly."

Caitrin swallowed, her hands clenching by her sides. "I can't bear the thought of never seeing him again … it feels as if there's a gaping hole in my chest where my heart should be."

Rhona put aside the embroidery she'd been working on. "Ye will see him again." Her jaw firmed then. "Have ye got any further with that plan of yers?"

Caitrin nodded, taking a seat opposite her. A large loom sat to her left, with a half-finished tapestry on it. Caitrin had been trying to work on it, but then restlessness had overtaken her. She picked up the tapestry beater, a wooden comb she used to push the strands of yarn into place, but didn't resume work. Instead, she traced her fingertips along the teeth of the beater.

"I've met all three of them now," she replied softly, staring down at the comb, "and later I'll decide who can best help me get Eoghan back."

"Any early thoughts?"

Caitrin glanced up. "Gavin MacNichol is a neighbor, and he makes regular trips to Duntulm … he might be a good choice."

Rhona frowned. "He's on good terms with MacDonald though, and might not want to fall out with him."

"Ye think I should choose someone more aggressive?"

Rhona shrugged. "Perhaps. MacKay looks like he has some fire in his belly."

"What about Ross Campbell? Would he help me?"

Rhona went still, her expression turning thoughtful. "I'm not sure what to think of him. Maybe it's just because I don't like Una. He's difficult to read." She grinned then. "Although Campbell's certainly the best-looking of the three. Liosa can't stop sighing over him."

Caitrin snorted. "I care not about looks." It was true. She wasn't searching for a man who'd make her knees go weak or one to fall in love with. Finding a husband wasn't her choice, but if she had to wed, it would be to a man who'd treat her well, who valued her happiness—and who realized how important it was for her to be with her child.

Rhona smiled. "Ye had better think on what to ask them later then," she said, rising to her feet. "Ye want to choose wisely."

Rhona then reached for a woolen shawl, wrapping it around her shoulders.

"Where are ye going?" Caitrin asked with a frown.

"It's nearing noon," her sister replied. "The men will be back at any moment. I'm going down to the stables to wait for Taran." She cast Caitrin an appraising look. "I'll find Liosa on my way and send her up … ye had better start getting ready for the feast."

Caitrin watched Rhona leave the solar, the door thudding shut behind her.

Loosing a sigh, Caitrin leaned back in her chair. She still toyed with the beater, turning it over and over in her hands, but made no move to resume her weaving. In truth, although she knew what she must do, she dreaded the coming feast and the hours of music and dancing that would inevitably follow.

She wasn't looking forward to making idle chatter and smiling till her face ached. She wasn't looking forward to pretending that she wanted a husband at all.

Alasdair swung down from the saddle, landing lightly on the cobblestones. The rain beat down on his head, and he blinked water out of his eyes. He'd thought the storm might abate during the journey back to Dunvegan, but if anything, the rain was even heavier than earlier. The roar of it filled his ears as it thundered down into the bailey.

Leading his horse into the stables, his boots squelching with every stride, Alasdair breathed in the odor of wet horse, dog, leather, and wool. Around him, men grumbled as they tied their horses up inside the stalls and began unsaddling them.

"Come on lads, finish up here and get inside." Malcolm MacLeod's voice boomed through the stables. "Soon ye shall be feasting and making merry."

Behind Alasdair, Boyd paused while unsaddling his horse and glanced over his shoulder at him. "Does MacLeod ever let anything dampen his spirits?"

Alasdair pulled a face. "Don't let his ready smile fool ye ... Malcolm MacLeod's not someone ye want to get off-side with."

"His daughter's imminent remarriage has clearly put him in a jovial mood."

"Aye ... MacLeod loves an opportunity to break out the ale."

Boyd pushed his wet hair out of his eyes before grinning at Alasdair. "I'm enjoying Dunvegan."

"Don't get too comfortable. We're leaving tomorrow."

Boyd's face fell. "So soon?"

"Aye." Alasdair turned from him and started rubbing down his horse. "Tell the others we'll be riding out shortly after dawn."

The events of the last day had made Alasdair realize that it had been a mistake to agree to stay on in Dunvegan. The sooner he returned to Duntulm and put Caitrin out of his mind, the better.

He'd just removed his stallion's saddle and bridle when a firm nudge to his left leg drew his attention. A wet, bloodied wolf-hound sat at his feet, gazing up at him with soft eyes.

Dùnglas.

Alasdair let out an amused snort. "What are ye doing here, lad?"

"Shouldn't that dog be in its kennel?" Boyd muttered. "It risks getting trampled on in the stables."

"Aye ... I'll take him back when I finish here." Alasdair would also see to the beast's shoulder while he was at it. Growing up, he'd helped look after his father's dogs. As a keen hunter, Eoghan MacDonald had taken much pride in his kennel of wolfhounds.

Alasdair finished seeing to his horse and then made his way out of the stables, Dùnglas limping along at his heel. His wet clothing was starting to itch. After he saw to the dog, he would stop by his quarters and get changed before joining the others in the Great Hall.

As he approached the stable entrance, Alasdair spotted a tall woman with fiery auburn hair. Rhona MacKinnon was standing just inside the doorway, a damp shawl wrapped around her shoulders, awaiting her husband.

Rhona's gaze seized upon Alasdair as he neared. Her attention shifted from him to the dog following him before she frowned.

Alasdair favored her with a nod.

"Finally found a friend have ye, MacDonald?" she sneered.

Alasdair cast Rhona an answering smile. "At least the dog knows its place ... milady."

Chapter Twenty-two

Dancing and Feasting

THE STRAINS OF a lute and a harp echoed through Dunvegan's Great Hall, rising above the rumble of voices.

Caitrin took a sip of wine, her gaze traveling down the rows of tables that filled the wide space beneath the dais.

She'd rarely seen the Great Hall so crammed. Her father's retainers and their families packed the long tables, as did his warriors. There were also a number of faces she hadn't seen in years, clansmen who lived throughout MacLeod lands.

They'd all come to witness Caitrin choose her next husband.

Inhaling deeply, Caitrin shifted her attention to the huge array of food that covered the table before her: platters of roast venison, a rich goat stew, and a selection of breads and braised vegetables. A great roast goose stuffed with apples and nuts dominated the table.

Caitrin helped herself to a morsel of goose. The meat was rich and delicious, although her nervous stomach took the edge off her enjoyment. She doubted she'd be able to eat much of the spread. Despite that she'd vowed to try and enjoy herself, anxiety now bubbled up within her.

So much depended on tonight.

Her three suitors sat opposite her this eve, all of them dressed in their best léines and braies. Each wore a diagonal sash of their clan-plaid across his chest.

To Caitrin's chagrin, her father had seated Alasdair MacDonald next to her this afternoon, to MacLeod's right. Apparently, his guest had brought down a huge boar during the hunt. Her father wouldn't stop talking about it.

"Such a fine pair of tusks shouldn't go to waste. I shall have the boar's head preserved and mounted for ye," MacLeod announced, raising his goblet to Alasdair in yet another toast.

Alasdair smiled, raising his own goblet. "Thank ye, Malcolm."

MacLeod grinned at him and turned to a passing servant. "Fill my horn with mead and bring it here." He then turned his attention back to Alasdair, his expression turning sly. "Let's see if ye can drain it in one go. Few men can."

Despite her nerves, Caitrin fought the sudden urge to smile. To her knowledge, only her father had ever managed to drain the horn in one go. He loved to challenge men to drinking contests. She doubted Alasdair would manage it.

Alasdair seemed unmoved by the challenge. He merely smiled and waited for the horn. Moments later, it arrived: the great curved ox's horn, tipped in silver. Years earlier, MacLeod had faced the rampant ox armed only with his dirk and slayed it before cutting off one of its horns as a trophy.

"Ye won't be able to drain that, MacDonald," Fergus MacKay called out. "Hand it to me, and I'll show ye how a real man drinks."

Alasdair ignored him. Then, raising the horn to his lips, he tipped back his head and began to drink.

The other men at the table called out, some cheering him on while others heckled. Impressively, Alasdair paid none of them any mind. Caitrin watched his throat bob as he swallowed the mead in steady gulps.

"Drink, drink, drink!" Boyd bellowed from the far end of the table. The feasting had barely started, and the warrior was already well into his cups. At the tables below the dais, men had risen to their feet, necks craning to catch a glimpse of the commotion going on above.

Caitrin's gaze widened as she watched Alasdair continue to drink. The horn was nearly three times the size of a normal tankard. He should have drained most of it by now?

Even her father was starting to look impressed.

Alasdair reared back then, yanking the horn away from his mouth. His gaze had gone glassy, and his face was paling. For a moment, Caitrin was sure he would be sick.

Her father grabbed the horn off him and peered inside. "Ye did it!" he said, his voice incredulous. "I don't believe it."

A roar thundered down the table as Alasdair's men shouted their approval. However, their chieftain looked unwell. He gripped the edge of the table, squeezing his eyes shut a moment. His throat bobbed as he forced down the last gulp of mead. Caitrin noted the sheen of sweat on his face.

"He hasn't won yet," MacKay boomed, a delighted grin spreading across his face as he eyed Alasdair. "He's about to puke his guts out ... look!" MacKay winked at Caitrin. "I'd move aside, milady. Ye don't want that pretty gown ruined."

Alasdair opened his eyes, his jaw tightening. To Caitrin's surprise, and disappointment, he appeared to recover. Inhaling deeply, he relaxed his grip on the table edge. He then straightened up and cast Fergus MacKay a sickly smile, his gaze glinting. "Yer turn?"

The feasting lasted a long while. After the meat dishes had been enjoyed, servants brought out wheels of aged cheese, platters of fruits, and raspberry tartlets. Mead, ale, and wine flowed—and the noise of conversation gradually grew more raucous.

Caitrin both ate and drank sparingly.

She wanted her wits about her for the dancing, when she would have the opportunity to speak to each of her suitors in turn.

At the table, those surrounding Caitrin all paced themselves differently. Her father downed food and wine with abandon, while Una picked at her meal like a sparrow. MacNichol and Campbell ate and drank moderately, while MacKay drained tankard after tankard of ale. Next to Caitrin, Alasdair ate slowly and barely touched the goblet of wine before him. After downing that horn of mead so quickly, Caitrin wasn't surprised. His face remained pale for some time afterward.

She and Alasdair didn't speak during the feast, choosing instead to ignore each other. Yet she was aware of his presence next to her, even when she was talking to one of her suitors. All three of them worked hard for her attention during the feasting. They teased each other, flattered her, and plied Caitrin with questions.

When the last of the food was cleared away, Caitrin was exhausted. She could easily have slunk away to her bower, but there was the dancing still to come. She wouldn't be able to leave for a long while yet.

The lutist and harpist changed their tune, instead shifting to a playful jig, while the tables were pushed back and the hall cleared.

A line of men and women then took to the floor.

"Lady Caitrin." Fergus MacKay rose to his feet, swaying slightly. "I'd like to have the first dance with ye, if I may?"

Caitrin nodded. She got up and stepped down from the dais, joining the others at the end of the line. Fergus followed, taking her hand, and then they began. Two steps forward, two steps back, and then a twirl. Caitrin knew all the steps, for she and her sisters had done this one many times over the years. This was a dance that all high-born lasses knew, for it was popular at handfastings and other celebrations.

After the twirl, Caitrin picked up her skirts and followed the other dancers around in a circle. She moved in short, gliding strides while keeping her back ramrod straight.

The music grew more strident. Caitrin twirled, stepped, and dipped, while the onlooking crowd started to clap. She loved to dance, and it felt good to move after the long feast. The music caught alight in her veins, and she let it carry her away.

Alasdair watched Caitrin move.

He was unable to take his gaze off her, tracking her across the dance floor as she glided backward and forward. She circled Fergus MacKay, the pair of them edging around each other, drawing together and then apart. He watched MacKay say something to her before Caitrin smiled back at him.

Alasdair sucked in a sharp breath.

Caitrin had never looked so lovely. She'd left her long pale-blonde hair completely unbound, although someone had threaded daisies through it. Rather than the sky-blue kirtle of the day before, she wore a gown of shimmering pale green.

It hurt Alasdair to look upon her. Each moment was torture, and yet he couldn't tear his gaze away.

"Tell me of yer home in Strathnaver," Caitrin asked as she circled her dance partner. "I have yet to visit the mainland."

Fergus MacKay flashed her a wide smile. Despite that he'd looked unsteady on his feet when he'd risen from the table, he danced with surprising grace. "My father resides at Castle Varrich, where I grew up," he replied. "But these days, I rule the lands around Borve Castle."

The dance brought them close, and MacKay's smile faded, his gaze growing intense. "It's a wild, beautiful coast, milady. I look forward to showing it to ye."

They circled around each other, back to back now.

"Do ye visit Skye often?" Caitrin asked.

"Every year or so," he replied. "Why?"

Caitrin twisted her head right, meeting Fergus MacKay's eye. "My son resides at Duntulm ... I don't wish to be parted from him."

"I'm afraid ye will be," he said softly, regret in his green eyes. "Ye shall bear my sons ... that will make it easier to forget the one ye left behind."

Caitrin dropped her gaze. Indignance pulsed through her. Did MacKay really think a woman could just forget such things?

The dance ended then, and MacKay led Caitrin back to her seat. Another dance started up, a lively jig that had most of the onlookers clapping their hands and stamping their feet as the dancers whirled.

Caitrin was glad she was waiting this one out. It gave her time to think.

Fergus MacKay had just made her decision easier. If she wed him, she'd never see Eoghan again. Sipping her wine, she deliberately swiveled around on the bench, facing the dancers, so that her back was to Alasdair MacDonald. It was easier to pretend he wasn't sitting next to her if she kept her back to him.

Once the dance ended, another gentler one commenced. And this time, Ross Campbell led Caitrin out onto the floor.

Una's brother was an excellent dancer. He moved with fluid grace, his midnight-blue eyes tracking Caitrin with a near predatory intensity.

"Milord," she admonished him softly as they drew close and she twirled around him. "Don't stare so ... it makes me uneasy."

Campbell laughed, and immediately Caitrin relaxed. The expression softened his face and eyes. "I apologize ... but it's because ye are a bonny sight, milady," he replied. "There are many men in this hall who are unable to take their eyes off ye."

Caitrin inclined her head, acknowledging the compliment. "Da tells me that ye serve the MacKinnon clan-chief at Dunan," she said lightly. "How long have ye been there?"

"I fostered at Dunan as a lad." They shifted apart for a spell then, as Caitrin and Ross danced to opposite sides of the floor. When they neared each other once more, he caught her eye. "Duncan MacKinnon is more of a father to me than my own."

Caitrin suppressed the urge to frown. She'd heard tales of Duncan MacKinnon—and none of them good. He was said to be a harsh man, one who made Malcolm MacLeod look soft-hearted in comparison. Rhona had told Caitrin that Taran had been pleased to leave Dunan and serve MacLeod instead. However, Campbell clearly held him in high regard.

"How exactly do ye serve him?" she asked.

"I'm Captain of the Dunan guard and the clan-chief's right hand."

Caitrin heard the pride in Campbell's voice, but also the edge. He wasn't used to being questioned by a woman, to having to explain himself to one. Ross Campbell was charming when he wanted to be, and yet Caitrin wondered if he wished for a demure wife who'd have little to say for herself. She sensed his loyalty would always lie with Clan-chief MacKinnon.

Such a man wouldn't help her get Eoghan back.

Chapter Twenty-three

The Bonniest Lass on Skye

"YE MUST BE tired, milady?" Gavin MacNichol asked with a smile. "Ye have only missed one dance so far."

Caitrin sighed, taking the chieftain's hand as they moved forward with the other dancers in a line. "Aye," she admitted. "My feet are aching."

"That's the problem with having three suitors all vying for yer attention."

Caitrin cut him a swift look and saw that he wore a wry expression. "Da thought it would be a good idea," she murmured. "To have all three of ye meet me over a short period ... as ye might have guessed, he's eager to see me wed again."

They left the line and circled their way, back to back, across the floor.

"He certainly is," MacNichol answered when they passed each other once more. "Although I remember ye telling me back in Duntulm that ye didn't want another husband?"

Caitrin met his eye. "I don't," she admitted. "But have ye tried refusing Malcolm MacLeod anything?"

MacNichol huffed a laugh. "He's informed us that we will hear of yer decision at noon tomorrow."

Caitrin tensed, irritation surging within her. She cut a glance across the hall at where her father sat, drinking horn in hand. Typical of him not to share that decision with her.

"Ye didn't know," MacNichol observed.

Caitrin shook her head. She moved away and twirled. When she returned to his side, Gavin MacNichol was frowning. "Ye have had a difficult time, lass. I'm sorry for that … I'd like to see ye happy."

Caitrin swallowed. His kindness unbalanced her. "It's difficult for me to be," she murmured. "When MacDonald has my son."

MacNichol's blue eyes clouded. "I heard about that," he admitted. "But I'd make sure ye saw him often … he'd grow up knowing ye were nearby."

Caitrin held his gaze, a lump rising in her throat. It was a kind offer, but it wasn't enough. She wanted Eoghan by her side. And yet, she was beginning to realize that Gavin MacNichol was indeed the only one of the three suitors she could consider—the only one she'd feel even comfortable with.

Drawing in a deep breath, Caitrin was about to speak when movement out of the corner of her eye drew her attention.

Alasdair MacDonald approached. He wore a determined expression.

Stopping before them, Alasdair met Gavin's eye. "May I interrupt, MacNichol?"

The two men's gazes fused for a moment, and the MacNichol chieftain frowned. Caitrin thought, hoped, that he might refuse. But then he gave a swift, curt nod. Gavin glanced over at Caitrin. "Till the next dance, milady."

Caitrin swallowed, casting him a pleading look.

MacNichol didn't heed it. Instead, he walked away, leaving Alasdair and Caitrin facing each other in the center of the dance floor, men and women circling around them.

Heat rose to Caitrin's cheeks. "What are ye doing?" she demanded between gritted teeth.

Alasdair flashed her a hard smile. "Dancing with the bonniest lass on Skye of course." He took her hand then and pulled her after him so that they fell in line with the other dancers. The feel of his fingers clasped through hers was a brand against her skin. She'd held the hands of all three of her suitors, but none had affected her like this. Alasdair's touch, the firmness of his grip as they halted, turned, and began to dance, made her pulse race like a bolting horse.

Caitrin knew that everyone upon the dais, her father included, would be watching them. They'd be wondering why MacDonald had interrupted one of her suitors—why he was dancing with Caitrin at all.

"What's the point of this?" Caitrin growled.

He gave a soft laugh. "I already told ye."

Alasdair let go of her hand then, his fingers trailing across her palm. Heat shivered up her arm, and Caitrin clenched her jaw. Picking up her skirts, she took mincing steps forward with the other women, bobbing with each stride.

When she completed the steps and made her way back to her partner, Caitrin was fuming. Her feet and back ached, and her heart was sore. She didn't have the patience for whatever game MacDonald was playing.

"Ye will anger my father," she hissed. "None but my suitors should be dancing with me."

Alasdair smirked. "Ye aren't wed yet, milady."

"They might object to yer insolence."

He laughed. "Which one? MacNichol has just bowed out, Campbell couldn't care less who ye dance with, and MacKay has drunk so much he can barely stand."

"Swine." Caitrin circled around him, doing slow turns as the music changed tempo. "All ye have done of late is torment me ... I shall be glad to see the back of ye."

"Aye, I can see ye are eager to find yerself a husband now we are in Dunvegan. All yer talk of remaining a widow was empty, wasn't it?"

Caitrin sucked in a breath. "I don't *want* to wed again."

He barked a laugh, moving around her as the music changed once again. "Liar. I've seen yer smiles, the looks ye give them. Which one will it be?"

Incensed, Caitrin rounded on him. "Bastard! How dare ye?"

Alasdair turned to face her. His mouth curved. His dark eyes blazed. "Don't be coy, Caitrin. We all know ye are no longer the blushing maid. The truth is ye can't wait to warm another man's bed."

The crack of Caitrin's hand colliding with Alasdair's cheek echoed across the hall.

The music stopped, and the dancers halted, swiveling to where Caitrin and Alasdair faced each other in the center of the floor.

Breathing hard and not caring that every eye in the Great Hall was now riveted upon her, Caitrin glared up at Alasdair. "Ye have a forked tongue, MacDonald," she snarled. "If it were up to me, I'd have it ripped out."

Alasdair took his seat once more upon the dais, aware that the atmosphere there had changed. The expressions around him weren't friendly.

MacLeod was glowering, and Caitrin's three suitors stared him down. MacNichol's usually affable face was hard, Campbell's eyes had narrowed, and the furrows on MacKay's brow looked deep enough to split open his forehead. Farther down the table, Rhona and Taran MacKinnon were glaring at him.

Alasdair ignored them all, although it was harder to ignore his stinging cheek.

Caitrin had struck him hard.

Her act had brought the festivities to an abrupt halt. However, as Alasdair picked up his goblet of wine and raised it to his lips, the music restarted. He glanced over his shoulder to see that the dancing had resumed as if nothing had happened.

Caitrin had returned to her seat next to him. She'd turned her back to him again, cradling a goblet of wine in her hands as she watched the dancing. Her shoulders were tense, her spine rigid.

The dancing continued for a short while longer before MacNichol rose to his feet and approached Caitrin. He favored her with a smile, ignoring Alasdair. "Shall we finish that dance?"

Caitrin nodded, rising to her feet and following him onto the floor.

Alasdair took another gulp of wine. A squeal of laughter reached him from the far end of the table. Boyd had just pulled a serving maid onto his lap, but the lass didn't seem to mind the attention. Her giggle rang out across the dais once more while Boyd nuzzled her neck, his hands reaching up to grope her breasts.

Alasdair shifted his gaze from his cousin, back to the dance floor, to where Caitrin and MacNichol circled each other.

He wasn't sure what had been going through his mind when he'd left the dais and strode onto the floor to interrupt their dance earlier. All he knew was that he'd been sitting there watching her with each of her suitors, laughing and smiling as they'd spoken to her—and, finally, he'd been unable to bear it. The beast within—a seething jealous animal that had tormented him all day—had driven him to his feet and across the floor toward them.

Alasdair looked away from the dancers and stared down at the dark wine in his goblet.

Idiot.

It was just as well he was leaving at first light tomorrow.

Chapter Twenty-four

Before It's Too Late

FINALLY, ALASDAIR TOOK his leave of the Great Hall. The dancing had ended, and the only folk still present were men drinking or playing at knucklebones or dice. Caitrin had left with her sister as soon as the last dance finished.

No one said anything as Alasdair rose to his feet.

MacLeod was deep into a game of Ard-ri with Campbell, while MacNichol looked on. The clan-chief's wife, Una, had retired with the other women. A few feet away from the game, MacKay had slumped face-first onto the table and was starting to snore loudly. Farther down the table, Taran MacKinnon was playing knucklebones with Darron—and Boyd was nowhere to be seen.

Alasdair's mouth thinned. No prizes for guessing where his cousin was. At least he'd enjoyed his evening.

Alasdair bid none of those upon the dais good-night, although Gavin MacNichol glanced up as he left the table.

Ignoring him, Alasdair walked out of the hall and into the cool entrance-way beyond. Cressets burned on the pitted stone walls, throwing out long shadows. The air there felt light and fresh after the muggy, smoky interior of the hall.

Taking the stairs up to the second level, Alasdair made his way along a narrow corridor toward his chamber. His limbs dragged, and his head hurt; he couldn't wait to close the door on the world for a few hours. He'd nearly reached his chamber when a voice at his back hailed him.

"MacDonald."

Swiveling around, Alasdair's hand immediately when to his side, where he usually carried his dirk. However, he hadn't worn it tonight and so his hand clutched at nothing.

Gavin MacNichol stood behind him. The chieftain's brow furrowed. "Apologies … I didn't mean to startle ye."

"Ye didn't," Alasdair replied tersely, cursing how edgy he'd become, another lingering effect of that bloody battle. MacNichol was the last man he wished to see right now. "What do ye want?"

"A few moments of yer time."

Alasdair frowned. "Now?"

"Aye." MacNichol motioned to the doorway a few yards behind him. "Step into my chamber … we can talk there."

Alasdair hesitated. He wasn't in the mood for a chat. However, Gavin MacNichol wore an unusually stubborn look on his face, and Alasdair sensed that the man wasn't about to walk away.

With a huff of irritation, Alasdair followed him into his chamber.

Rectangular-shaped with a tiny shuttered window on the far wall, the bed-chamber was an almost exact replica of the one Alasdair was staying in. A large bed took up one corner and two high-backed chairs faced a small hearth, where a lump of peat burned. Outside, the rain pattered on the wooden shutters.

MacNichol lowered himself into a chair and stretched out his long legs before him, crossing them at the ankle. "Take a seat."

Alasdair approached the fireside and stopped before it. "I'd prefer to stand. Say yer piece, and let's be done with this."

Gavin MacNichol eyed him before giving a weary shake of his head. "I'm not blind, MacDonald."

Alasdair's gaze narrowed, although he didn't respond.

"I should have seen it earlier," MacNichol continued. "I don't know why I didn't. Ye are in love with Lady Caitrin."

Alasdair stiffened. To mask his discomfort, he scowled. "No, I'm not."

MacNichol gave a soft laugh. "Aye, ye are. I know the look. I've been there myself."

"Well, ye are mistaken," Alasdair drawled, stepping back from the fire. "Is that all ye have to say?"

"No." MacNichol's tone hardened. "Why are ye letting the lass go?"

Alasdair folded his arms across his chest. "MacLeod wants Lady Caitrin to wed again. It has nothing to do with me."

"Then why the Devil didn't ye take her for yerself? Ye could have saved us all a trip."

Alasdair drew in a deep breath, his anger rising. However, he deliberately left the question unanswered.

MacNichol's gaze narrowed. "Ye are stubborn and proud, MacDonald. Careful, or it'll be yer downfall."

Alasdair went still. "What's any of this to ye?" he growled. "Lady Caitrin is likely to choose ye … isn't that what ye want?"

MacNichol snorted. "I don't want another man's leavings. Caitrin will choose me because of what I offer, not for love. I've already wed once for duty. I'll not do it again."

The frank admission made Alasdair pause. "I thought ye were happily wed?"

Gavin MacNichol held his gaze for a long moment. "Eventually … aye. But Innis wasn't my choice. I loved her younger sister, but that wasn't who our families wanted me to wed."

"And where's her sister now?"

MacNichol's gaze clouded. "She took the veil at Kilbride."

Silence fell in the chamber. Alasdair shifted uncomfortably. He wasn't sure how to respond, or what the man wanted from him exactly. He wished only to leave.

"I don't tell ye this for sympathy," MacNichol continued, his tone sharpening, "but as a warning. Ye stand upon a crossroads. If ye don't decide which road to take, fate will do it for ye ... and ye will have to live with the consequences for the rest of yer life."

Alasdair snorted. "Ye forget that the lady in question hates me."

Gavin MacNichol raised a dark-blond eyebrow. "Does she?"

"Aye, ye saw for yerself tonight."

MacNichol gave a dry laugh. "I might not be blind, but *ye* are. The moment ye took her hand tonight, Caitrin's cheeks flushed. We all saw the way she looked at ye."

"In loathing?"

The chieftain shook his head, his mouth curving. "Love and hate are close cousins, lad. Talk to her ... before it's too late."

Caitrin was sitting by the fire, staring at the dying embers, when someone knocked on the door to her bed-chamber.

She frowned. It was late. After returning from the Great Hall, she'd thought that she'd fall into bed exhausted. However, she'd been unable to relax.

The day's events had left her drained yet restless. Fury still churned in her belly at what Alasdair had done, how he'd treated her. She'd hoped he'd leave the hall after she slapped him—but he hadn't. Instead, she'd been forced to ignore him for the rest of the evening, all the time painfully aware of his presence.

She hated how responsive she was to him, how the touch of his skin against hers had set her blood aflame. She hated him, and yet her body betrayed her.

Caitrin's throat constricted then. Tomorrow Alasdair MacDonald would be the least of her concerns—for then she'd have to choose a husband.

Thud. Thud.

Again, someone knocked. Rising to her feet, Caitrin padded barefoot across to the door. Dressed in her night-rail and robe, she wasn't in a state to welcome visitors. However, she guessed it would be Liosa or Rhona coming to check on her. She wished they wouldn't fuss.

Caitrin opened the door and froze.

Alasdair MacDonald stood there. Hair tousled, he wore a slightly wild expression.

Time paused for a moment as their gazes locked, and then Caitrin reacted. She stepped back and moved to slam the door in his face.

Alasdair shifted forward, jamming his body against the door and preventing her from closing it on him.

"Get out," Caitrin growled. Rage slammed into her, and she shook from the force of it. She couldn't believe the man had the nerve to try and barge his way into her bower. "I'll count to three, and if ye aren't gone by then, I'll scream this keep down."

"Caitrin," he rasped, his dark eyes searing hers. "I need to speak to ye. Just let me say my piece, and I'll go … I give ye my word."

"What? Here, in my bed-chamber? Have ye lost yer wits?"

"Aye." The pain in that one word made her pause. "And that's why I implore ye to hear me out. *Please*, Caitrin."

Chapter Twenty-five
Make Ye Mine

A LONG MOMENT passed. Caitrin stared into Alasdair's eyes, witnessing naked desperation. What was wrong with the man?

"Make it quick then," she growled, "and then go."

He nodded.

Slowly, she released the door and stepped aside, allowing him to enter her bed-chamber. His presence dominated the small space, and Caitrin immediately regretted letting him in.

Alasdair moved over to the fireplace before turning to face her. His eyes were haunted pools in the fire's soft glow. "I've been cruel to ye," he said finally. "And I'm sorry for it."

Caitrin pulled her night-rail close and frowned. "Ye came here to apologize?"

Alasdair's features tightened. "I know this won't be easily put right."

She drew herself up, her temper simmering. "Ye are right ... it won't. Ye have taken my son from me. I'll *never* forgive ye for that."

His throat bobbed. "Ye are angry with me."

"I don't need ye to state the obvious, MacDonald." Fury pulsed through Caitrin. "And if that's all ye have come to say, ye can get out now."

His face went taut. He stared down at her, his eyes suddenly bright. "I shouldn't have separated ye from Eoghan."

"So ye realize that now, do ye?"

A shadow moved in his eyes. "No, I knew before ... I just didn't care."

Caitrin's temper flared hot. "Because I wouldn't kiss ye?"

He ran a hand down his face before he muttered a low oath. "Ye make me sound contemptible."

"That's because ye are." Caitrin stepped back. Her heart now thundered against her breast bone. "Leave now, Alasdair. We're finished here."

But he didn't move. He merely stared at her, his face so bereft that an arrow of compassion speared Caitrin's chest. She couldn't stand the man, yet the pain in his eyes made her catch her breath.

"Leave," she repeated, her voice rising as panic seized her.

Alasdair moved then, but not toward the door. Instead, he stepped closer to her and, unexpectedly, went down on one knee.

Caitrin sucked in a breath. "What the Devil are ye doing?"

"I'm sorry, Caitrin." His voice was raw. The words sounded like they'd been ripped from him. His eyes glittered with tears. "If I could, I'd go back in time and undo it—all of it. Give me a chance, and I'll prove to ye that I'm not the rogue ye think I am. I'll spend the rest of our lives proving it to ye."

Caitrin's lips parted in shock. "What are ye saying?"

A beat of silence followed.

"I love ye, Caitrin ... I always have," he rasped. "I thought I'd mastered it ... but the moment I returned to Duntulm and saw ye, I knew I'd been lying to myself."

Shock rendered Caitrin momentarily speechless. When she finally found her tongue, she realized she was trembling. "Ye truly are a hateful man, Alasdair MacDonald," she whispered.

He gazed up at her, naked pain upon his face. "I know."

"Love is an act, not just a word." Her voice shook as she spoke. "If ye love me, why have ye put me through so much misery?"

"I have no excuse ... only cowardice." A nerve flickered in his cheek. Tears glittered on his long dark eyelashes.

Caitrin swallowed as her own vision misted. "Why didn't ye say something months ago?"

He drew in a shuddering breath. "I was about to ... on the night I kissed ye in my solar."

"So, this is *my* doing?"

He shook his head. "No ... it's entirely mine." His gaze ensnared hers then. "Do I repulse ye, Caitrin?"

The question caught her off-guard. She stared down at him, her lips parting. When she managed a response, her voice was barely above a whisper. "No. Why would ye think that?"

"Ye shrank from me that night."

Caitrin swallowed. "I panicked," she replied huskily. "I was determined never to let another man control me." She broke off here, brushing away a tear that now trickled down her cheek. With everything that had happened since, her decision seemed pointless now. Soon she'd be a wife again, and her life as chatelaine of Duntulm would be nothing but a memory.

Alasdair's gaze guttered. "I thought ye couldn't stand to touch me."

Caitrin wrapped her arms around her torso, hugging herself tight. It wasn't cold inside her bower, but suddenly she shivered. "I tried to explain myself the following day," she said. "But ye never gave me the chance."

A deathly hush followed her words. Despair welled up within Caitrin. What an awful mess all of this was.
"Please get up, Alasdair," she whispered.

Seeing him on one knee before her reminded Caitrin of that fateful day, nearly three years earlier—and of the proposal that she'd spurned.

He didn't move. "Will ye wed me, Caitrin?"

Caitrin stopped breathing.

"I'll love ye and cherish ye … for as long as I have the breath to cool my porridge. And I will never try to separate ye from Eoghan again."

Silence drew out between them. When Caitrin replied, her voice was brittle, pleading. "Please, Alasdair … get up."

He complied this time, rising to his feet before her. However, the desolation she now saw in his eyes suddenly made it difficult to breathe. With a jolt, she realized that she cared whether Alasdair suffered or not.

Despite everything—she cared.

"Ye will not wed me?" he asked softly.

She met his eye. "If I refuse, will ye still deny me Eoghan?"

They stared at each other for a long moment, before Alasdair answered. "No … as soon as I return to Duntulm, I will send him to ye." He paused then. "I see it's too late now … ye hate me."

Caitrin swallowed. She'd told herself many times over the past days that she detested him. She wanted to rail at him, to tell him that she wished him dead, yet the words wouldn't come.

"I don't hate ye," she whispered brokenly. She squeezed her eyes shut as more tears welled. How she wished she did hate him. "I too have done things I'm sorry for."

"Ye have nothing to apologize for," he rasped.

Caitrin opened her eyes, not bothering to wipe away the tears that now trickled down her cheeks. "We were good friends once, but I destroyed our friendship," she whispered. "I laughed in yer face when ye proposed to me … it was a cruel, thoughtless thing to do. Ye deserved better."

Their gazes fused. Alasdair didn't answer, and so she continued.

"When ye returned to Duntulm it didn't take me long to realize ye are ten times the man yer brother was. Had I seen that years ago, I could have spared us both a lot of pain."

Alasdair's mouth twisted. "As could I … if I hadn't been so bitter."

"Ye have been through a lot in the past years," she said softly. "I admire yer strength."

Alasdair shook his head. His gaze dropped to the flagstone floor between them, and a tear trickled down his cheek. Watching him, Caitrin's throat constricted.

Long moments passed, and then, wordlessly, he moved toward her, bridging the gulf between them. Reaching out, he gently took hold of her wrist.

The feel of his fingers, warm and strong, against her skin made Caitrin draw in a sharp breath. Gaze still averted, he drew her hand toward him, before turning it over and placing his lips upon the fluttering pulse inside her wrist.

Caitrin stopped breathing.

His lips seared her skin. She felt naked standing before him.

Alasdair gently trailed his lips down from her wrist to the palm of her hand. He kissed her gently there, holding her hand against his face. Instinctively, Caitrin spread her fingers against his cheek. It was wet. She curved her fingertips under the lean line of his jaw and felt his pulse, pounding as fast as hers.

Caitrin closed her eyes as her own tears slid silently down her face.

She'd been resisting this for months now. She couldn't deny it any longer. She couldn't keep lying to herself, telling herself that it was better to remain alone. Like the waxing moon and the turning of the seasons, this thing between them couldn't be stopped. While they both drew breath, it would torment them.

Caitrin's lips parted, but the sigh that escaped her quickly turned into a gasp when Alasdair pulled her into his arms. Yet, instead of kissing her, his lips trailed over her face, brushing away her tears. The touch, feather-light, yet overwhelmingly sensual, made her limbs tremble.

"Ye are everything to me," he whispered as his lips trailed down her jaw. "I can't pretend anymore."

And then his mouth captured Caitrin's, his lips slanting hungrily over hers.

The kiss was wild, devouring. Caitrin let out a soft moan. She reached out with her free hand—for he still gripped the wrist he'd kissed—her fingers splaying out over his heart.

Alasdair ended the kiss then, his breathing ragged. He stared down at her. "The thought of ye wedding another tears me up inside."

Caitrin stifled a gasp. His voice sent shivers of need across her skin.

He pulled her hard against him this time, cupping the back of her head with his hands while he kissed her again. Caitrin leaned into him, her body turning molten as his tongue parted her lips. She'd never known a kiss like this, had no idea a kiss could make her pulse with raw need.

When Alasdair drew back once more, she struggled to draw breath.

"Tell me to stop, and I will," he said, his voice ragged, his eyes aflame. "Otherwise I'm going to make ye mine."

Chapter Twenty-six

Mo Leannan

CAITRIN GAZED UP at Alasdair. His words had rendered her speechless.

"Do ye wish me to leave ye be?" A nerve flickered in Alasdair's jaw. He held her in the cage of his arms, and she felt tension ripple through him. He thought she would push him away, send him from her.

Caitrin drew in a trembling breath. "No," she whispered. "Stay."

That was all he needed.

Alasdair lowered his head and claimed her mouth once more, pulling her against him. The heat of his body hard against hers was searing. Caitrin reached up, her arms entwining around his neck as she sought to pull him closer still.

His hands slid down her back as he kissed her, his touch firm and sensual. The feel of his hands exploring her body pushed all thoughts, all cares from her mind. The world shrank to the feel of his tongue, his lips, to his hands that now shifted to her breasts, opening her robe and untying the laces of her night-rail. Moments later, the garments fell to the floor.

Caitrin stood naked before him.

Breathing hard, she watched his gaze devour her.

Motherhood had changed her figure, made her breasts fuller, her hips a little broader. Small puckered stretch marks marked her belly, and she forced herself not to cover them with her hands. There wasn't any point in hiding from him.

She glanced down at her body to see her breasts strained toward him, her swollen pink nipples aching for his touch.

When she looked back at Alasdair, she watched him wet his lips, his high cheekbones flushing. He heeled off his boots and shrugged off his léine. Then he unlaced his braies and let them drop to the floor.

His body, long and lean, made her suck in a breath—as did the sight of his shaft. Fully erect, it strained up against his belly. Her knees trembled as a shiver of fear went through her. The only man she'd ever lain with was Baltair. Before now she'd only ever known roughness and brutality at a man's touch. However, when Alasdair reached for her, pulling her gently into his arms, the fear dissipated.

The feel of their naked flesh touching caused her to whimper. His skin was so hot, she wanted to taste it. She bowed her head to his neck and gently bit the tender skin there.

Alasdair growled, his chest rising and falling sharply while she continued her exploration, her tongue tracing the whorls of hair on his chest before she discovered that his nipples pebbled under her touch. She nibbled one, and he gasped. The male musk of his skin was intoxicating. She suddenly felt dizzy with want.

Alasdair's hands went to her hair, and his fingers tangled in the soft curls. Then he pulled her up and kissed her again. This time, it was slow and sensual—a kiss that made Caitrin melt into his arms. The feel of his arousal pressed up against her belly made shivering excitement pool in the cradle of her hips. Restlessness rose within her. She needed more.

Alasdair picked her up, his hands sliding under her buttocks, and carried Caitrin to the narrow bed.

Together, they collapsed onto the mattress. Tearing his mouth from hers, he bent his head to her breasts and suckled them, drawing each nipple deep into his mouth. He sucked hard until she groaned under him, before continuing his leisurely progress down her body. Then he spread her legs and knelt down between them.

Caitrin groaned, arching back against the cool coverlet. Her body thrummed with pleasure now, radiating out from a hot pulse at her core. His tongue, his fingers, made her forget her own name. She felt boneless, just a molten pool of want. Her body began to quiver.

Softly, she moaned his name.

He rose up between them, spread her legs wider still, and positioned himself at the entrance to her womb. Caitrin glanced down between them, her breath catching at the sight of his shaft pressing against her damp nest of blonde curls.

"I'm going to take ye slowly, mo leannan," Alasdair breathed. Sweat coated his body. His hair fell like black silk over his broad shoulders. "I want to make this last."

Caitrin could only groan in response. *My lover*. She didn't care what he did, as long as he was inside her.

He entered Caitrin then, inching into her, stretching and filling her. And then he began to move in long, easy strokes.

Throwing her head back, Caitrin gave a long shuddering moan and embraced the waves of pleasure that now pulsated out from where their bodies joined. Alasdair changed position, hooking her legs over his shoulders before he continued his deep, slow, and deliberate thrusts.

The look on his face, the strain as he struggled to keep a leash on his control, excited her beyond measure. She wanted to see him unravel, just as she was.

Caitrin let go of any lingering inhibitions and angled her hips up to meet each thrust, bringing him deeper still. She arched back and let her groans fill the bower, writhing against him.

It had never felt like this before—she now understood what all the fuss was about. Why her sisters had gotten coy, secretive expressions on their faces when they'd spoken of lying with their men.

It was magic, an enchantment she gave herself up to willingly.

"Caitrin," Alasdair gasped, his voice raw with need. His hands cupped her buttocks as he thrust hard into her now, his self-control slipping. Caitrin cried out, pleasure radiating out in deep, throbbing waves from the cradle of her lower belly.

Then Alasdair drove into her once more, and a rush of heat exploded inside her as he gave a throaty cry.

Trembling on the bed, Caitrin looked up to see that Alasdair was bent over her. His sweat-slick body quivered. He was struggling to catch his breath. Reaching out, Caitrin brushed the hair out of his eyes. Panting, Alasdair raised his chin, and their gazes fused.

It was a long, hot look, infused with more meaning than either of them could articulate.

Caitrin awoke to the sound of anguished groaning.

Pushing herself up onto one elbow, her gaze fell upon Alasdair. The last of the glowing embers in the hearth softly illuminated the narrow bed where they lay. Alasdair was asleep next to her on his back, but he was not at peace. He writhed and twitched, his skin gleaming with sweat. His features were twisted into a grimace, and his hands clenched and unclenched by his sides. He appeared to be in the grip of a violent dream.

As Caitrin observed him, he flinched before crying out.

"Alasdair."

He paid her no mind, his body going rigid, and then his head jerked from side to side. "No ... no."

"Alasdair!" She reached out, gripped his shoulder, and shook him.

His eyes snapped open. He stared up at Caitrin, but it was as if he wasn't even seeing her.

"Alasdair?" Her voice rose in concern. "What is it? What's wrong?"

Gradually, the wildness faded from his eyes. A moment later he focused upon her, and his face relaxed. "Did I wake ye?"

Caitrin's mouth quirked. "Aye … and likely half the keep."

He muttered a curse and closed his eyes, running a hand over his face. "Sorry … I have bad dreams sometimes."

Caitrin watched him, her brow furrowing. "Since the battle?"

"Aye."

Caitrin's frown deepened. "Tell me of them."

His eyes flickered open, and he cast her a pained look. "Ye don't want to hear of such things."

She huffed. "Let me be the judge of that."

Alasdair heaved a deep breath and rolled over onto his side, facing her. "They're always the same," he began hesitantly. "I'm right back there in the mist and the mud. The English are running at me … like ghosts through the fog. All I can hear is the screams of men as they die … and I know I'll fall soon, skewered on an English blade."

Caitrin watched him steadily. "But ye didn't."

His mouth twisted. "Maybe I should have. I've not been right since, Caitrin. I jump at shadows, I can't sleep, and sometimes my hands shake like I'm an old man. I might not look it, but I'm broken … on the inside where no one but ye can see."

Caitrin's breathing constricted at these words. She reached out, her hand clasping his. "I can't imagine how ye must have felt," she murmured. "How it must feel to see all those men fall around ye … but I don't think ye are broken. Just like a wound to the body, this too will heal."

He huffed, although his eyes glittered. "Will it?"

"Aye." She squeezed his hand. "Ye won't have to face it alone now."

Their gazes met and held. His throat bobbed. "Are ye saying that ye—"

"Aye," she cut him off with a wobbly smile. "I will wed ye, Alasdair MacDonald."

He stared at her for a moment, before joy spread across his face, chasing away the lingering horror of his nightmare.

Alasdair reached for Caitrin. When their faces were just inches apart, he gave her a tender smile. His eyes shone with tears. "I meant what I said earlier," he said softly, "about loving and cherishing ye to my dying breath. All I've ever wanted is ye, Caitrin, and yet all I've done of late is make ye suffer. I want to make it up to ye … but I don't know where to begin."

Caitrin stared back at him before a slow answering smile curved her lips. Reaching up she traced his lower lip with her fingertip. "Ye can start by making love to me again," she whispered. Her cheeks flushed at her own boldness, but she didn't stop.

Instead, she let her hand travel down his jawline and neck to his chest. Her fingers then slid down the taut plane of his stomach, before they wrapped around his shaft. It pulsed in her hand, hot and hard, straining toward her. "After that, we shall see."

Chapter Twenty-seven

Forgiveness

"THIS IS UNEXPECTED." Malcolm MacLeod viewed Alasdair and Caitrin with a jaundiced eye before his gaze shifted to the three men who also stood in his solar: Gavin MacNichol, Ross Campbell, and Fergus MacKay. "Do any of ye have anything to say about this?"

A heavy silence filled the solar, broken only by the patter of rain against the shutters. The bad weather had settled in, turning the world grey and misty. The huge hearth to Alasdair's left roared this morning, throwing out much-needed heat. A great stag's head mounted above the fire glared down at the chamber's occupants.

MacNichol broke the silence first. "I have no objection," he said, his mouth quirking into a rueful smile. "Who am I to stand between two lovers?"

Alasdair met his eye, and a look passed between the two men.

Next to MacNichol, Campbell wore an inscrutable expression, although his gaze was hard. "I've nothing to say," he said tersely, casting MacLeod an irritated look. "Other than ye have wasted my time."

MacLeod's heavy brow furrowed. "I didn't know MacDonald had an interest." He cast Alasdair an accusing look then. "Why didn't ye tell me ye wanted to wed my daughter?"

"I was under the impression she didn't want me," Alasdair replied, holding his eye. "I was wrong." He glanced over at Caitrin then. Her face was tense, her blue eyes wary. She'd been nervous about this meeting. He didn't blame her, for their future rested on what was decided here.

The pair of them stood shoulder to shoulder as they faced her father. Wordlessly, Alasdair reached out and took her hand, interlacing her fingers with his. Caitrin's answering squeeze reassured him.

"Campbell's right," MacKay growled. "Ye have wasted all our time. I didn't travel here to be made a fool of."

Alasdair cut MacKay a sharp look. "No one's made a fool out of ye, Fergus. Lady Caitrin was free to choose between us ... and she has."

"Aye ... but I wager the lass always knew she'd choose ye."

"No, I didn't," Caitrin replied. Her voice was soft, although with a steely edge just beneath. "I met with all of ye in good faith."

MacKay glared back at her. "Ye have made a mistake choosing him. I could have given ye Strathnaver ... a vast tract of land, far superior to any on this barren rock."

His comment made MacLeod stiffen. Alasdair too tensed at MacKay's insult but held his tongue. He was too happy this morning to let anything ruin it. He understood MacKay's bitterness. The man was disappointed—he was lashing out.

"Let them be," MacNichol cut in, his voice weary. "Lady Caitrin has made her choice, and we must accept it."

Fergus MacKay spat out a curse. "Ye may, but I don't. The Devil take the lot of ye ... this is the last time I have anything to do with the MacLeods of Skye."

With that, MacKay strode from the solar, slamming the door behind him with a force that made the chamber shudder.

"Well ... that's an important relationship ye have just cost me, daughter," Malcolm MacLeod said sourly. "It's just as well ye are wedding a MacDonald and strengthening the link between our clans ... or I would be very displeased with ye right now."

"Ye do realize that MacKay was always going to be a poor loser?" MacNichol pointed out. "He was sure Lady Caitrin would select him."

Campbell snorted at this, raising a dark eyebrow as he cast the MacNichol chieftain a disbelieving look. "That oaf? He never stood a chance."

Alasdair smiled, while MacLeod's glower eased. Campbell's comment had succeeded in easing the tension in the solar. Alasdair gently squeezed Caitrin's hand and glanced at her. He was glad to see that much of the tension had ebbed from her face. She looked up, meeting his eye, and smiled.

MacLeod huffed out a breath before crossing to the sideboard, where he reached for a jug of wine and set out five goblets. "A toast is in order then," he rumbled, pouring out the wine.

He handed out the goblets, pausing once he'd passed Caitrin hers. He fixed his daughter in a level stare. "Is this truly yer wish, lass?"

Caitrin nodded. She smiled once more, a soft expression that made her eyes darken. The sight made Alasdair's breathing quicken. "Aye, Da. It is."

"Very well." MacLeod held up his goblet. "Let us toast to yer handfasting." He paused then, his gaze narrowing as it pinned them both to the spot. "There will be no time for second thoughts, mind. If ye wish to wed, then there will be no delay. Ye shall be handfasted in Dunvegan chapel tomorrow at noon."

Rhona had gone very quiet.

She and Caitrin were sitting in the women's solar. Rhona was working upon her tapestry, while Caitrin wound wool onto a spindle. It was late afternoon, and usually, at this hour they would have taken a walk together in the gardens. However, rain still fell outdoors, so they were forced to remain inside the cool, damp stone walls of Dunvegan Castle.

When the silence finally got too much, Caitrin put down her spindle, fixing her sister with a level stare. "Out with it."

Rhona glanced up from her weaving. "What?"

"Ye have something to say to me. I am waiting."

Rhona huffed, favoring her with a rueful look. "Words fail me, sister ... I'm struck dumb."

"That's a rarity," Caitrin replied with a snort. "I should annoy ye more often."

"Cheeky wench," Rhona growled. Their gazes met, and her features tightened. "Of late, ye keep yer own counsel. Sometimes I think I hardly know ye."

Caitrin inclined her head. "Because I didn't say anything about Alasdair?"

"Aye. Ye had plenty of opportunities to tell me how ye truly felt about him ... but ye didn't. Don't ye trust me?"

Caitrin loosed a sigh. She heard the hurt in her sister's voice and was sorry for it. "It's hard to speak of something ye haven't even admitted to yerself," she said after a pause.

Rhona's gaze narrowed. "Ye didn't know how ye felt?"

Caitrin shook her head, dropping her gaze. "When I knew Alasdair before, we were friends. I didn't see him in any other way. But when he returned to Duntulm, something changed between us. We both fought it initially. Alasdair still resented me, and I was determined to continue as chatelaine ... after Baltair I promised myself I'd let no man rule my life again."

"But what Alasdair did to ye." Rhona was scowling now. "It was unforgivable."

A wry smile tugged at Caitrin's mouth. Her sister could be dogmatic at times. She was like their father:

certain lines could never be crossed, and once they were, there was no going back.

"I thought so too," Caitrin admitted softly. "There have been times over the past few days, if ye had given me a dirk, I'd have happily stabbed him through the heart with it."

Rhona's grey eyes grew wide. "And ye are going to wed this man?"

Caitrin sighed. "Aye … I can't describe it, Rhona. I started the day hating him … but after he came to my chamber and told me how he felt … and explained himself … my feelings changed."

"So ye aren't doing this just to get Eoghan back?"

Caitrin shook her head. "Alasdair agreed to return Eoghan to me, whether or not I decided to wed him." She paused here, meeting her sister's gaze. "I'm doing this because I want to."

Rhona exhaled sharply. "I just hope ye are seeing things clearly."

"Surely ye understand, Rhona?" Caitrin replied with a shake of her head. "On yer wedding night with Taran, ye were set to hate him forever … and yet by the next morning yer feelings toward him had completely changed."

Rhona's brow furrowed. "That was different."

"How? He entered those games without telling ye, knowing that ye would feel betrayed. Ye were then forced to wed a man ye didn't want." Caitrin paused here. "Yet one night alone together made all the difference."

Rhona actually blushed then, dropping her gaze. When she looked up, there was understanding in her eyes. "It did," she said softly.

Silence stretched between the sisters then, as each retreated into their own thoughts. Finally, Caitrin picked up her spindle once more and resumed winding wool. "Forgiving Alasdair was much harder than hating him," she admitted softly. "But I realized I would know no peace until I did."

Alasdair pulled up the hood of his cloak and exited the keep, making his way down the slippery steps to the bailey below. The rain fell in heavy sheets, sweeping across the courtyard in waves. It didn't seem to have let up since it had begun the previous day.

Crossing the cobbled bailey, Alasdair made his way toward the stables. However, instead of taking the left door into where the horses were kept, he ducked through a low doorway into the lean-to where MacLeod housed his hounds.

The smell of wet dog assaulted his nostrils as he entered. The lean-to was open on two sides, letting in light and a little rain. The dogs didn't seem to mind though. Most of them were asleep, curled up together at the back of the space, although they stirred when Alasdair appeared.

Tails wagging, many lurched to their feet. The first to reach the edge of the enclosure was a young, leggy wolf-hound with a wiry grey coat.

Dùnglas jumped up against the wooden boarding lining the enclosure, whining with delight at the sight of Alasdair.

"Easy lad." Alasdair smiled as he tried to fend off the dog's clumsy feet and wet tongue. He leaned down and examined the injury to the wolf hound's shoulder, pleased to see the stitched cut had started to scab over now.

Gently, he pushed Dùnglas back into the enclosure. However, the hound tried to get back up again. Its tail was wagging so hard now that its whole body moved from the force of it.

"Looks like ye have found yerself a new friend."

Alasdair glanced over his shoulder to see Taran MacKinnon standing behind him. Wearing a rain-splattered leather cape, his short hair slicked back against his scalp, the warrior was an intimidating presence.

Alasdair huffed a laugh. "Aye ... yer wife thinks the dog is the *only* friend I'll make here at Dunvegan."

MacKinnon's mouth curved. "Ye would be right there. Rhona would like to see ye gelded."

He moved closer, his gaze shifting to where Dùnglas had climbed up onto his hind legs again so that he could get to Alasdair. "Are ye looking for a new hound?"

Alasdair shook his head. "I've already got plenty of them back in Duntulm."

"One more won't make a difference," MacKinnon replied with a shrug. "Dùnglas is a funny one ... since Adaira left, he's never bonded with anyone else, and he keeps apart from the other dogs. I think he'd be happier elsewhere."

Alasdair absently stroked the hound's head. "I suppose I could take the dog back with me ... if ye don't want him?"

MacKinnon nodded, as if the matter was settled, before he crossed his arms and turned to face Alasdair. "I hear there's to be a wedding here tomorrow."

Alasdair's mouth quirked. "Aye ... I'm sure ye are invited."

"I don't care if I am or not," MacKinnon replied with a snort. His gaze narrowed then. "I take it the lady is willing?"

Alasdair raised an eyebrow. "Of course ... I'd not force Caitrin to wed me."

"Good to hear," MacKinnon grunted.

Chapter Twenty-eight

Vows

"YE ARE BLOOD of my Blood, and Bone of my Bone."
Alasdair MacDonald's voice echoed through the silent
chapel. "I give ye my Body, that we Two might be One. I
give ye my Spirit, 'til our Life shall be Done."

Caitrin held his gaze as he spoke. Her skin prickled at
the words; they were the same ones she'd heard
Lachlann Fraser say to her sister in Duntulm kirk barely
ten months earlier.

Adaira had wept as Lachlann made his vows—but
Caitrin was dry-eyed. She'd never wept easily in front of
others. She was too private, too proud. A small group
had gathered behind them in Dunvegan's chapel: her
father and Una, her brother, Iain, Rhona and Taran, and
Alasdair's men.

Caitrin had been aware of their gazes upon her as the
ceremony had started, but as Alasdair finished his vows,
and she began hers, she forgot they had an audience.

She couldn't tear her gaze away from Alasdair's; the
intensity in his peat-brown eyes made the rest of the
world fade. The sincerity in his voice made her throat
tighten.

"Ye are now man and wife," the priest announced when Caitrin had completed her vows. He was smiling as he unwrapped the length of plaid that bound their hands. The priest met Alasdair's eye briefly. "Ye may kiss yer bride now."

Caitrin's breath stilled when Alasdair stepped close, gently cupped her chin, and raised her face to his. He then gave her a soft, slow, lingering kiss that made the small party watching the ceremony cheer.

Alasdair pulled away, favoring Caitrin with a sensual smile that made her pulse quicken.

"Come, wife," he murmured. "Take my arm."

Alasdair held out his elbow to her, and she took it. Together they walked down the aisle and out of the chapel.

The wail of a highland pipe echoed through the Great Hall of Dunvegan, accompanying the handfasting feast. The noise inside the hall was so great that Caitrin could barely hear herself think. In truth, she preferred the lilting music of a harp to the screech of the highland pipe, yet with the feasters making such a noise, the gentler sound of the harp would have been drowned out anyway.

Before her lay a great spread of pies, cheeses, fruit, and oatcakes dripping in butter and honey. The large pies were filled with left-over meat, vegetables, and boiled eggs, and topped with a thick suet and oaten crust. The cooks, Fiona and her daughter Greer, had done well at such short notice, especially since they'd had to prepare another feast just two days earlier.

The aroma filling the hall was divine, and unlike at the last feast, Caitrin actually had an appetite for the fare before her. It was hard to believe only two days had passed since she'd sat here, her stomach in knots, dreading having to choose a suitor.

None of the three men were at the feast. MacKay had left in a rage shortly after he'd stormed from MacLeod's solar. MacNichol and Campbell had both left at dawn the morning after.

"Wine, Caitrin?" Alasdair leaned forward, raising his voice to be heard over the din. He held up a ewer of spiced bramble wine.

Caitrin nodded, smiling. "Thank ye."

They sat together at the center of the table upon the dais. Alasdair's elbow brushed against hers as he bent forward to refill her goblet. Before them sat a platter of two different pies; it was tradition for husband and wife to dine off the same platter at their wedding feast.

Caitrin was reminded then of her handfasting feast to Baltair. They too had been wed in the chapel at Dunvegan, as her father had wished, and the feasting had gone on late into the night. She'd been happy that day, glowing with hope and pride at her handsome husband. Yet that glow had only lasted a short while. Later, when Baltair took her maidenhead, her happiness shattered. Even then, knowing it was her first time, he'd been brutal.

"Ye seem pensive, Caitrin," Alasdair observed. The din in the hall was such that he had to lean close to speak to her. The scent of leather and clean male skin enveloped her, and she breathed it in. "Is something amiss?"

Caitrin shook her head, pushing aside her memories of the past. Baltair was dead; she would keep him that way. He had no place at this table.

"Just reflecting a little," she replied, taking a sip of wine, "and getting used to the idea of being a wife again."

Alasdair's gaze fused with hers then, and just like during the wedding ceremony, their surroundings disappeared—even the wail of the highland pipe and her father's booming voice.

"Baltair was a fool," Alasdair said, his expression turning fierce. "He didn't know how lucky he was."

Alasdair reached out, entwining his fingers with hers. His touch made Caitrin's breathing quicken. She felt as if she'd only just had a taste of him the night before last. It wasn't enough. They had not lain together since and already it seemed like an eternity. She ached for him.

Caitrin watched Alasdair's pupils dilate and knew that he'd been affected by the touch the same way.

"I have my faults, Caitrin," he continued, before his mouth twisted into a self-recriminating smile. "More than I'd like to admit ... but I'll never ignore ye ... never frighten ye. I'd do anything in my power to make ye happy."

Caitrin held his gaze, a lump rising in her throat. Something deep inside her breast—something that had been tightly knotted ever since she'd wedded Baltair—unraveled.

"Ye already have," she whispered.

Caitrin collapsed upon the bed with Alasdair. There, they lay spooned together, panting and sweat-slicked, his arms fast around her. A soft sigh escaped Caitrin. Her body felt weak and boneless, her senses completely scattered. She enjoyed the sensation and the abandon that had caused it.

They'd been hungry for each other.

The handfasting feast had seemed to go on for an age, after which there had been dancing. Eventually, they'd been able to take their leave, although not without fanfare.

Much to the delight of onlookers, Alasdair had scooped Caitrin into his arms and carried her from the Great Hall. Face flaming from the men's bawdy comments and laughter, Caitrin had huddled against Alasdair's chest.

However, once they'd reached the chamber where they would spend their first night as man and wife, her embarrassment faded.

They'd come together like beasts, tearing off each other's clothes, before Alasdair pushed her down on all fours on the bed and took her.

"I liked that," she murmured when her breathing had slowed.

"Me too," he replied sleepily, placing a kiss on her shoulder.

"The effect ye have on me, Alasdair ... ye only have to touch my hand, and my whole body answers."

He kissed her shoulder once more, trailing his lips up to her earlobe. Caitrin's eyelids fluttered with pleasure as his tongue explored the shell of her ear. "It's the same for me," he whispered back.

Alasdair's arms tightened around her. Caitrin felt his body relax against hers, his leg slung over her hips protectively. She closed her eyes, enjoying the warmth of his body curled against hers. Alasdair's breathing grew slow and even, and she realized that he'd fallen asleep. A heavy languor pressed down upon her too.

Outside, she could still hear the hiss of the rain. She didn't care about the gloomy weather though, or that they would have to set off for Duntulm in it the following morning. Soon she would be reunited with Eoghan, but right now she was wrapped in her husband's arms.

A soft smile curved Caitrin's lips. At this moment, she was exactly where she wanted to be.

Rhona watched her sister ride out of the bailey. Caitrin sat astride a grey palfrey, a delicate mare with a mincing gait. She rode alongside her husband, Alasdair MacDonald. He towered above her upon a bay courser. A grey wolfhound loped along beside his horse, its gaze keen.

"Isn't that Adaira's dog ... Dùnglas?" Rhona asked, glancing at where Taran stood beside her.

"Aye," he replied with a smile.

"Why is he leaving with MacDonald?"

"Dùnglas took a shine to Alasdair ... I thought the hound would be happier elsewhere."

Rhona favored her husband with an incredulous look before she shifted her attention back to the departing riders. A light rain fell this morning, and the clouds hung low over Dunvegan. All of the MacDonald party wore woolen traveling cloaks and had pulled up their hoods.

As she descended the incline toward the Sea-gate, Caitrin turned, her gaze catching Rhona's. She then smiled and raised her hand in farewell. Rhona waved back, her vision misting.

Caitrin turned away, and a moment later, she disappeared through the gate. Shortly after, the rest of the party from Duntulm followed, the clip-clop of their horses' hooves ringing against the wet stone.

"Don't look so worried, love. She will be fine."

Rhona swallowed before glancing up at Taran. He was watching her, a soft look in his eyes. "Really," she said huskily. "Can ye be sure of that?"

"No ... but ye can't be certain she'll be miserable either."

Rhona huffed. "I thought ye didn't like him?"

"I hardly know the man," Taran replied evenly, "but now that he has done right by yer sister, I'm prepared to revise my opinion of him."

Rhona's mouth thinned, before her gaze shifted back to the Sea-gate, almost as if she expected Caitrin to reappear at any moment. "If I ever find out he's mistreated her, I'll ride to Duntulm and sink a dirk into his guts," she growled.

"There will be no need for that, mo ghràdh," Taran replied, amusement lacing his voice. "Ye can see MacDonald adores her."

Rhona drew back, favoring Taran with an arch look. "What's wrong with ye this morning?"

Taran smiled, his eyes crinkling at the corners. To most folk, he had a frightening face, made even more so by a formidable expression. But to Rhona, he was the most handsome man she'd ever seen. It was nearly a year since they'd been wed, and with each passing day, she grew to love Taran MacKinnon more.

"Nothing," he replied. "Only that I know what it's like to lose yer heart to a woman ... long before she knows ye exist."

Rhona felt chastened by that, remembering how she had seen Taran before they'd been wed. He'd been her father's faithful warrior, her servant, and a friend of sorts. But she hadn't seen him as a man. "Ye think it's a good match then?" she asked, still unconvinced.

Taran nodded before he slung an arm around her shoulders and turned her back toward the keep. The others, who'd come out to see the MacDonald party off, had all dispersed, including MacLeod and his wife—driven indoors by the wet weather. "Perhaps. But only time will tell," he replied before he leaned in and kissed her. "Come on ... let's get out of this rain."

Chapter Twenty-nine

Sing for Us

ALASDAIR STOLE A glance at the woman who was now
his wife

It didn't seem real.

He had much to thank Gavin MacNichol for—the man
had made him see sense, had made him look truth
squarely in the eye. He'd taken a risk. His visit to Caitrin
could have gone terribly wrong. She could have rejected
him and thrown him out of her bower. She could have
called for her father's guards and caused an ugly scene.

But she hadn't.

Something had shifted within him since that night. It
was as if a bitter thorn that had been festering within his
flesh had finally been lanced. He felt lighter, freer. He
hadn't realized just how big a burden he'd been carrying.
Ever since making the decision to take Caitrin back to
her father, he'd struggled with it. What a relief it was to
cast the weight aside.

They were riding east, across a stretch of bare hills.
The rain clouds hung over them in an oppressive grey
curtain. Shortly after leaving Dunvegan, they'd been
soaked through. Strangely, Alasdair didn't mind. He felt

as if he'd been reborn; all the things that used to matter didn't.

Glancing right, he saw that Dùnglas was managing to keep up with him. The wound to its shoulder was healing well. The wolfhound trotted along, tongue lolling. It had shadowed him ever since leaving Dunvegan. Alasdair smiled. He'd almost forgotten about taking the dog with him, but when he'd led his horse out of the stables that morning, Dùnglas had been there, sitting upon the cobbles in the rain, waiting for him.

It was as if the hound knew he was leaving and was determined not to be left behind.

Alasdair glanced up, his gaze sweeping the road ahead. To the southeast, he spied great brooding peaks just visible through the shroud of rain and mist, but they weren't heading that way. By the end of the day, they'd cross into MacDonald lands and then turn north for Duntulm.

For home.

Alasdair cut Caitrin another glance, his gaze lingering on her profile as she looked ahead. Sensing his gaze upon her, his wife shifted her attention to Alasdair.

"What is it?" she asked, her lips curving in a way that made him wish they were alone. During the two nights they'd spent together, Caitrin had surprised him; she was lustier and more sensual than he could have ever hoped or dreamed. She had given herself to him wholeheartedly.

Alasdair smiled back. "Just gazing upon my wife's beauty."

Caitrin huffed although her eyes gleamed. "Ye have a honeyed tongue, Alasdair. I'm wet, bedraggled, and smell of wet wool and horse."

"Aye ... but ye are still the bonniest lass I've ever set eyes on." He gave her a long look then that made her cheeks pinken. "Or ever will."

She cleared her throat, embarrassed by his declaration. Yet he saw from the twinkle in her sea-blue eyes that she'd responded favorably to it. "Ye are a rogue, husband. The world is filled with fair-faced women. How do ye know ye won't meet one prettier?"

"None lovelier than ye, Caitrin," he replied. "That I promise ye."

As dusk neared, they made camp at the bottom of a shallow valley. The rain continued falling in a steady patter upon the already soaked earth. Caitrin dismounted from her palfrey, her already soaked boots squelching on the wet grass. They stood in a grove of beech trees, where the men started to erect an awning between three trees for the party to shelter under, and another a few yards away for the horses.

The bedraggled wolfhound they'd brought from Duntulm shook out its wet coat and sat down under a tree, watching the men work.

"If this continues, we'll have to build ourselves an arc and row the rest of the way to Duntulm," Boyd MacDonald grumbled as he removed a roll of hide from behind his saddle. "We'll be lucky if we find any dry wood for a fire."

Darron MacNichol snorted, relieving him of his roll. "Well, I'm sure if anyone can, it is ye. Off ye go and find us some then."

Boyd's lip curled. As a member of the Duntulm Guard, he now took orders from Captain MacNichol and had no choice but to do as bid.

Watching the brief interaction between the men, Caitrin noted that there was little in the way of friendship between them. She remembered the scene back at Beltane and wondered if their rivalry over Sorcha MacQueen's affections had anything to do with it.

At the thought of Sorcha, warmth filtered over Caitrin. This time tomorrow she'd be warm and dry and back in Duntulm—with Eoghan in her arms. They'd been apart for only a few days, but it felt like months to her. She was impatient to see him again.

Once the awning had been erected, Caitrin helped the others roll out dry sheets of hide around a small hearth area. Grateful to be out of the rain, Caitrin removed her sodden cloak and hung it up on a branch. It was sheltered here, although with the air so damp, she doubted her cloak would dry much overnight.

Boyd and a couple of other men returned presently with armloads of firewood, although some of it was damp. While the others settled themselves on the hide, Darron crouched down next to the hearth and got a fire going. He used a flint and steel to light a pile of tinder that he'd carried with him wrapped in an oiled cloth. It took a few tries, and a bit of ribbing from the likes of Boyd, but he eventually managed to light a fire.

Caitrin watched the bright gold tongues of flame licking at the damp wood and released a sigh. It wasn't a cold evening, but the air was heavy with moisture. The fire was a beacon of color and warmth, a ward against the encircling grey.

They ate a simple meal of oaten bread, butter, and boiled eggs washed down with ale. Caitrin sat shoulder-to-shoulder with Alasdair, listening to the rumble of conversation around the fireside. Despite that her clothing felt damp and itchy against her skin, and that an uncomfortable night awaited her, a warm sensation of well-being settled over her.

With a jolt, she realized that the feeling was happiness.

She'd not felt like this in a long while. After Baltair's death, once she'd taken up the role of chatelaine, Caitrin had thought she'd been content in her new life. In reality though, she'd been living in dread, for she'd known that at some point a man—be it her father or Baltair's brother—would shatter her peace.

Now, there was no dread. She was the Lady of Duntulm once more, but this time she'd not cower before her husband. The bond between her and Alasdair was still new, yet she had a knowing deep in her bones that he'd be good to her.

Once the supper had ended, the men started passing around skins of ale. Caitrin took a delicate sip from one before casting a look at her husband. The hound he'd brought with him had somehow sidled up to the fire and now sat pressed up against Alasdair's right side. The dog appeared so content it almost looked as if it were smiling.

"Should I be jealous?" she asked, stifling a laugh.

Alasdair met her eye, his mouth curving. "Don't mind Dùnglas ... he seems to think I'm some long-lost relative."

"Just as long as he doesn't want to share yer bed when we get home."

Alasdair snorted. "No chance of that."

"Curse this rain." Boyd's voice interrupted them from across the fire. "We need some cheer to chase away the gloom." He turned his attention to the young warrior who'd sung the bawdy songs on their journey to Dunvegan. "Come, Finlay, give us another one of yer tunes."

"Those aren't songs fit for a lady's ears, Boyd," Alasdair pointed out.

His cousin snorted. "Lady Caitrin won't mind."

Darron cleared his throat. "I remember ye having a good voice, Alasdair. Why don't ye sing for us?"

Boyd's eyes widened, and he cut Alasdair a reproachful look. "All those months together and ye never let on ye could sing."

Alasdair shrugged. "There wasn't much cause for it, was there?"

Caitrin inclined her head, focusing on Alasdair. He actually looked a little embarrassed. "Go on," she murmured with a smile. "I'd like ye to sing for us."

He met her eye and gave her a pained look. "Ye would?"

"Aye ... if it means I don't have to hear of swiving lusty tavern wenches."

Her comment brought bursts of surprised laughter from the surrounding men. Alasdair raised an eyebrow, and Finlay's cheeks glowed red.

Caitrin said nothing more though, and finally, Alasdair loosed a defeated breath. "Very well, wife ... here is a song more suitable for yer ears."

A pause followed, and then Alasdair began to sing. He had a low, slightly husky voice, and sang a slow ballad, one that Caitrin had never heard before.

"Oh the summer time has come
And the trees are sweetly blooming
And wild mountain thyme
Grows around the purple heather.
Will ye go, lassie, go?

And we'll all go together,
To pull wild mountain thyme,
All around the purple heather.
Will ye go, lassie, go?

I will build my love a tower,
By yon clear crystal fountain,
And on it I will pile,
All the flowers of the mountain.
Will ye go, lassie, go?"

Alasdair finished his song, his voice fading into silence. The fine hair on the back of Caitrin's forearms prickled, and she let out a slow breath, realizing that she'd forgotten to breathe while he sang.

"That was beautiful," she whispered.

He ducked his head, smiling. "Ye enjoyed it then?"

"Aye."

Across the fire, Boyd snorted. "Ye have a fine voice, I'll give ye that cousin ... but did ye have to choose something so ... feeble?"

Alasdair threw back his head and laughed. "I know plenty of other songs."

"Why don't ye sing us one?" Boyd grinned at Caitrin then. "None that'll offend yer lady's ears, mind."

They rode into Duntulm under the drumming rain, approaching the fortress from the south. However, when he crested the top of the last hill, Alasdair pulled his courser to an abrupt halt.

"What is it?" Caitrin pulled up her palfrey next to her husband, her gaze following the direction of his.

She didn't need him to answer, for an instant later, she saw for herself what the problem was.

When they'd left Duntulm, the Cleatburn had been a meandering stream that cut east of the village, spanned by an old humpbacked stone bridge.

It was now a turbid torrent, covering the meadows and the outlying cottages. Sod roofed dwellings peeked out of the rushing water, and the bridge was completely gone. Villagers were wading through the water, trying to salvage what they could and rescue livestock from the flooded meadow.

Alasdair cursed, gathered his reins, and urged his horse down the hill. Dùnglas bounded along behind him, and Caitrin followed. The mare broke into a brisk canter, her hooves cutting into the wet turf. Caitrin pulled her up at the bottom of the hill, just in time to see Alasdair leap down from his horse, tear off his cloak, heel off his boots, and stride toward the water.

"Alasdair!" Caitrin called after him, wondering where on earth he was going.

And then she saw her.

The young woman was drifting downriver toward the sea, clinging to a tree trunk. Her cries floated across the hillside, barely audible over the roaring of the water.

Darron rushed past Caitrin, hot on Alasdair's heels, the others close behind him. However, by the time they reached the water's edge, the chieftain had already plunged in and was swimming in long strokes toward the lass.

"Get some rope," Darron shouted.

Caitrin sprang down from her horse and rushed to one of the horses the men had abandoned, retrieving a heavy coil of hemp rope. She then picked up her skirts and hurried to the water's edge, where Dùnglas sat whining, staring after Alasdair.

Darron took the rope from Caitrin and handed one end to Boyd, who was looking on, bemused by both men's actions. "Keep ahold of the end," Darron ordered. "I'm going to see if I can get the rope out to Alasdair."

With that, Captain MacNichol waded into the water after his chieftain.

Chapter Thirty

Irreplaceable

CAITRIN STOOD ON the water's edge, her heart in her throat. The Cleatburn raged like a beast. No one should be swimming in the torrent, least of all her husband.

"Alasdair!" Darron had waded in to waist height. "Catch the rope!"

The chieftain twisted, attempting to tread water as the rope sailed toward him. It hit the churning water with a slap, and Alasdair lunged for it.

Panic surged through Caitrin when he went under, disappearing from view. "Alasdair!"

Dùnglas stood up and started barking, his hackles rising.

For a sickening heartbeat or two, there was no sign of Alasdair, and then he appeared, surfacing like a seal just yards from where the woman still floated downstream, the rope clutched in his hand.

He reached the young woman—who was now sobbing in fear, for she clearly couldn't swim—and wound the rope around the tree trunk.

"Ready!" he called to Darron.

The other men in the party had taken hold of the rope behind Captain MacNichol, and together they all heaved the log, with its two passengers, into shore. A crowd had now gathered at the water's edge. An elderly woman stepped up beside Caitrin, sobbing. "That's my Hilda. Ye found her … I thought her lost!"

Alasdair helped the young woman up onto the shore. She was shivering and weeping, but when she spied the old woman, she left Alasdair's side and ran to her. "Ma!"

Alasdair rejoined the others then, still out of breath from his swim. Water ran in rivulets down his body. His sodden clothing clung to him. His hair was slicked back, accentuating the lean angles of his face.

Dùnglas approached the chieftain, tail wagging, and nuzzled against his leg. Alasdair glanced down at the wolfhound before giving an exasperated snort. "Bloody useless dog." However, he still reached down and stroked its wiry coat.

Caitrin stepped forward. "I thought I'd lost ye," she gasped, unable to keep the anxiety out of her voice. "When ye went under … I …"

Alasdair held her gaze before a smile curved his lips. "I'm a strong swimmer, Caitrin. I'd never have gone out there otherwise."

Caitrin punched his arm. "I didn't know that, did I?"

His gaze clouded. "Did I worry ye?"

"Aye." She was close to tears now. "Don't scare me like that again."

Wordlessly, Alasdair pulled her into his arms. It didn't matter that he was soaking wet; after the morning's travel so was she. The drum-beat of his heart against her ear calmed her.

After a moment she pulled back, pressing into his side, as Alasdair looped a protective arm around her shoulders. He then turned his attention to his men. "Get the villagers up to the keep. We'll house them there until the water recedes."

"Aye, milord," Darron replied with a nod. He then moved away, marshaling his men to do the chieftain's bidding.

Together, Alasdair and Caitrin turned to face the swollen Cleatburn.

"It's stopped raining," Caitrin noted, raising her gaze to the sky. "For the first time in days."

"Just as well," Alasdair murmured. "Or there would soon be nothing left of the village."

Caitrin's gaze swept across the churning water, to where the bridge had once stood.

"All that work ye did on the bridge over the winter," she said with a sigh, "and the river has destroyed it."

Alasdair huffed a laugh, his grip around her shoulders tightening. "Bridges can be rebuilt, love," he murmured. "But some things are irreplaceable."

Sorcha hurried out into the bailey, Eoghan balanced on her hip. She was pleased to see the rain had finally stopped although the sky was still the color of lead.

Picking her way around the large puddles, Sorcha approached the bedraggled crowd that had just entered the muddy courtyard. Caitrin was among them, her blonde hair curling in wet tendrils around her face. She walked, hand in hand, with Alasdair MacDonald, leading their horses behind them. A lanky grey wolfhound trotted along at the chieftain's heels.

Sorcha halted, gaze widening. The chieftain and Lady Caitrin holding hands—this was a sight she'd never thought to see.

When she spied her hand-maid, Caitrin cried out, leaving Alasdair's side.

"Ye are back!" Sorcha greeted her. "I can't believe it."

"Aye." Caitrin threw her arms around Sorcha and Eoghan and hugged them both tight. Drawing back, she smiled, her eyes gleaming. "What a sight ye both are. Let me have a look at my wee laddie."

Sorcha handed Eoghan to her. Caitrin spun the lad around, laughing as he squealed in delight. Sorcha saw then that her mistress's cheeks were wet with tears. Eoghan wrapped his soft arms around his mother's neck as she hugged him once more. Caitrin buried her face in his soft dark hair and inhaled deeply.

"How I've missed ye, Eoghan," she said softly, her voice choked with emotion. "Yer smell, the chirping laugh ye make when ye are happy … how ye say my name."

"Ma," Eoghan gurgled happily, not understanding what his mother had just said.

"I know sweetheart," she whispered, and Sorcha started to weep at the love she saw shining in her mistress's eyes. "I'm home."

Caitrin carried Eoghan away, heading back toward the steps leading into the keep, while Sorcha attempted to compose herself. She didn't want the chieftain's men gawking at her or making fun. The others were approaching now, and she suddenly felt self-conscious for weeping.

Captain MacNichol was heading her way.

"Welcome home, MacNichol." Sorcha scrubbed at her wet cheeks with the back of her hand and favored him with a watery smile.

"Good day, Sorcha." He stopped before her, and although he was rain-soaked and mud-splattered, she realized with a jolt just how handsome he was. His leather braies and léine were plastered against his hard, muscular body, and his wet blond hair was pulled back at the nape of his neck. "We return with happy news, as ye can see."

Her gaze searched his face. "What happened?"

He stepped close, glancing over his shoulder to make sure they weren't being overheard. "I'm not really sure," he murmured. "One moment we're watching Clan-chief MacLeod parade suitors before his daughter, the next we're standing in Dunvegan chapel watching MacDonald and Lady Caitrin wed."

Sorcha's eyes widened. "They're married?"

"Aye, the day before last."

Sorcha gasped. "But I thought they hated each other?"

Darron's mouth lifted at the corners. "Clearly, they didn't."

Sorcha was about to reply when a loud voice boomed across the bailey. "Good day, bonny Sorcha."

She glanced right to see Boyd MacDonald striding toward her. Like Darron, he was wet and dirty from his journey. However, he wore his usual irrepressible smile.

"Greetings, Boyd," she replied warmly. "It's good to see ye back too."

Boyd grinned. "How about a kiss then ... to show me how pleased ye are to see me?" He stepped close, and Sorcha immediately shrank back.

"What's this?" Boyd's grin turned mischievous, and he reached for her.

Sorcha ducked out of reach, stepping back into a muddy puddle in her haste to avoid his grasping hands. She didn't enjoy being grabbed at like she was a spring lamb he was trying to catch.

"Coy, are we?" Boyd's grin turned into a leer.

"Leave the lass be, MacDonald," Darron rumbled, a warning note to his voice. "Clearly, she doesn't want to kiss ye."

Boyd snorted, drawing back. His gaze narrowed as it settled upon Sorcha. "That's not very friendly, lass."

Sorcha swallowed and took another step back, not caring that she now stood ankle-deep in cold water. Her pulse raced. She'd been happy to see both Darron and Boyd—but the latter's behavior had put her on edge. Boyd had never taken such liberties before.

"I'd better get back inside," she murmured, picking up her skirts so that they didn't drag in the muddy water. "Lady Caitrin will need my help."

With that, she turned and hurried away.

It was loud inside the Great Hall of Duntulm. The roar of voices echoed through the space like storm-driven waves pounding a rocky shore. Extra tables had been carried in, for all those villagers who'd been temporarily rendered homeless by the flood. Servants carried out tureens of thick salted pork and cabbage stew, served with large loaves of coarse bread.

Caitrin took a sip of wine and let out a long sigh, glancing across at her husband. Alasdair sat upon his carven chieftain's chair, goblet of warmed wine in hand, surveying the sea of hungry village folk beneath him. The air was heavy with the smells of food, wet wool, and peat smoke. It wasn't a pleasant odor, but no one seemed to mind. They were all just happy to be somewhere warm and dry, and to fill their bellies.

The rain had stopped now at least, and with any luck, the Cleatburn would quickly recede. Then work could start on repairing the damage the flood had caused.

When the last of the food and drink had been served, Alasdair rose to his feet.

"People of Duntulm." His voice echoed through the Great Hall, quietening the din. "Today might not seem like a cause for celebration, but I have news to share with ye." Alasdair glanced down at Caitrin then, his eyes shining. He then shifted his attention back to the sea of faces beneath the dais. "Three years ago ye welcomed Lady Caitrin to these lands. Ye have seen her strength, her justness, and her capability. I inform ye now that this woman, whom I know ye all love and respect, is now my wife. She will rule Duntulm at my side."

Shock rippled across the hall. Nervousness tightened Caitrin's belly as she looked on. Alasdair's words had filled her with joy, yet what if the people here didn't love her as much as he believed?

An instant later she realized her fear was unfounded.

A roar went up, as men and women rose to their feet and raised their cups in the air.

"To the chieftain and his lady!" Alban MacLean shouted, his leathery face creased with joy.

Raucous cheering followed, shaking the hall to its foundations. Smiling, Alasdair reached down, pulling Caitrin to her feet so that she stood next to him. Then, he placed an arm around her shoulders, drawing her close.

Caitrin's vision misted. She'd never expected such a response. Meeting Alasdair's eye she grinned. "Ye are well-liked here," she said, raising her voice so he could hear her over the din.

His smile widened. "Aye ... and so are ye."

The cheering settled and the feasting began. Caitrin and Alasdair took their seats once more. Helping herself to some stew, Caitrin felt warmth seep through her. The atmosphere in the hall was more joyous than Yuletide. A simple meal sat before them, but it didn't matter. It was moments like these that made life worth living.

The stew was delicious and the bread fresh and nutty. Wine flowed, and laughter echoed high into the rafters.

Eventually, her belly full, Caitrin leaned back in her chair. She wrapped her fingers around the goblet of wine she held. Like Alasdair, she'd changed into dry clothes upon arriving home, but there had been no time to relax in their quarters together. They'd both come straight back downstairs as there had been much to organize before supper.

"I feel as if the damp has drilled into my bones," Caitrin said with a sigh.

"Aye," Alasdair replied, massaging a stiff muscle in his shoulder. "I'm looking forward to a hot bath later."

Caitrin shot him a smile. "I'll ask Sorcha to have one brought up to yer bed-chamber."

"*Our* bed-chamber," he corrected Caitrin, before leaning in and kissing her. "I was hoping ye would join me."

Chapter Thirty-one

All We Need Is Time

THE SIGHT OF the huge iron bathtub, filled with steaming water, made Caitrin release a sigh of pleasure. She sniffed then, catching the scent of rose and lavender. Sorcha had added oils to the water.

The tub sat in the midst of Alasdair's bed-chamber—or what was now their marital bed-chamber. It was the same one she'd shared with Baltair, and Caitrin had been worried that setting foot inside the chamber again would raise unpleasant memories. Yet, this eve, it didn't.

Finally, it seemed as if Baltair's ghost had stopped haunting her steps. For the first time since his death, Caitrin's body didn't tense when she thought of him.

It was cozy and warm inside the chamber. The shutters to the single window had been closed tightly, and a fire burned in the hearth. A few feet from where Caitrin stood, she watched her husband disrobe.

Alasdair undressed with the unconscious self-confidence that only men seemed to possess. Most women were prone to cower, to try and cover their breasts with their hands, but a man merely tossed his clothing aside and stood there in his naked glory, without a care.

Caitrin was glad of it, for her gaze feasted upon Alasdair, taking in the long, hard planes of his body and the way the firelight danced across his skin.

Throwing aside his braies, Alasdair turned to her. "Are ye going to join me in the tub?"

Caitrin's mouth quirked. "Are ye sure there's room in there for the both of us?"

A slow smile spread across his face. "Aye."

Without shifting her gaze from his, Caitrin started to unlace the front of her kirtle. It had been a long, tiring day. They'd just retired to their bed-chamber. Once supper had ended, Caitrin had tucked Eoghan into bed, and Alasdair had made sure all the villagers whose homes had been flooded had bedded down in the Great Hall. However, as Caitrin undressed, the day's fatigue lifted from her.

She'd been looking forward to this moment, to finally being alone with Alasdair.

The rest of the evening belonged to them.

Alasdair stepped into the iron tub and lowered himself into the hot, fragrant water. "I'll smell like a lass after this," he complained, wrinkling his nose.

Caitrin laughed. "Apologies ... Sorcha is used to preparing a bath for me. I'll tell her to be less generous with her scented oils in future."

Naked, her slender limbs and gentle curves glowing in the gilded light of the hearth and the candles that burned around them, Caitrin walked toward the bathtub. Alasdair watched her, transfixed, his mind suddenly going blank.

Every time he saw Caitrin naked he felt like a gauche youth, a simpleton who didn't know what to do with such a sight except gape.

"God's bones," he breathed finally. "Ye are so beautiful it hurts to look upon ye."

Caitrin's mouth curved. She then stepped into the bath and sank down into the water opposite him.

They stared at each other for a long moment, a veil of steam encircling them. Alasdair shifted so that his legs encircled Caitrin, and she was able to stretch out her legs before her. "See," he said with a grin. "I told ye we'd both fit."

Caitrin arched an eyebrow before reaching for a soft cloth and cake of lye and holding them out to him. "Come on then, let's bathe before the water cools."

Alasdair inclined his head, smiling. "I'd like ye to wash me."

She huffed a laugh. "I'm sure ye don't need my assistance."

He gave her a sultry look. "What I need and what I want aren't the same thing, my love ... will ye?"

She appeared almost shy then, dipping her head so that her hair fell in loose pale waves around her face. Of course, despite that she'd been wedded before, Caitrin was new to love play. He sensed her sudden nervousness. Even so, she obliged, moving onto her knees so that she could reach him properly.

Dipping the cloth into the water, she soaped it before beginning to wash his shoulders and chest.

The feel of her touch sliding across his skin made Alasdair let out a long sigh. He leaned back, resting the back of his head against the rim of the tub, and gave himself up to the sensation.

Caitrin seemed to be taking her task seriously. She lifted up his arms, washing under them, before soaping his arms and hands. Then she returned to his chest and began a leisurely path down to his stomach. Then she stopped.

Alasdair's eyes flickered open to see that she was staring down at his groin. His gaze shifted to where his shaft strained up out of the soapy water.

Caitrin glanced up at him. "Can I?"

"Ye don't even have to ask," he replied, his breathing quickening. "I'm all yers."

Caitrin smiled, her gaze dropping once more to his arousal. Then she wet the cloth, soaped it once more, and began to slide it up and down his shaft.

Alasdair groaned. His head fell back as he gave himself up to the sensation. Then, moments later, the cloth disappeared, and he felt her fingers encircle him. He reopened his eyes to see her attention fixed wholly upon his rod, her lips parted as she pleasured him.

Lust slammed into Alasdair like a charging bull. The blend of innocence and desire in this woman undid him.

With a growl, he pulled her up so that she was above him, her legs spread over his erection. Then, guiding her hips, he lowered Caitrin onto him. He inched into her, watching her face as he did so. He loved how a flush appeared on her cheeks, how her eyes widened, the deeper he penetrated.

When he pulled her down so that he was fully seated within her, she gave a soft cry, her chest now rising and falling sharply.

Alasdair drew in a slow, deep breath, shifting his attention down to her breasts. They were delicious: small and pert but with large pink nipples that were as firm and sweet as ripe strawberries. He angled his hips so she leaned toward him, allowing him to feast on her breasts. He drew a nipple deep into his mouth and sucked till she moaned. Suckling her, he reached down and gripped her hips, gyrating them so that they began to gently move together.

Caitrin gasped, her lithe body trembling in his grip.

Alasdair groaned against the breast he suckled. He loved how quickly she responded to him, how little it took for him to bring her to the edge.

It excited him beyond measure.

They were so aware of each other that even a heated glance across a crowded room was enough to arouse him. The feel of being buried deep inside her was enough to bring him to the brink of madness.

Tearing his mouth from her swollen nipple, he gazed up at Caitrin. She was lost in a haze of pleasure, neck arched back, eyes closed, and an expression of rapture upon her face.

"Caitrin," he rasped. "My love."

She opened her eyes and gazed down at him. "Alasdair," she whispered, her breath hitching. "Mo chridhe."

My heart.

Alasdair sucked in a breath. This was the first time she'd uttered such an endearment to him, the first time she'd openly acknowledged that she felt as he did.

He reached up, pulling her down for a kiss. Their mouths collided, hungry and devouring. Alasdair gripped her hips, lifting her. He then slid her up and down the length of his shaft with relentless determination. He wanted to take her over the brink, to see her shatter.

Caitrin cried out into his mouth, her body shuddering now. But still she rode him, the bathwater splashing over the sides of the tub onto the floor. Neither of them paid it any mind, and when Caitrin finally sobbed his name, Alasdair's cries joined hers.

Caitrin stretched out on the bed, smiling. She felt as if she was floating, untethered from the earth.

"What are ye looking so pleased about?"

Her eyes flickered open to see that Alasdair had propped himself up on an elbow and was staring down at her.

Caitrin's smile widened. "If I say, ye will be insufferable."

His mouth twitched. "How so?"

She reached out, her fingertips tracing the whorls of dark hair on his chest. "Ye are a wonderful lover."

He did smile then, as she'd known he would, delight twinkling in his eyes. "Why, thank ye, milady."

"I mean it."

He captured her hand in his and brought it to his lips, kissing her fingers gently. "I know ye do. Although I don't think I can take all the credit ... ye play yer part."

Silence stretched between them. Caitrin stared up at him, her smile fading. "Do I? Sometimes I worry that ye must think me cold … emotionally that is …"

He inclined his head. "Why would I think that?"

"Because I hold back my feelings … I know I do." She swallowed. "I don't think I've ever trusted a man … any man."

His gaze widened. "Even yer father?"

Caitrin huffed. "Especially him. He's behaved better of late, but any woman who puts her faith in Malcolm MacLeod's loyalty is a fool. Ye know what he did to my sisters."

Alasdair nodded. Releasing her hand, he reached out and stroked her cheek with the back of his hand. "I want ye to trust me," he said softly, "and I will work to earn it. Even if it takes me the rest of my life."

Chapter Thirty-two

Duntulm Fair

One month later ...

CAITRIN WALKED AMONGST the crowds in Duntulm village. A sense of contentment settled over her like a warm cloak. Of all the festivals that marked the year, this one was her favorite: Duntulm Fair. Her home of Dunvegan held a similar festival a little later in the summer, yet she preferred this one.

Folk from miles around came for the festival, swelling Duntulm's population to nearly five times its usual size. The screech of a highland pipe echoed through the streets, although the sound was almost drowned out by the excited chatter of conversation.

Caitrin walked slowly, aware that she had a footpad. Instead of Darron shadowing her—for Alasdair had relieved him of that duty as soon as they'd returned to Duntulm—a leggy wolfhound loped along at her heels. Dùnglas had become a constant presence in their lives of late. Eoghan loved him, and the hound now lived indoors, sleeping in a basket in the chieftain's solar at night, and following his master and mistress around during the day as they went about their duties.

Caitrin had thought the dog might get underfoot and annoy her, but it hadn't. She enjoyed going out for walks with Dùnglas at her side. The hound was also a constant reminder of Adaira.

Surveying her surroundings, Caitrin noted how tidy and prosperous the village looked. Greenery, boughs of pine and hawthorn, decorated the humble cottages, and the streets were filled with stalls boasting the best of the summer produce. She was pleased to see that there remained no sign of the devastating flood of a month earlier. The Cleatburn had now returned to its usual flow, and Alasdair and his men had built a make-shift wooden bridge over it, while they started work on a new stone bridge. One that would hopefully withstand the test of time.

Eoghan perched in a sling on Caitrin's back, chubby arms waving at passersby. It was a joy to wander here, enjoying the kiss of the sun on her face. The weather leading up to the fair had been grey and wet, but this morning the day had dawned bright.

Caitrin stopped to buy herself a square of rich cake dripping in butter and honey. She had to eat it quickly, lest the honey dripped over her clothing. Dùnglas sat gazing up at her wistfully as she finished the cake and licked honey off her fingers.

"Don't look at me like that," she admonished the dog. "There will be plenty of scraps for ye later."

Caitrin moved on down the crowded street. She walked by men having arm-wrestling contests. An excited crowd swirled around them, shouting encouragement. Not far from the waterfront, a pretty lass with a crown of daisies in her hair danced with other maids before a clapping crowd. Caitrin stopped to watch the dancing, as did many young men. Most of the lads were gawking at the lass with the crown of flowers—this year's Summer Queen.

Amongst the crowd, Caitrin spotted many of those who worked within Dunvegan keep. Galiene had even managed to drag cook out from her lair. Briana watched the dancing with a grin on her face, her hands full of sticky cake. Sorcha was there too. Caitrin's hand-maid had joined the dancers. She laughed with the other lasses as she spun and dipped, her hair flying behind her.

Spotting Caitrin, Sorcha broke away from the dancers and joined her. She linked her arm through Caitrin's, and they moved on, toward the shore. "Will ye watch the men race, milady?" she asked.

"Of course," Caitrin replied with a smile.

She hadn't always felt this way. Baltair used to take part in the race, and she'd made a point of staying away, browsing the stalls while he competed. It was tradition that the MacDonald chieftain took part.

But this year was different. This year Alasdair was competing.

Caitrin caught the gleam in her handmaid's eye. "I imagine ye won't bother attending?" she asked, feigning innocence.

Sorcha favored Caitrin with a coy smile. "I wouldn't want to miss watching a dozen handsome men strip down to their braies, would I?"

Caitrin laughed. Her hand-maid could be almost prudish at times, but then surprise her with a bawdy comment like this.

The two women made their way down to the shore, Dùnglas padding along behind them. Garlands and bright buntings of meadow flowers and heather decorated the streets, leading down to the wooden jetty where small boats bobbed in the tide.

Caitrin stopped, her gaze shifting out across the sparkling water. "How far will they swim?"

Sorcha pointed to where a small blue boat bobbed with the incoming tide. "Out to that dinghy and back."

They stopped talking then, realizing that the race was about to start: a row of men were undressing ready for it.

Caitrin's attention immediately strayed to Alasdair. He had his back to her as he pulled his léine over his head, revealing his long, finely muscled back, narrow waist, and broad shoulders. He turned then, tossing his léine aside, and her attention traveled to the dark hair covering his chest, tapering down to his belly.

Despite that she'd seen him naked countless times now, the sight made heat pool in Caitrin's lower belly.

Shifting her focus to Sorcha, Caitrin saw her hand-maid was watching Darron MacNichol. The warrior had also stripped down for the race as he chatted to Alasdair. Farther down the line, Boyd MacDonald readied himself to race. Tall and lean, his blond hair tied back, Boyd glanced over his shoulder. His gaze rested upon Sorcha until he caught her eye, forcing her to shift her attention from Darron. Then he winked.

The men moved down to the waterline, their bare feet slipping on the loose shingle, and then in a flurry, they dove into the water.

Caitrin stifled a gasp. Despite that it was summer, the water would still be freezing.

The swimmers struck out toward the boat. It was hard to tell who was in front. The water foamed around them. However, as they circled the boat, the swimmers drew apart.

Sorcha gripped Caitrin's arm. "Look, the chieftain and Boyd MacDonald are in the lead."

Caitrin raised her hand to shield her eyes from the sun, squinting. "Aye ... it'll be a close race too."

Cheering echoed out across the water. Most of them were calling Alasdair's name.

As if hearing them, Alasdair inched forward. He swam in long confident strokes, moving ahead of Boyd.

Caitrin clapped her hands, her voice joining the rest of the watching crowd. Likewise, Eoghan started to squeal with excitement, his chubby arms and legs waving in the sling. Dùnglas started to bark then, adding to the chaos.

Caitrin clasped her hands together as the swimmers drew close. She was sure Alasdair would win, but then, just yards from shore, Boyd put on a spurt of speed and reached the beach just before him.

Cries of disappointment echoed over the shore, Caitrin's among them.

Boyd staggered up onto the beach, wiping water from his eyes. Oblivious to the fact that everyone had been cheering on the chieftain, he wore a wide, victorious smile.

Alasdair followed him out of the sea. Spying Caitrin among the spectators, he made his way toward her. "I'm slowing down," he gasped as he reached the women. "Time was, no one could beat me."

Boyd stepped up beside him. "That's only because ye had never raced me." He then grinned at Sorcha. "I'm half-selkie, didn't ye know?"

Caitrin frowned. She wondered, if that was the case, why Boyd hadn't dived in to help that woman on the day they'd arrived home from Dunvegan. If her memory served her correctly, Boyd had remained on the shore holding the end of a rope while Alasdair risked his life.

Alasdair snorted before waving to the men who were pouring out cups of ale from barrels on the jetty. "Get Boyd a drink, he's earned it." He then turned his attention back to his wife. "I'm glad ye came to watch the race," he said, before giving a sheepish smile. "Even if I didn't win."

"I don't care about that." Caitrin stepped close, pushing Dùnglas out of the way. The hound had a habit of wrapping himself around Alasdair's legs whenever it got the chance. She stretched up and kissed his wet lips. "Ye were still magnificent."

Sorcha took a bite of pie, savoring the rich flavor of venison. It was a treat she only got to enjoy a few times a year. This midsummer's fair was the best she could remember. The good weather had brought in huge crowds.

The pie was hot, and Sorcha ate it gingerly, careful not to spill the filling down the front of her kirtle. Pale blue, the color of a summer's sky, it was the prettiest one she owned; she didn't want to ruin it. She stood in the shade between two cottages at the edge of the festivities. As she ate, Sorcha's gaze skirted the crowd.

The chieftain and his lady were enjoying the fair together. Lady Caitrin still carried Eoghan on her back, although the lad had now fallen asleep. She and Alasdair watched the dancing. Heads bent close, they laughed over something.

It warmed Sorcha's heart to see them so happy. One day, she too hoped to find such contentment.

Finishing her meal, Sorcha brushed pastry crumbs off her fingers. Her gaze shifted away from the chieftain and his wife, continuing through the crowd. She realized then that she was looking for Darron. Ever since his return from Dunvegan, they'd been spending more time together. He often sought her out when she'd finished her chores, and over the last week, they'd shared an ale in the Great Hall before retiring for the night.

Sorcha had found herself starting to think about him—a lot.

Instead of spying Darron in the crowd though, her gaze alighted upon Boyd. He was approaching her.

When he'd first arrived in Duntulm, Boyd MacDonald had drawn her eye, with his arrogant swagger and boyish smile. But these days Sorcha wasn't so sure of him. His manner, once charming, had developed an aggressive edge to it. Discomfort settled over her when he stopped before her.

"I was wondering where ye had got to," he greeted her.

"Why?" she asked innocently. "Were ye looking for me?"

He grinned. "Aye … thought ye might like to congratulate me properly for my win."

"I already have."

He laughed. "I'd like more than a few words, lass. How about that kiss ye keep promising me?"

Sorcha stiffened. "I have promised ye no such thing."

Boyd moved closer, and Sorcha instinctively shifted back into the space between the two cottages. That was a mistake because it took her out of view of the crowd of folk filling the market square.

"Ye don't need to tell me," he said, lowering his voice intimately. "I can see ye want it."

"Nonsense." Sorcha kept her voice light although inside she felt a frisson of alarm. "Ye are quite mistaken, MacDonald."

"I don't think so."

Sorcha tried to edge around him. She'd had enough of such talk. He was making her uncomfortable, and she wished she hadn't let him take her out of view of the crowd. "I think I'll return to the dancing."

"I'll still have that kiss though." He grabbed her arm. His fingers bit into Sorcha's flesh, and he shoved her back against the white-washed wall. "Ye have been tempting me for months now."

His mouth came down on hers roughly, cutting off the scream that rose in Sorcha's throat. Without thinking, she brought her knee up, jabbing him in the cods.

Boyd ripped his mouth from hers and let out a hiss of pain.

She thought it would be enough to make him let go, but it just seemed to enrage him. His grip tightened, and he dragged her down the alley between the two dwellings.

Fear slammed into Sorcha, and she began to struggle. "Let go of me!"

His hand slammed over her mouth to stifle her protests. He threw her up against the wall, his free hand fumbling with her skirts. "Keep yer mouth shut," he growled, "and spread yer legs for me."

Sorcha didn't obey him. She couldn't shout for help, for his hand prevented her, but she started to struggle wildly, clawing at him. Boyd MacDonald wasn't a big man, but he was lean and wiry, and much stronger than her.

Terror pulsed in her breath as she felt his hand on her thighs, raking her skin. He was trying to wedge his thigh in between her legs. He was going to rape her, right there, just yards away from where folk were enjoying the fair. Sorcha wasn't strong enough to fight him off.

And then, as suddenly as he'd grabbed her, Boyd jerked away.

Sorcha sagged against the wall to see Darron drag Boyd backward by his hair. Then he spun him around and punched him hard in the face. Boyd staggered, blood pouring from his nose.

Cursing loudly, Boyd righted himself. "Keep out of this, MacNichol," he rasped, wiping away the blood with the back of his hand. "It's my turn now to have some fun with the wee whore."

Darron growled before his fist shot out once more. He hit Boyd in the eye, and the man went down like a lump of peat, where he lay groaning.

Captain MacNichol then crossed to Sorcha. His face was pale and taut as he stared down at her. "Did he hurt ye?"

Chapter Thirty-three
Willing

ALASDAIR SURVEYED BOYD under hooded lids.

"Do ye have anything to say in defense of yerself?"

Boyd stared back at him before folding his arms across his chest. Darron had made a mess of his face. His nose had been flattened, his nostrils were encrusted with blood, and his left eye was purpled and had already swollen shut.

Boyd's response, when it came, was spoken in a growl. "I thought the lass was willing."

"Willing?" Darron growled from behind them. "Ye were trying to rape her."

Alasdair's gaze remained focused upon Boyd. "Were ye?"

A chill silence settled over the market square. They stood in the midst of the wide space, a large crowd of village folk looking on. The merriment and dancing had ceased the moment Darron had dragged Boyd out by the hair into the center of the square.

Boyd's mouth thinned. "No."

The hiss of an enraged intake of breath interrupted them. Sorcha stood next to Caitrin. The handmaid's face was ashen although her eyes were ablaze. "He dragged me out of the square, threw me up against a wall, and tried to force himself on me," she said, her voice shaking with the force of her rage. "I was *not* willing."

Boyd shrugged. "And ye would trust the word of that MacQueen bastard over mine?"

Alasdair drew in a long, measured breath. Boyd was starting to sorely test his patience. He wasn't sure how much longer he'd be able to keep a leash on his temper. "And what of Darron. Are ye calling him a liar too?"

A nerve flickered in Boyd's cheek. "MacNichol has had his eye on the lass for months ... he's just jealous I got in first."

"Dog," Darron snarled. "I'll blacken yer other eye." He stepped forward, hands clenched by his sides, but Alasdair halted him with a hand to the arm.

Turning back to Boyd, Alasdair fixed him with a hard stare. "I brought ye into my home and gave ye a place in my guard. Is this how ye repay me?"

Boyd's lip curled. "There's no need to be over-dramatic, cousin. Don't work yerself up over some goose-brained slut."

Alasdair went still, his fists clenching at his sides. The anger inside him coiled like a serpent readying itself to strike. "That's it, Boyd," he growled. "Ye are out of chances."

His cousin shrugged, his battered face creasing into an expression of scorn. "If ye say so, *milord*."

"I do. Ye are to leave Duntulm. Today."

Shock turned Boyd's face slack. "Ye are sending me away?"

Alasdair nodded. "I'll send word to yer kin in Glencoe. They shall know what ye have done, and that ye are on yer way home."

Boyd stared at him—and a moment later something ugly moved in his blue eyes.

Without warning, he lunged for Alasdair, his right fist swinging for his face.

Alasdair was ready for him, for he'd been waiting for Boyd to turn nasty when he realized the game was up. Alasdair grabbed Boyd's wrist, moving back with the blow. Then he brought his knee up sharply and drove it into his assailant's gut.

Boyd collapsed onto the ground, where he coughed and wheezed as he struggled to regain his breath.

Alasdair turned his attention to Darron. "Escort Boyd south, out of sight of the keep," he rasped, "and make sure he doesn't come back. He's a disgrace to the clan."

Darron's mouth thinned, his gaze glinting. "With pleasure." The captain and another warrior heaved Boyd to his feet and dragged him from the square.

Alasdair watched as they led him away, rage pulsing through him like a Beltane drum.

Caitrin didn't take her gaze from her husband's face.

Alasdair was staring after Boyd, his face hard, gaze burning. His skin had pulled tight over his cheekbones. Caitrin had never seen him look so angry.

Heart pounding, she released Eoghan from the death-grip she'd been holding him in. The lad was uncharacteristically subdued, as if picking up on the surrounding tension.

"Alasdair?"

Tearing his gaze from where Boyd had just disappeared, dragged away by the guards, Alasdair met her eye. Around them, the people of Duntulm started to talk amongst themselves in low, excited voices.

"Sorry ye had to see that," he murmured, his gaze softening.

Caitrin raised an eyebrow. "I've seen worse."

Alasdair's gaze widened before his mouth curved. "Of course ye have ... ye are MacLeod's daughter after all."

"Aye ... I've witnessed my father beat men half to death for crossing him."

Alasdair huffed. "And there was me holding myself back on yer account."

Caitrin held his gaze. "I'm glad ye did. Ye have seen enough blood and violence, Alasdair." She paused then, her mouth curving. "Don't worry ... Darron's likely to give him a parting gift before he sends him south."

Her husband smiled then, the expression chasing away the lingering anger in his eyes. "Aye."

Caitrin turned her gaze then to the young woman who stood silently beside her. Sorcha's usually sunny face was pale, her eyes bloodshot and swollen from crying. She stared down at her clasped hands, her expression haunted.

"I did nothing to encourage him," she whispered. "I promise, milady."

Caitrin's chest constricted at the pain in the girl's voice. Reaching out, she pulled Sorcha into a hug, difficult since Eoghan now wriggled in her arms. "I know ye didn't," she murmured. "He didn't need an excuse. Don't blame yerself."

"But I shouldn't have let him corner me."

"Ye weren't to know he'd behave so. Don't worry ... ye are safe now."

Alasdair stepped close to the hand-maid, his brow furrowing with concern. "Do ye need to see a healer, lass?"

Sorcha shook her head. She drew back from Caitrin, extracting Eoghan's fingers from her hair. The lad had grabbed a handful of the handmaid's dark tresses. Meeting Alasdair's eye, she offered him a wan smile. "I'm well, milord," she replied. "Just shaken."

Caitrin had worried that the incident with Boyd would cast a shadow over the day. Yet not long after Boyd was dragged away, the fair continued as if nothing had happened. Laughter and singing drifted across the market square once more.

However, there were a few folk who were subdued in the aftermath.

Sorcha returned to the keep early, while Alasdair and Caitrin left the crowds, making their way east of the village to where the stone bridge over the Cleatburn was taking shape.

Alasdair carried Eoghan now, for Caitrin's arms and back had started to ache. Pride shone in Alasdair's eyes, and the lad was delighted to have his uncle carry him. He squealed and burbled gibberish, pointing at things as they walked. Dùnglas padded after them, although the dog was distracted by clumps of heather and rocks he felt compelled to lift his leg at.

Caitrin stopped on the western bank of the Cleatburn and surveyed the bridge. The half-built structure was twice the size of the old bridge. It was made of basalt blocks of stone and thus much sturdier than its predecessor, spanning the water in a graceful curve.

"Alasdair ... did ye design this yerself?" she asked.

"There's a beautiful bridge in Inbhir Nis," he replied. "It's much bigger than this one, but I studied it while I was there."

Caitrin tore her gaze from the structure and glanced over at him, smiling. "Just as well ye did. It's remarkable."

Alasdair smiled back. "Like that bridge, we built this one with a pointed arch. It makes it less likely to sag at the crown ... it'll also put less strain on the supports."

Caitrin nodded. She was impressed by his knowledge. "When will it be finished?"

"In a month, I'd guess ... if the fine weather holds, we'll be able to work faster." Alasdair grimaced then, grabbing Eoghan's hand as the lad grabbed hold of his hair and yanked.

Watching them, Caitrin smiled once more. She liked seeing Alasdair and Eoghan together. The family resemblance was there, although Alasdair's features were more hawkish than his nephew's.

I wonder when we shall have our first bairn.

The thought made warmth spread across her chest. She looked forward to giving him children: sons or daughters, she didn't mind which.

She thought then of her sisters. Rhona's belly would have become noticeable by now. When would Adaira and Lachlann start a family?

A tiny kernel of sadness lodged in Caitrin's breast then, as she thought about her sisters. She loved her life here at Duntulm, her marriage, and her son. Yet Rhona and Adaira were a part of her. She suddenly missed them with a force that made her chest ache.

"What is it, love?" Alasdair's voice brought Caitrin out of her reverie. She glanced up to see he was watching her. "Ye look leagues away."

She smiled. "I was just thinking about my sisters ... I miss them."

Alasdair's mouth curved. "Well then ... we should organize another visit to Dunvegan ... and perhaps a trip to Argyle."

"Really?"

"I'll see what I can do. We should cross to the mainland before the cold weather sets in."

A smile spread across Caitrin's face. The past month since their wedding had been an exciting, wondrous time. It was as if she'd been reborn; all the hurts of the past slowly faded into the mist. She woke up every morning, curled up in her husband's arms and wondering how it was possible to feel so happy.

She'd told Alasdair that she found it difficult to trust, but as the days passed, she found herself opening up to him more and more. With him she didn't need to be wary, to keep an eye out for dark moods or a vicious temper.

Alasdair still suffered nightmares—even if they had started to become less frequent and intense. The tremors in his hands had ceased of late, but sometimes she still caught him staring off into the distance—caught up in unpleasant memories. The wounds he'd brought home with him from war were gradually starting to heal.

Caitrin's vision misted. Alasdair wasn't like the other men she'd known. As much as she loved her father, Malcolm MacLeod was not a man who treated any woman, even his wife, as an equal. He had no use for conversation with them, preferring the company of his men and a horn of mead. Baltair had been much harsher than her father though. MacLeod at least suffered the opinions of his daughters, even with bad grace at times. Baltair had forbidden her from expressing her views entirely. She'd learned that lesson quickly upon coming to live at Duntulm.

But with Alasdair, there were no rules she had to follow, no subjects she had to avoid. She could be herself completely, and he loved her for it.

The friendship they'd once shared as bairns, the ease in each other's company, had been reforged—and with it a deeper bond. Something that had taken root inside Caitrin's breast and grew stronger with each passing day.

Caitrin stepped close to her husband. Then, going up on tip-toe, she leaned in and kissed him. "I love ye, Alasdair MacDonald," she murmured. "Sometimes the force of it overwhelms me."

He stared down at her, his dark eyes gleaming. "Ye don't know how I've longed to hear those words," he murmured, his voice catching. "I was beginning to think I never would."

Caitrin cupped his face with one hand while taking hold of one of Eoghan's grappling fingers with the other. "I've known for a while now ... I've just been waiting for the right time to say it." Her mouth curved then. "Ironic really ... for I once thought I loathed ye."

He huffed. "Gavin MacNichol told me that love and hate are close cousins."

"They are." Caitrin then inclined her head. "What passed between the two of ye?"

"What do ye mean?"

"I saw the look he gave ye that morning in Da's solar. He said something to ye."

Alasdair favored her with an enigmatic smile. "Nothing of importance."

Caitrin drew back. "Very well ... keep yer secrets then."

His smile widened. "There aren't any. We just had words that's all." His expression turned rueful then. "I was jealous of MacNichol, ye know? I thought ye would choose him."

"I would have," she admitted. "If ye hadn't made yer feelings known."

Their gazes fused. "It took everything I had to go down on one knee before ye again," he murmured. "I'm not sure what I'd have done if ye had sent me away."

"Ye were brave to say what ye did," Caitrin replied softly. "I'm so glad ye took the risk."

He smiled. "Ye have a tender heart, wife."

Caitrin stared up into his eyes, her fingers stroking the line of his jaw. "Aye, and it belongs to ye."

Chapter Thirty-four

A Man of My Word

CAITRIN TOOK A seat at the table, next to her husband.

The noon sun warmed her face, and a sea breeze tickled her scalp. Three weeks had passed since Duntulm Fair, and the Cleatburn Bridge was now complete. To celebrate, Alasdair MacDonald had put on a feast. All the folk of Duntulm—from the high to the low—had been invited.

Alasdair rose to his feet, raising the tankard he held into the air. Caitrin glanced over at him, admiring his strong profile, lean features, and flowing raven hair. Alasdair looked every inch a chieftain today, especially since he wore the MacDonald sash over his léine.

They sat at the center of a long table that had been erected in the center of Duntulm village's market square. Locals, both from the village and the keep, packed its length on both sides.

Once Alasdair stood up, the chatter of excited conversation died down, and all eyes settled upon their chieftain. Caitrin saw the respect in the men's eyes and the appreciation on the women's faces. Alasdair had won their hearts, as he had hers.

"People of Duntulm." Alasdair's deep voice traveled across the square. "Thank ye all for joining us here. Today we celebrate our new bridge, but also much more. I want to thank ye all for the support ye have given me and my kin over the years. We've had difficult times—famines, wars, and sickness—but ye have stayed here, farmed this land, fished these seas, and kept our people strong. I will not forget it. By sea and land, the MacDonalds stick together."

"By sea and land!" A roar went up. Men and women raised their tankards.

When Alasdair sat back down, Caitrin flashed him a smile. "Well spoken."

An excited chatter rose around them as the feasting began.

His mouth curved. "We MacDonalds have a way with words."

Caitrin snorted. "And a self-confidence that knows no bounds."

He laughed. "Admit it … it's just one of the many things ye love about me."

"Conceited cockerel," she muttered, smiling. Of course, he knew she did.

"Ye look radiant today," Alasdair said as he handed her a goblet of sloe wine. "I don't think I've seen the smile leave yer face since dawn."

Caitrin laughed and took a sip of wine. "On a day like this, I have much to be happy about."

"And what's that?" he asked, a teasing edge to his voice.

"A sunny sky, fine food and wine, and a handsome man by my side," she replied. "What more could a lass ask for?"

Alasdair grinned. "The lady is easy to please it seems."

Caitrin didn't reply, instead merely favoring him with an enigmatic smile. She wondered then if she should ask him about the trip he'd promised they'd take to Argyle. He hadn't said anything since the day of the fair, and as summer crept on, she wondered if he'd forgotten.

Her gaze shifted down the table then, taking in the faces of the servants, retainers, farmers, and artisans who made up their community. A sense of belonging settled over her. She wasn't born here, on Skye's isolated northern tip, and yet this place was her home much more than Dunvegan ever had been.

Under the table, something nudged her knee. Caitrin glanced down to see that Dùnglas sat at her feet. She glimpsed his dark eyes and whiskery muzzle and smiled. The dog was hoping someone would drop a tasty morsel down to him. With a sigh, Caitrin picked up a piece of pork from the platter before her and dropped it under the table.

"Ye will encourage the hound to beg," Alasdair warned.

Caitrin glanced up guiltily. "I can't stand it," she replied with a contrite smile. "When he looks at me with those soulful eyes, I can deny him nothing."

Alasdair huffed. "I shall have to try that with ye in future ... and see how far it gets me."

Caitrin shook her head in mock chagrin before her gaze returned to farther down the table, where Darron MacNichol and Sorcha MacQueen sat together. The pair were deep in conversation, oblivious to the feasting and drinking going on around them. It was a heart-warming sight. For days after Boyd's attack, Sorcha had been out of sorts: pale and tense. But from the looks of things, she'd now put the ordeal behind her.

Caitrin nudged Alasdair with her elbow. "It looks like we might have a handfasting in Duntulm before long."

His gaze followed Caitrin's down the table before he glanced back at her. "Are ye match-making, wife?"

"No," Caitrin said innocently, spearing a piece of pork with a knife. "Just making an observation. Look at them, Alasdair ... and tell me they won't be wed by the spring."

The cèilidh started mid-afternoon. Once the long tables and scraps of food had been cleared away, a man pulled out a fiddle and began to play, while his wife sang a bawdy song about a farmer's wife, her foolish husband,

and her two lovers. The song had folk laughing and clapping along by the second verse.

Caitrin watched Darron and Sorcha run into the midst of the dancers. Their faces were flushed from wine and the sun. Darron twirled Sorcha around, while she laughed.

Caitrin observed them wistfully, tapping her foot to the music.

"We never finished that dance," Alasdair's voice intruded. "Ye slapped my face and sent me on my way instead."

Caitrin turned to him, her mouth curving. "What a shrew ye have wed."

He smiled, holding out his hand to her. "May I have *this* dance, milady?"

Caitrin inclined her head. "Of course, milord."

He led her out into the dancing, and a moment later they were caught up in it, whirling, stepping, and turning in time to the music. Caitrin danced until her feet ached and she felt light-headed. After that, she returned to the table and took a restorative sip of wine.

Galiene arrived then with Eoghan. Caitrin took the lad from the woman and bid her go and find some food and drink, and enjoy herself. Eoghan looked around, his chubby face eager, his blue eyes bright with curiosity. Caitrin gave him a chunk of bread, and he began to chew at it. Eoghan then looked up at Alasdair before grinning.

"Dair."

Alasdair smiled at the lad's attempt at his name. He couldn't yet manage long words, but he'd become quite talkative of late. "Dair!"

Caitrin's throat constricted when Alasdair reached out and ruffled Eoghan's thick black hair. There was genuine affection in his peat-brown eyes when he looked upon his nephew. "Ye are a good-natured lad, aren't ye?"

Eoghan dropped the chunk of bread he'd been mauling and held out his hands to Alasdair. "Dair!"

Alasdair laughed and took him from Caitrin. The lad clutched at Alasdair's léine and sash, squealing with delight when his uncle rose to his feet and bounced him in his arms. Alasdair then glanced down at Caitrin with a grin. "I think someone else wants a dance. We'll be back soon."

Caitrin watched Alasdair and Eoghan make their way into the dancing, her gaze misting with love as she watched them.

Alasdair was a good father to the lad. She hadn't expected him to treat Eoghan like a son, yet he had. Eoghan would grow up loved at Duntulm.

The celebrations stretched out and would continue long into the night. However, Alasdair, Caitrin, and Eoghan left when the bairn started to get tired. Leaving the laughter and music ringing out across the hillside behind them, they climbed the hill back to the castle. Eoghan was asleep, slumped against Alasdair's chest. Dùnglas trotted along, trailing the couple like a shadow.

A cool wind skirted across the hill and mist had crept in from the sea. Although this day had been a fine one, Caitrin imagined that they'd awaken to a foggy morning the following day. That was how it was upon Skye. No two days of weather were alike.

They'd nearly reached the brow of the hill, and the drawbridge that spanned the deep ditch encircling Duntulm's curtain wall, when the bellow of a hunting horn reached them.

Caitrin stifled a gasp. She knew that horn. It was one she'd grown up with, had heard every time her father took his men and dogs out on a hunt.

Turning south, her gaze alighted upon a company of riders approaching over the brow of the nearest hill. Pennants of gold, grey, and black, threaded with red, fluttered in the breeze.

Caitrin's heart soared at the sight.

She swiveled on her heel, her gaze meeting Alasdair's, and saw that he wore a knowing smile.

"Ye invited Da?"

"Aye, as well as Rhona and Taran MacKinnon. They were supposed to arrive yesterday, in time for the feast, but it looks like they were delayed. It matters not, for the boat doesn't leave for two days."

Caitrin stilled. "The boat?"

Alasdair stepped close, reaching up with his free hand to cup her cheek. "Ye didn't think I'd forgotten, did ye? We're taking a trip to Argyle to see yer sister, and I've invited Rhona and Taran to join us."

Caitrin stared at him a moment before joy exploded in her breast. She threw herself into his arms, accidentally waking Eoghan who gave a low whimper and snuggled back into Alasdair's chest.

Kissing Alasdair hard on the lips, Caitrin beamed up at him. "Ye remembered!"

He smiled down at her, his gaze filled with tenderness. "Aye ... and I'm a man of my word."

Epilogue

I Made Ye a Promise

CAITRIN'S FIRST GLIMPSE of Gylen Castle was of a stone tower etched against a grey sky, surrounded by an emerald blanket of green.

Clutching at Rhona's sleeve, Caitrin pointed east. "Look ... there it is!"

The sisters stood at the bow of the large boat that sailed across the choppy waters of the Firth of Lorne. A brisk breeze had whipped up the surface of the water, making the boat roll. Rhona and Caitrin clung together for stability, clutching the railing.

The castle perched upon a rocky outcrop, commanding a view for miles around. Although it formed part of Argyle, Gylen didn't actually sit upon the mainland. It sat instead upon the rocky Isle of Kerrera, just off the coast.

Caitrin's mother's people resided here—Clan MacDougall. Adaira had assured Caitrin in her letters that their uncle had given her and Lachlann a warm welcome, and that they enjoyed their life at Gylen. But even so, Caitrin felt nerves flutter in the pit of her belly.

She hoped that Adaira and Lachlann truly were happy here and that no unpleasant surprises awaited them.

"It's impressive," Rhona said, pushing her unruly auburn hair out of her eyes. "I'd thought Adaira must be exaggerating."

Caitrin smiled. She'd imagined the same, for their sister could be prone to over-enthusiasm. The tower that rose from the grey-stone keep had graceful lines. It was very different to the more bulky and squat silhouettes of Dunvegan and Duntulm.

"Adaira has no idea we're coming." Caitrin's gaze dropped to the approaching rocky shore. A long wooden jetty jutted out to meet them. "I can't wait to see her face."

"Hopefully, she's at home," Rhona replied. One hand rested on her belly as she spoke; it had started to swell now under her kirtle, visible when the wind pushed her clothing against her form.

"I hadn't thought of that," Caitrin said with a frown. "But I'm sure our uncle will entertain us until she returns."

Rhona huffed. "I'll be glad to get off this boat. It's rolling makes me queasy."

Caitrin nodded, casting her sister a sympathetic smile. It had been a rough ride across from Skye. They'd had to weather two rain squalls and a constant wind that had quickened the journey but made it more uncomfortable.

Rhona held her gaze, her storm-grey eyes piercing. "I haven't had the chance to say much to ye, Caitrin. We never seemed to have a moment alone once we arrived at Duntulm, but I'm truly happy for ye. I look at yer face now, and I see my sister again."

Caitrin's mouth quirked. "I feel a different woman," she admitted. "But I haven't gone back to who I was before I wed Baltair. That girl is gone forever."

Rhona's eyes clouded. "I must admit that I had my doubts. I thought ye mad for wedding MacDonald. I'm happy to see I was wrong."

"So am I," Caitrin replied.

Rhona favored her with an arch look. "Taran did tell me all would be well between ye. He's been insufferably smug to be proved right."

"He's a wise man yer husband," Caitrin said with a teasing smile. "Taran says little but notices much."

"Ready to disembark?"

Caitrin glanced over her shoulder to find Alasdair standing behind them, a coil of oiled rope in hand. Dùnglas sat at his side, tail wagging. Since the hound had once belonged to Adaira, they'd decided to bring him with them to Gylen Castle. Behind Alasdair, Taran and two others were readying the boat to dock, trimming the sail and maneuvering it toward the jetty with long oars.

"Aye," Caitrin replied before grinning. "I don't think Rhona or I have a love for the water."

A short while later, Caitrin MacDonald stepped onto Argyle soil for the first time. Her legs wobbled under her as she made her way up the wooden jetty. They took a few moments to adjust to a solid surface, and she was glad of her husband's steadying arm.

Alasdair carried Eoghan strapped to his back. The lad was restless, hands waving as he wriggled against the restraints. Now that he could stand, pulling himself up on any solid object he could find, Eoghan no longer liked being carried.

Dùnglas ran ahead, eager as them to be on land again.

The small party made their way up the path from the jetty, carrying leather bags and satchels with them. The road up to the castle wound over rocky headland, although beyond Caitrin spied grassy hills dotted with cottars' huts and grazing sheep. It was a peaceful spot, if a little windswept.

They'd almost reached the gates, which were open this afternoon, the jagged teeth of the iron portcullis raised, when a small figure appeared. She was a comely young woman with long walnut-colored hair, dressed in flowing green. Picking up her skirts, she broke into a sprint, her slippered feet flying over the stony path.

Caitrin's breath caught. *Adaira.*

Her youngest sister collided with Rhona first and threw her arms around her. Adaira's face was wet, her hazel eyes gleaming, as she pulled back. "I can't believe it! Ye came!"

Rhona laughed, knuckling away a tear of her own. "Of course we did. I made ye a promise, didn't I?"

A lean grey wolfhound bounded up to Adaira then, nearly knocking her off her feet.

"God's bones," Adaira gasped, averting her face from its eager tongue. "Who's this?"

"Don't ye recognize wee Dùnglas?" Rhona asked, laughing. "He's a bit bigger than when ye saw him last."

"Dùnglas?" Adaira pushed the hound off her before reaching down to pat him. The dog's tail whacked against her skirts as he pressed against her. "Ye have grown into a beast!"

"He lives at Duntulm now," Caitrin said, "but I thought ye would like to see him again."

"Aye." Adaira's gaze shone as she shifted her attention to Caitrin.

Stepping around Dùnglas, she crushed her sister in a tight hug. For a small woman, Adaira's grip was fearsomely strong. Drawing back from the embrace, Adaira's gaze searched Caitrin's face, curiosity lighting in her eyes. Although Caitrin had sent no word of her marriage—or had yet said anything about her change in circumstance—Adaira knew. Caitrin saw it in her expression.

Adaira's attention shifted to Caitrin's left, where Alasdair stood with a now grizzling Eoghan on his back. "Alasdair MacDonald?"

Caitrin glanced back to see Alasdair smile at Adaira. "Aye, greetings Lady Adaira. It has been a while."

Of course, the pair had met briefly when Alasdair had visited Dunvegan intent on wooing Caitrin. It seemed like a lifetime ago now.

"Alasdair is now chieftain of the MacDonalds of Duntulm," Caitrin said gently, turning her attention back to her sister.

Adaira dropped into a neat curtsy. "Milord."

"He and I are wed," Caitrin added.

Adaira's eyes grew huge. Her gaze flicked between them both. "Ye wed and didn't invite me?"

Caitrin favored her with an apologetic smile. "The circumstances of our marriage were … unusual, Adi." She looped her arm through her sister's and steered her toward the gates. "Come … my belly needs settling after that rough crossing, and if Eoghan doesn't get out of that sling soon, he'll turn Alasdair deaf."

Up ahead, another figure appeared: a tall man dressed in leather braies and a crisp linen léine. He walked with a loose-limbed, confident stride, a smile creasing his handsome face. Fiery auburn hair, of an even brighter shade than Rhona's, blew around his face.

Lachlann Fraser.

Caitrin cut a glance back to Adaira. "Ye are happy, Adi?"

Her sister nodded, her expression glowing when she too glanced up to see her husband approach. "Very," she replied softly.

They continued up the path toward where Lachlann had stopped and waited for them. Adaira now clung to Caitrin's arm as if she feared her sister would run off. "I want to hear the whole story about ye and Alasdair," she insisted in a low voice. "Ye are to leave nothing out."

Caitrin laughed and shared a grin with Rhona, who'd fallen into step next to her. Alasdair walked behind them with Taran as they approached the gates.

"I'd forgotten how bossy ye can be," Rhona chastised Adaira, still grinning.

Caitrin met Adaira's eye and smiled. "I'll definitely need to take a seat and have a good platter of food and drink before me. This tale is a long one."

The End

From the author

I hope you enjoyed the conclusion to THE BRIDES OF
SKYE. This has been my first 'quick-release' series. I
actually managed to release all three books a month
apart in April, May, and June 2019! Whew!

Writing a revenge story is much more complex than I
thought it would be! It's not a theme I embark on that
often, but I'd been waiting for the opportunity to get my
teeth into such a tale. Caitrin and Alasdair gave me the
chance! Often seething resentment is built on
misunderstandings, and so I gave our lovers plenty. A
young man's ego is a fragile thing, having Caitrin laugh
at him when he proposed would have been hard to take,
and then when she marries his brother shortly after the
damage is complete. Likewise, when Alasdair separates
Caitrin from her son, he does something that's very hard
to forgive.

THE ROGUE'S BRIDE is a highly character-driven story.
I enjoyed exploring how far we'll let our past dictate our
future, and delving into the nature of forgiveness. Caitrin
and Alasdair were both unhappy at beginning of the
story, and I really wanted to give them a HEA. Of course,
you met Caitrin back in Book #1, when she was married
to Baltair, so I hope her story was worth waiting for!

I had to do a bit of research into PTSD for this story.
Such things hadn't been diagnosed back in medieval
times, but PTSD existed all the same. As those of you
who've read other novels by me will know, I like to write
about flawed heroes. Alasdair had a lot to contend with,
not just the bitterness of losing the woman he loves to
his brother, but the trauma of war as well.

The Battle of Neville's Cross was a real battle. It took
place on 17 October 1346, just half a mile from Durham,
England. As explained in the novel, the battle was a

crushing defeat for the Scottish. The invading Scottish army of 12,000 led by King David II was defeated with heavy losses by an English army of approximately 6,000–7,000 men led by Lord Ralph Neville. King David survived the battle and was taken prisoner by the English. For those Scots who did survive and manage to flee with their lives, the memories of that fight would have been harrowing.

The novel's main setting, Duntulm, is an actual castle set high upon a cliff on The Isle of Skye's windswept northern coast. It was the MacDonald stronghold for many years. These days it's nothing more than a ruin, but enough remains that I was able to get a clear picture of what the keep would have looked like.

Jayne x

About the Author

Award-winning author Jayne Castel writes epic Historical and Fantasy Romance. Her vibrant characters, richly researched historical settings, and action-packed adventure romance transport readers to forgotten times and imaginary worlds.

Jayne has published a number of bestselling series. In love with all things Scottish, Jayne also writes romances set in Dark Ages Scotland ... sexy Pict warriors anyone?

When she's not writing, Jayne is reading (and re-reading) her favorite authors, cooking Italian feasts, and going for long walks with her husband. She lives in New Zealand's beautiful South Island.

Connect with Jayne online:
www.jaynecastel.com
www.facebook.com/JayneCastelRomance/
https://www.instagram.com/jaynecastelauthor/
Email: contact@jaynecastel.com